Dear Reader,

When I was on a cruise to Alaska, I played *What's My Line* on the ship. My fellow passengers never guessed that I was a romance author!

However, they might have had a clue if they'd been around when I met the man running the bagel concession on the dock in Ketchikan. Since I look for book ideas everywhere I go, I asked him, "How did you end up doing this?"

He replied that he'd started out selling bagels in Key West, Florida, which is about as far away from Alaska as you can get and still be in the United States. Since the tourist business dwindles in Key West in the summer, he looked for another venue and landed in Ketchikan, where there's lots of great native salmon to put on the bagels as well as cruise ships to provide a steady stream of customers.

I bet he'd be surprised to learn that he was amazingly transformed into the heroine of *Kisses in the Rain*, Martha Rose. As for the hero, Nick, well, keep reading....

With love,

Pamela Browning

PAMELA BROWNING

is the award-winning author of many bestselling romances for Harlequin. Her books consistently win high ratings from reviewers and readers alike. She lives in North Carolina, where she indulges her fondness for bagels and chocolate-chip cookies every chance she gets!

Books by Pamela Browning

Harlequin American Romance

Cherished Beginnings #101
Handyman Special #116
Through the Eyes of Love #123
Interior Designs #131
Ever Since Eve #140
Forever Is a Long Time #150
To Touch The Stars #170
The Flutterby Princess #181
Ice Crystals #194
Kisses in the Rain #227
Simple Gifts #237
Fly Away #241
Harvest Home #245
Feathers in the Wind #287
Until Spring #297
Humble Pie #354
A Man Worth Loving #384
For Auld Lang Syne #420
Sunshine and Shadows #439
Morgan's Child #451
Merry Christmas, Baby #516
The World's Last Bachelor #565
Angel's Baby #600
Lover's Leap #632
RSVP...Baby #788
That's Our Baby! #818
Baby Christmas #854
Cowboy with a Secret #874

& BACHELORS USA

Pamela Browning
Kisses in the Rain

HARLEQUIN®

TORONTO • NEW YORK • LONDON
AMSTERDAM • PARIS • SYDNEY • HAMBURG
STOCKHOLM • ATHENS • TOKYO • MILAN • MADRID
PRAGUE • WARSAW • BUDAPEST • AUCKLAND

This book is for my parents,
Jack and Helen Katter,
who know how to throw a party.

HARLEQUIN BOOKS
225 Duncan Mill Road, Don Mills,
Ontario, Canada M3B 3K9

ISBN 0-373-82250-2

KISSES IN THE RAIN

Copyright © 1987 by Pamela Browning

Visit us at www.eHarlequin.com

Printed in U.S.A.

Chapter One

Martha Rose munched thoughtfully on the chocolate-chip cookie that was her breakfast and considered the hills on the other side of the Golden Gate Bridge. It had rained yesterday, the storm rolling in off San Francisco Bay and starting a few mud slides west of town. Mud slides, earthquakes, heavy fogs—San Franciscans took all in stride. Martha didn't think she'd ever get used to it.

The question today was whether or not to take a raincoat or umbrella when she set off in search of a job. From this tiny sun deck hanging off the back of her friend Polly's rented house halfway up Telegraph Hill, Martha thought the bay looked exactly like a picture postcard; the blue was bluer than ever, the greens were greener, and the few clouds scudded across a sky that dazzled the eye with its intensity. For once—and this was unusual—there wasn't even fog. It looked like a perfect May day.

Martha reached for another chocolate-chip cookie and bit into it as Polly's curly blond head appeared around the edge of the door.

"I'm running late, Martha. I've got to go. What are you going to do today?" Polly stepped outside so that she could cadge a cookie from the plastic bag.

"I'm going to answer a couple of newspaper ads. See if I can find a job. The usual."

"Why don't you join Sigmund and me for dinner tonight? We're going for pasta."

"Um," said Martha, using a full mouth as an excuse for not answering right away.

"You can think it over. I'll be home right after work—*if* that awful Mrs. Claussen doesn't come in and start pestering me about the furnishings for her yacht." Polly was an associate with a prominent interior-design firm, and Mrs. Claussen was her worst client.

"That Mrs. Claussen of yours rolls in as regularly as the fog, doesn't she?"

"There's no fog today. Maybe that's a hopeful sign."

"Here's to a Claussen-free day," said Martha, raising her glass of milk in a toast.

Polly rolled her eyes and laughed. "If only I could count on being that fortunate. Good luck with your job hunt." With that, Polly rushed back inside the house. Martha heard the rapid click of Polly's heels on the wooden floor as she left for work.

Martha settled back in her chair and reached for another cookie. Then she put it back. She'd better start thinking about staying slim, especially since the ad in last night's paper that had most interested her had stated: *Wanted: Model Type with B.A. Degree in Business.*

Martha's bachelor of arts degree was indeed in business, and she'd modeled for a department store while she was in college. The ad more than interested her—it intrigued her. It seemed to promise a different kind of job from the ones she'd been offered since she'd arrived here.

She sipped her milk slowly and surveyed Polly's neighbors on the decks of the pastel-colored houses descending in tiers below. Many of the people were gulping down a last cup of coffee before running off to work. Perhaps by next week Martha would be doing that, too. She fervently hoped she'd find a job she liked by that time.

Maybe Martha was aiming too high, but she didn't think so. She wanted a job in the retail business, a job with a future in management. Since her graduation from college four years ago, she'd worked at a major department store in the accounting department, then switched to sales when she'd realized that she enjoyed contact with the customers. A year later she'd left to manage a boutique in Kokomo, Indiana, but she'd become restless when she'd realized that it was a dead-end job.

"Come out to San Francisco," Polly had urged during one of the therapeutic long-distance telephone calls during which they'd regularly poured out their hearts to each other. "We can be roommates again, just like we were in college."

To Martha, that had sounded like a wonderful idea. She'd missed Polly. They'd been close friends since they were both eighteen, the age at which Martha had first left her home in small-town Greenleaf, Indiana, to attend the university. If there was anything that Martha valued above all else, it was her friends. Besides, Polly had recently broken up with her boyfriend of two years, and Martha thought Polly needed support.

Without thinking much about it, telling herself cheerfully that she was nothing but a creature of impulse, Martha had bade her friends in Kokomo goodbye. She knew she'd keep in touch; it was the way she was. She'd given away the parched houseplants she'd never remembered to water and headed west from Kokomo with everything she owned crammed into a U-Haul-It trailer. The trailer had swayed laboriously all the way to California behind her aging Volkswagen Rabbit.

Martha had wished she'd never heard of a U-Haul-It trailer by the time she'd gotten lost on some of San Francisco's most crooked streets. She'd thought she'd never escape from the mad maze of hills and houses; she'd been a nervous wreck by the time she'd reached Polly's house on Telegraph Hill.

"How do you stand it?" she'd blurted to Polly, who had greeted her at the door with a reviving glass of wine and, unexpectedly, a new beau, with whom Polly was apparently madly in love.

"Oh, you'll get used to it," said Polly, grinning up at the new man, whose name was Sigmund.

But for the past two weeks Martha had doubted that she'd ever grow accustomed to this town. She loved San Francisco; who wouldn't? But she didn't know if she really wanted to live here. She was used to the essentially homogeneous population of Kokomo.

She'd never forget the Sunday when Polly and Sigmund and she had all walked to Golden Gate Park together. Martha didn't even try to hide her amazement at some of the characters who entertained on Beach Street or Market Street; there was a man who billed himself as the Video Jukebox, walking around inside a huge cardboard packing crate until someone shoved a dollar in the slot, at which time the man would stop and strum a tune on his banjo as he peered out a cellophane-covered hole near the top. Not only was there a Video Jukebox, there were mimes and jugglers and Dixieland Bands, all adding to the spontaneity for which the city is famous.

"We sure didn't have anything like this in Kokomo" became a catchphrase that she could always count on to start Polly laughing, and usually Sigmund would join in, too, because it seemed as though everywhere Polly and Martha went, Sigmund tagged along.

Friends were one thing; friends' boyfriends were another, and this boyfriend wore a pink crystal suspended from a chain around his neck, claiming he used it to amplify his thought consciousness. He had another crystal on the engine of his car to help it run, and a third very large crystal on his living-room table for reasons Martha couldn't fathom.

Martha supposed she should be thankful that Sigmund wasn't a Video Jukebox, but after two weeks being part of a threesome had begun to feel distinctly uncomfortable, and Martha couldn't wait to move out of Polly's house on Telegraph Hill and into an apartment of her own so she could give up her fifth-wheel status. She had a feeling that Polly wouldn't want for a roommate for long. Sigmund was obviously eager to fill the bill.

Now Martha sighed and wrapped up the rest of the chocolate-chip cookies. They were the best chocolate-chip cookies she'd ever tasted; she replenished her supply every couple of days at a little kiosk not too far from Fisherman's Wharf. They were probably the best thing so far about San Francisco. Chocolate-chip cookies were so homey. So ordinary. So Indiana-ish. They made her feel a little bit more at home in this oddball environment.

It occurred to Martha as she pulled the sliding glass door closed behind her that she hadn't asked Polly if she thought it was going to rain today. Her hair, a sure barometer of damp weather, curved across her head in a carefully studied wave. When the weather was damp, it sprang into tight ringlets. No ringlets this morning, so the humidity must be low.

After another dubious look at the mountains beyond the bridge—they looked clearer than ever, she thought—Martha put on her best suit. It had cost her plenty, even with her discount at the boutique. It was bright turquoise with a pencil-slim skirt and a jacket with a fashionably flared peplum. The color made her eyes, which were gray, look like clear aquamarines, and it made the red highlights in her dark brown hair seem even brighter.

Martha took special care with her eyeliner, smudging the corners just so. She also touched up a chip in the rose nail enamel on her right forefinger. Not that she ever looked scruffy. Polly claimed that Martha "radiated chic." But Martha was convinced that no one could radiate chic with even one chip in her nail polish.

Martha didn't know what the author of the newspaper ad had in mind when he specified a "model type," but she could definitely be a model. Not a photographic model, perhaps, because she didn't have the bone structure for it. But she was suited to tearoom or runway modeling, and she was experienced at both. Surely she'd have a chance at this job if she wanted it.

She decided to walk to the address specified in the ad. The office was not far from Fisherman's Wharf, where she went often. As she deftly dodged cable cars in her high-heeled shoes, Martha thought about the jobs she'd already turned down so far.

The first job she'd refused had been a sales position with a furrier, a shifty-eyed little man who had made it clear that his designs were not necessarily the ones hanging on the racks of his store. There was a job as manager at an up-and-coming boutique in fashionable Ghirardelli Square, but when she'd inquired into the job duties she'd found out that after hours, when the store was closed, the manager and salesclerks were required to vacuum the floor and clean the rest rooms on a rotating basis because, as one of the salesclerks confided behind a cupped hand, "the owner's too stingy to hire a janitorial service."

Martha had briefly considered working for a local department store, one of the biggest in the city. After interviewing there and touring the office, she had decided that so many junior executives would have seniority over her that it would be difficult for a newcomer to rise through the ranks.

No, Martha wanted to be part of a smaller operation, one that would grow. She liked the retail business and she liked working with people. She had good business sense, and after all she had a degree in business administration. Somehow—she knew it—she'd find the right job for her.

The ad she held in her hand led her to a neat office building, nothing fancy, nothing big. She rode in an elevator to the fifth floor, where she found a door labeled Sidney Pollov Enterprises.

The secretary looked her carefully coordinated outfit over with interest, spirited Martha's résumé into Mr. Pollov's office and informed Martha that Mr. Pollov would be with her in a few minutes.

Martha scanned the office with a practiced eye. Absolutely nothing gave away the purpose of Sidney Pollov Enterprises. By the time she was ushered into his office, Martha still didn't have a clue about the kind of job being offered.

Sidney Pollov jumped to his feet when she entered and reached over his cluttered desk to shake her hand. When they were seated across from each other, he leaned forward enthusiastically. He was a round-faced, boyish type, and she guessed his age to be about thirty-eight or so. He wore a natty three-piece suit, which was unusual in this city where everything was always so casual.

"I've read your résumé," he said. "You might be just what I'm looking for. You have a business degree from the University of Indiana, is that right?"

"Yes," she answered, her curiosity rising. She wondered if he was a Hollywood talent scout. But then why would she have to have a degree in business for this job?

"And you've worked in retail, I see." He thumbed through her résumé and frowned. "I don't suppose you've ever had any experience in food service."

"Food service?"

"Cooking, working in a restaurant, waiting tables, that kind of thing."

This line of thinking bewildered her even more. "No, I've always worked in the kind of places that sell clothes," she said. "Except for when I had a job with the city parks department when I was in high school."

"What'd you do?"

"I led nature walks. I was a Girl Scout, you see, and I knew about camping and local plant life."

"Mmm. And did you like it?"

"I liked being outdoors. I liked the kids I worked with, too."

He took in the glossy manicure, the slim skirt and the high heels. "You certainly don't look like the outdoor type," he said. "Tell me, do you like working with people?"

"Oh, yes. In my last job, I enjoyed seeing the customers every day."

"You didn't get tired of them? They didn't annoy you with their demands?"

"Never. I wanted to make sure everyone was satisfied when they left our shop."

"I see." His eyes twinkled at her unexpectedly. "How tall are you, Miss Rose?"

"I'm five feet seven inches," she said, wondering what that had to do with anything.

"You'd barely fit," he said, tapping his pencil on the pad on his desk. "Five-seven's the absolute max."

She couldn't help bristling. "Your ad called for a model type," she said. "Models are supposed to be tall."

"I know, I know," he said. "You'll notice I only said model *type*. I didn't actually say a model. Did you think this was a modeling job?" His dark-eyed gaze seemed to pierce into her.

"I had no idea," she admitted. "I wondered. Usually people who want to hire a model don't care whether she has a degree in business administration."

He stood up, swinging forward in his chair with an enthusiasm that startled her.

He said, "Come over here."

He beckoned with one hand and pulled aside the filmy window drapery with the other, revealing a view of Fisherman's Wharf. "See that red shack near the entrance to the wharf? The Bagel Barn?" asked Sidney.

She did, barely. It was surrounded by a crowd of people.

"Do you know what it is?"

"Sure," she said. "It's a bagel concession. I've even bought a bagel there once or twice."

"Did you like the bagel?"

"It was delicious," she said, looking back at him with a frankly puzzled frown.

"I'm glad you liked it. I own the place."

Martha blinked. "Is *that* what Sidney Pollov Enterprises is?"

He nodded, watching her shrewdly. "I own Bagel Barns all over the country. Mostly in tourist places like Cape Cod, Key West, San Diego, Padre Island, you know. Places where people need a quick bite to eat and want something substantial without going the old hamburger-and-French-fries route. I sell several different kinds of bagels and juice, coffee, tea."

Martha collected herself. Whatever she'd expected, she hadn't dreamed that Sidney Pollov sold bagels for a living.

"You still interested?"

"I'm not sure where this is leading," she hedged. Sidney Pollov chuckled and dropped the curtain. Whatever he was, he was certainly jolly.

"Sit down, Martha—you don't mind if I call you Martha? You can call me Sidney if you want to get even." He hiked his pant legs and sat down once she was again seated in the chair across from him.

"What I have here is a chain of Bagel Barns," he said, pushing a list across the desk. Martha picked it up and saw that it was a complete list of all the Bagel Barns in the country. According to the list, Sidney owned Bagel Barns in Memphis, Virginia Beach, Panama City, Sun Valley, Savannah, Vail, San Antonio and too many other places for her eyes to register in the few moments she had to look at the list.

"Now, what I'm hiring is somebody to open up a new Bagel Barn—somebody with a good business head on her shoulders. I want a woman because women are pretty. My Bagel Barns are located in sight-seeing and vacation places, and a beautiful woman adds to the scenery. That's important to people on vacation, believe me."

"Do you know how chauvinistic that sounds?" she said.

Sidney shrugged. "Well, that's the way I feel about it. Most men are too big to fit in the booth. I prefer beautiful women to run my Bagel Barns. I like to wear black socks with all my clothes and I put too much salt on my steak, too, but that's the way I like it, and I'm entitled to my personal preferences. Bagel Barns are my business. I started from scratch with my mother's bagel recipe and one Bagel Barn a couple of years ago right here in San Francisco. Since they're mine, I can do what I want. What do you think of that?"

Martha shrugged. She found Sidney amusing. "I think if you're the boss, you've probably earned the right."

Sidney slapped his knee. "Smart girl," he said.

"Woman," retorted Martha. She'd already decided that she didn't want to sell bagels for a living.

"I guess you don't like chauvinists," Sidney commented with a wry look.

"I'm not a die-hard feminist, if that's what you mean. I think you're misguided to think that women sell bagels better than men."

He laughed again. He laughed a lot. She thought he regarded her with new respect.

"Can we talk about the job, Martha? I mean, that's why you're here, right?"

"I don't know," she said doubtfully. "I'm not sure I'm interested."

"What if I make it worth your while?" That shrewd look again; it surprised her, interspersed as it was with so many smiles and so much laughter.

"How much worth my while?" she inquired with what she knew was a distinctly skeptical rise of the eyebrows.

"Listen to what I have to say, Martha, that's all I'm asking."

He looked so sincere that she gave him her full attention.

"It's a fairly simply operation," Sidney went on. "We use our own bagels, but I order all other supplies. I get my lox from a place in Los Angeles. Jelly I order, cream cheese, all of it. The operator of each Bagel Barn submits an order to me every week. I ship the supplies the fastest way. Each operator has to keep careful records, of course."

"Which is why your employees have to have experience in retail, right?"

"Sure. It helps to know a lot about the way a retail business works. And pleasing the customers is important, real important. I want everyone to know that when they eat bagels from a Bagel Barn they also get a pleasant smile and a cheery thank you from a pretty girl—er, woman, woman," he said hastily when she shot him a meaningful look.

"Go ahead," she said.

"That's about it. Do you want the job?" Sidney leaned back in his chair and clasped his hands behind his head.

"Just like that?"

"Sure. I like you. You've got a good background and you're pretty. Plus you look good in a dress."

"I don't understand why you need a person with a degree in business administration to sell bagels in a Bagel Barn," said Martha. "Anyway, you haven't mentioned a salary."

"I'm not just looking for a salesperson, Martha. I'm looking for someone who can be my vice president and administrative assistant here at Sidney Pollov Enterprises. Who can travel around the country and untangle problems that arise at my various Bagel Barns. I've got forty-four Bagel Barns all over the country."

"So many!"

"They open in Cape Cod in the summer and close in Cape Cod in the winter. They open in Key West in the winter but close in Key West in the summer. I have to travel, Martha, you wouldn't believe it. Last week I had to run down to New Orleans and hire a new person to operate the local Bagel Barn because the last one quit. Took me a week, and in the meantime everything else went to pot. Can you travel?"

"Yes, if necessary."

"Good. That's important. You'll be in charge of hiring. Managing my personnel is another worry. These girls—women, I mean. They have problems. They want to tell me about their kids, their husbands, and I don't have time to hear it. I have a wife and four kids that I love very much. I want to spent more time with them, and this business is killing me."

Martha took a deep breath. "You still haven't mentioned a salary."

He named a figure that made Martha's eyes pop.

"After you've learned the business, in six months or so, you'll get a raise. In a year, if we're both happy with the arrangement, I'll cut you in on the profits. I'm going to have to hire regional supervisors before long. Then you can supervise the supervisors."

"You'll cut me in on the profits? Do you mean it?"

"Sure. You help build it up, you deserve it. Soon you can run the Bagel Barn division of Sidney Pollov Enterprises. I'm going to expand; I'm going to open a chain of Chinese take-out places soon. Hey, Martha, I need you."

"Sidney, this is all...just a bit more than I expected," she said.

"I'll put everything in writing just to keep it kosher."

It was sounding better all the time. This looked like a ground-floor opportunity, certainly better than anything else she'd found.

"When would I start work?"

"Monday."

Martha thought about how she could now move out of Polly's house, leaving the field clear for Sigmund and his crystals. She thought about her dwindling savings account. She thought about moving into a cute little apartment in one of the city's historic old wooden houses. A pink one.

"Then you leave Monday. Is it settled? You'll work with me?" He looked pathetically eager.

"Leave? You didn't say anything about leaving."

"Well, I guess I forgot to mention it. You know I need you to set up the newest Bagel Barn. I've done all the groundwork. All that needs doing is to get the place started, hire a helper and run it all summer. That way you get a good idea about how a Bagel Barn works and know what the problems are. Nothing like hands-on training experience, I always say."

The man's rambling was exasperating to say the least. It was a constant challenge to hold him to the topic at hand.

"But Sidney, where? Where is this newest Bagel Barn?"

"Ketchikan, Alaska," he said.

Martha stared at him. The vision of her own apartment in one of San Francisco's historic wooden houses crumbled away, leaving her with the image of an igloo, which was not her idea of a habitable dwelling for a sophisticated, college-educated woman of twenty-seven.

"Alaska?" she said, unable to believe it.

"Alaska," he replied.

As far as Martha was concerned, he might as well have said, "The end of the world."

Chapter Two

Martha felt unexpected awe at the vastness of the Alaskan landscape as her plane, a regularly scheduled airliner, penetrated the shroud of fog overlying the city. To Martha, in the brief glimpse she caught of it as the plane bounced down on the runway, Ketchikan didn't look like much. Squat, square buildings, precariously perched on the rocky shore, seemed to lean off the edge of Revillagigedo Island into the water of the Tongass Narrows. Across the Narrows were the docks where she would begin setting up the newest Bagel Barn.

"Chistochina, Yakutat, Levelock, Nome," Martha chanted under her breath as the plane taxied toward the terminal. These were the names she'd read on a map of Alaska, and she liked the way they rolled off her tongue. She'd taken to reciting them over and over to herself on the flight from San Francisco in a kind of litany of reassurance.

She rode a ferry from the airport, which was located on a separate island, across the Narrows to the neighboring island whose name was conveniently shortened to "Revilla" by the locals. *If only Polly could see this country,* Martha thought wistfully as she took in the majestic mountains and the utter immensity of the land, but then she had second thoughts. Polly had clearly thought that Martha was crazy to be going.

"You can't be serious," Polly had said when Martha told her about Sidney's stunning offer.

"But I am serious," Martha had said calmly.

"Then *he* can't be serious. What on earth is in Ketchikan, Alaska, anyway?"

"The newest Bagel Barn. Sidney says that big cruise ships stop in Ketchikan all summer long. He says that it's a great place for a Bagel Barn. He says—"

"Please don't tell me anything else that Sidney says," groaned Polly. "Obviously the guy has quite a line of persuasion." She plumped up her pillow; she was propped up in bed.

Martha peered up at Polly from her perch on the floor, where she sat with her hands locked around her knees. "I believe in him, Polly," Martha said quietly. "He's making a success of his own original idea. He needs my help."

"But how are you going to handle selling bagels to tourists all summer? It's not something you've ever done before. Maybe you'll hate it. Do you realize that you've been chewing on the skin next to your thumbnail again? You know that's one habit of yours that drives me crazy."

Martha inspected her thumb; the skin beside the nail resembled shredded wheat. She always chewed on the skin beside her nails when she was nervous. She clamped her other fingers around the offending thumb so that Polly wouldn't have to look at it.

"Martha, are you sure you haven't bitten off more than you can chew?"

When Martha started to laugh, Polly colored and said, "I didn't mean that as a joke. It's just that I don't understand how you can give up the sybaritic pleasures of San Francisco for igloos, polar bears and who knows what else?"

"This is spring-going-on-summer. There aren't any igloos and polar bears in the southeastern Alaska panhandle, at least from what Sidney tells me. Sidney says—"

"No more 'Sidney says,'" warned Polly darkly.

"It won't snow in Ketchikan in the summer, and it's a tourist town. There's lots of rain, though. I need to take all the rain gear I can get my hands on. It rains an average of a hundred and sixty-two inches a year, can you believe it? Why, even Seattle only gets a dry thirty-nine inches."

"Ketchikan is a tourist town and it rains all the time. Lovely. Martha, are you sure you know what you're doing?" Polly's eyes, very serious now, searched her friend's face.

"Yes, Polly. After all, I'm a creature of impulse. Now are we going to go to sleep or are we going to stay up all night lamenting my decision to work for Sidney?''

"I guess we'd better get some sleep. My Mrs. Claussen is coming in first thing tomorrow morning.''

With that, Polly had subsided into a wide yawn and Martha had retreated to the guest room, but it wasn't as though she was sure that she'd done the right thing. All night her eyes kept flicking open; she'd look at the clock and think, *Ketchikan, Alaska?* before trying, mostly unsuccessfully, to go back to sleep.

But here she was on a ferry in Ketchikan, smoothing the wrinkles out of the full skirt of her rayon dress and swearing that she'd never buy anything made of rayon again. What made manufacturers of expensive ready-to-wear think that rayon was a suitable fabric for anything? When she'd been in the position of ordering clothes for the boutique, she'd refused to stock anything made of rayon or one of its blends. She'd only brought this particular dress because she was bringing every dress she owned to wear when she worked at the Bagel Barn. Dresses with a little red-checkered apron were the Sidney-approved uniform.

Martha was actually looking forward to running a Bagel Barn and the experience of living in what Alaskans jokingly referred to as their state's Banana Belt for four months. She never minded cool weather, and she found rainfall refreshing except for the fact that it made her hair curl too tightly. The scenery, what she had seen of it, was wonderful. She thought of visiting Alaska as an exciting adventure.

She was met at the ferry dock by the representative of the local rent-a-dent company, who handed her the keys to a cumbersome Lincoln that had seen better days. The man, whose name was Ernie Nogoluk, was friendly and helpful. He went out of his way to give her directions to the small apartment that Sidney had rented for her.

"It's not like you can get too lost," he said. "The road out of town doesn't go anywhere."

"I beg your pardon?" Martha said, impatiently brushing unwelcome curls off her forehead. She'd had her hair straightened only last month, and now look at it.

"What I mean," said Ernie Nogoluk, "is that the road isn't

connected with another road. It stops. The only way into Ketchikan is by air or sea.''

"I remember reading that," said Martha. A light rain began to fall; car headlights crisscrossed through the fog.

"I hope you enjoy your stay in Ketchikan," he said.

"I'm sure I will," Martha replied before driving away in the rain. As she fumbled with the unfamiliar windshield-wiper switch, she thought to herself, *I'd better enjoy Ketchikan. It's not as though I can just drive away from it.* It was a strange feeling, knowing that her movements were limited to a stretch of road along the coast of Revillagigedo Island, and that road no more than thirty-five miles long. Despite her underlying sense of excitement, she didn't remember ever feeling more alone in her life.

She drove slowly through streets slick with rain, peering with interest at the neat boxy buildings and the flower-festooned lampposts that added a welcome bit of color to the wet and gloomy landscape. She found the duplex apartment without any trouble. It was located in a green shingled house not far from a park; the house was built on stilts.

"Probably so it won't flood," Martha muttered to herself as she wrestled her two big suitcases up the open wooden stairs in the rain.

Inside, the apartment had one bedroom, a neat efficiency kitchen with all the necessary equipment and a combination living-and-dining room. The big picture window overlooked a park with tall Sitka spruce trees and winding foot trails, and brightly colored tulips graced the front yard. Martha immediately turned on the heat in hopes of dispelling the chill in the air. She wondered who lived in the other apartment of the duplex. She certainly hoped it was someone pleasant. Newly aware of her aloneness in this strange place, she thought she'd like to meet people who might become friends.

After Martha unpacked, she put on an old pair of flannel pajamas and fell into the comfortable double bed. The apartment hadn't warmed up much, and there was nothing to eat until she could go shopping in the morning. Her supper consisted of two chocolate-chip cookies. Martha munched them with the damp bed covers pulled up to her chin for warmth. The cookies reminded her of home.

"I'm a creature of impulse," she reminded herself just before she fell asleep, and she barely had enough time to wonder just what her impulsiveness had gotten her into now.

PUTTING UP a Bagel Barn on the Front Street dock in a drizzle was definitely not one of her talents, Martha decided the next day as she struggled with the sides and roof of the thing. It was a bleary rain that blurred the outlines of the mountains in the distance and even the stores across the street. Martha blamed herself for believing Sidney when he told her that erecting a Bagel Barn would be easy.

"The bolts are already in place; a smart, resourceful girl— uh, woman—like you should have absolutely no trouble," Sidney had said when he'd showed her how to do it. Never mind that showing her how had taken place in his garage in Berkeley with his two oldest children helping. He had assured her that the Bagel Barns were designed for a woman to put together all by herself.

Clearly Sidney—or, for that matter, Martha herself—hadn't anticipated that in Ketchikan Martha's fingers would be numb with cold, that her hair would keep escaping from the hood of her rain poncho or that more than one bolt would be missing from the standard Bagel Barn assembly kit. What should have taken her two hours had now taken more than four, and there was no end in sight. She didn't know what she would do when it came time to bolt on the roof.

She would have quit midway through the task except that she wanted the Bagel Barn to be open tomorrow when the *Trondheim*, the biggest cruise ship to call at the Ketchikan port, would anchor in the harbor.

"Looks like you need some help," remarked a boy who had been watching her from a dry spot beneath the overhang at the nearby Chamber of Commerce information booth.

"Either that or I'd better wait until it stops raining to finish this job," huffed Martha, peering at him through the mizzling rain from behind a sodden lock of hair. He was a short teenager with dark, slanted eyes, an olive complexion and a wide smile.

The boy laughed. "If you wait for it to stop raining, you may never finish the job," he said. "Let me see what I can do."

With that he stepped into the rain, bent over, made an expert adjustment to the bolt with which Martha had been struggling for the last ten minutes and thus closed the gap between the recalcitrant side and front walls of the Bagel Barn.

"How would you like a job helping me put up the rest of the booth?" Martha asked in desperation.

His smile widened even more. "That would be great."

"I'll pay you," she said.

"You wouldn't have to." The boy shifted back and forth on his feet.

"Twenty dollars if you'll help me put the roof on," she offered.

"It's a deal, lady."

"My name's Martha. And yours is—?"

"Randy. Randy Gallahorn."

"Okay, Randy. I'll stand on the ladder and you can hand the roof pieces up to me. Then, when I have it balanced, you can bolt the roof to the sides."

They proceeded, and the teenager's efficiency almost halved the time needed to bolt the lightweight barn-shaped roof in place. Martha paid Randy his twenty dollars, and as she plugged the small refrigerator and toaster oven into the electrical outlet provided by the city, Randy lingered. He looked reluctant to leave, standing quietly with his shoulders hunched against the light drizzle and watching her as she worked.

"There," she said with satisfaction. "All finished and ready to lock up. I'll open the Bagel Barn tomorrow."

"Are you going to need any more help? I mean I've been looking for a job, and if you could use me—" His eyes petitioned her hopefully.

"Why," Martha said, "I *will* need some help once I get things going. I'll need someone to work here with me when there are a lot of customers, and I'll need someone to take over for me when I can't be here. Have you ever worked in a restaurant?"

"I'm afraid not," Randy said.

That shouldn't be a strike against him. Neither had she. "Well, this isn't exactly like a restaurant," she told him. "I suppose you know how to toast a bagel."

"A bagel? What is it?"

Martha blinked. "You've never eaten a bagel?" She, who had grown up eating bagels at home, bagels with cream cheese, bagels layered with lox and capers and onions, bagels with peanut butter, bagels slathered with butter and honey, could not imagine this. Still, the boy looked like an Alaskan Native, probably Tlingit Indian. A large community of Tlingits lived here, Sidney had told her.

Randy shook his head sheepishly. "I'm not even sure what a bagel is," he said.

"In that case, let me fix you one." Martha reached into a plastic bag, popped a bagel into her toaster oven and tore open a package of cream cheese from the refrigerator. "Would you like lox on it?"

"Lox?" He looked confused.

"It's fish. Salmon."

"Oh, I've had salmon before. I've had lots of salmon," he said. "This town started out as a fishing village, you know, and it still is. We call Ketchikan the Salmon Capital of the World. Sure, I'll try it."

Martha expertly assembled the bagel.

"You mean you brought your own salmon?" he asked as Martha layered on the lox.

"Sure," she said. "My boss orders it."

Randy looked doubtful, but he took the bagel anyway. Martha waited for Randy's assessment.

"Well, what do you think?" she said after he'd tucked away a few bites.

"I think bagels are going to be a big hit," he said with either enthusiasm or gratitude; she wasn't sure which.

Randy had said exactly what Martha wanted to hear. It occurred to Martha at this point that the boy might be really hungry. He'd said he needed a job. She required a helper, and he'd already proved himself to be efficient as well as helpful. His small size meant that he'd fit into the limited working space. She could do a lot worse than to hire Randy Gallahorn, she decided.

She fixed him another bagel. "Come back tomorrow at nine in the morning if you really want a job," she told him as he wolfed it down. "You and I can learn how to run a Bagel Barn together."

"Yes, *ma'am*," Randy said enthusiastically. He grinned at her for a moment before loping away, and she noticed a spring in his step that hadn't been there before.

It wasn't until later that she thought about Sidney's requirements that people buy bagels from pretty women at his Bagel Barns.

"Rubbish," she mumbled to herself as she closed and locked the Bagel Barn and stood back to admire the way it looked on the dock of Ketchikan. It was a bit incongruous, a little red barn standing against the background of the boats in the harbor and the cloud-covered mountains beyond, but she was proud of it. She was looking forward to working there. Sidney and his silly ideas were the farthest thing from her mind.

THE MAN WAS WATCHING HER the next day when the tourists came charging off the tender from the cruise ship *Trondheim*, which was anchored out in the harbor. He was a tall man, with cheekbones like ridges and a jaw like a rock. With his weathered face and bronze-brown hair hanging slightly over his shirt collar in back, he was attractive in a rugged sort of way. In fact, he was downright handsome. He radiated an aura of raw sexuality that made Martha do a quick double take.

He leaned casually against a flower-bedecked lamppost as he sipped from a Styrofoam cup, and Martha thought to herself, *He's just the kind of man I expected to find in Alaska.* According to Polly's information, there were ten men for every woman in this state. Did that mean that she could look forward to meeting nine more guys just like him? A shiver of anticipation ran through her at the thought.

But then Martha became busy heating water for tea for the tourists, fretting over cream cheese that was a bit too hard to spread well and worrying that she might not have enough change. She sent Randy to the bank for some rolls of dimes and quarters and started toasting bagels.

The next time she looked, the lamppost was managing to hold itself up without the support of the man who had been there, and he was nowhere in sight. Martha sighed, but brightened quickly when she remembered that there would be nine more men just like him. That was something to look forward to indeed.

Her first customers, a couple with a teenage daughter, were something of an event. Martha saw them hurrying up the ramp, and she knew they'd stop. They looked hungry.

"Hey, look, Duffy, let's get a bagel."

"Good idea, Stace. There wasn't much time for breakfast. Monica, how do you want yours?" The man, who was wearing a Stetson hat, smiled down at his wife, with whom he held hands.

The daughter stepped up to the Bagel Barn. "I'll have mine with cream cheese and lox, please. And some apple juice."

"We'll have two with just cream cheese, and one spiced tea and one peppermint tea," the man said.

As she spread the cream cheese, Martha listened to them chatter about the cruise and the whales the passengers had seen during the ship's voyage along the scenic Inside Passage from British Columbia. They were clearly enjoying their trip and everything about it.

"Are there really whales?" Martha asked skeptically before counting out the man's change. Sidney hadn't mentioned whales.

"Oh, lots," replied the daughter. "You mean you've never seen any?"

"No, I just got to Ketchikan yesterday. In fact, you're the Bagel Barn's first customers. I've given you a ten-percent discount in honor of that."

"Why, thanks," said the man with a grin.

"I hope you see lots of whales," said the daughter before flashing Martha a bright smile. It was then that Martha recognized her as a young amateur skater whom she'd often seen competing on television.

"And I hope you have a wonderful cruise," Martha replied before turning to greet her next customer.

After that Martha stayed busy. Many of the cruise-ship passengers had slept too late for breakfast, and evidently there'd been a long wait in the ship's salon as they'd queued up for tickets to get on the tender. They were hungry and they were thirsty. Sidney had been right; this was a wonderful place for a Bagel Barn.

There wasn't a lull until eleven o'clock, when the cruise-ship passengers thinned out, but by that time a smattering of shop-owners from nearby businesses catering to the tourist trade wandered over for a coffee break. The sky was overcast, but it wasn't raining, and benches scattered here and there among tubs of bright petunias provided a pleasant place to sit and watch the boats moving in and out of the harbor.

Then the lunch business started, and many of the customers were curious townspeople who had watched the Bagel Barn go up the day before in the pouring rain as they walked or drove past.

"I said to myself, there's a lady who must be an Alaskan. You didn't even let the rain stop you," said an elderly, bearded man who stopped to buy a cup of tea.

"I had to open today," said Martha with a laugh. "I promised my boss. Anyway, they tell me it doesn't often stop raining."

"It only rains twice a year in Ketchikan. January through June, and July through December." He laughed uproariously at what Martha suspected was one of the more hackneyed local jokes.

Martha sent Randy home at three when business tapered off because the ship was about to pull anchor and sail. She would have closed up, but she wanted to clean off the counter and rearrange her supplies. She had been so busy all day that she'd tossed empty wrappers around and dropped crumbs on the counter.

She was planning to bring her portable tape player to play soothing music tomorrow when the man she had noticed leaning against the lamppost earlier strolled up.

"Are you closed?" he asked.

Martha wheeled around in the enclosed place and, unused to it, knocked her head on a wooden support at the top.

"Oh, I'm sorry if I startled you," he said as a whole galaxy of stars and planets whirled and clashed inside Martha's head. When the star wars quieted, she opened her eyes to look into a pair of the brownest eyes she'd ever seen. Even if the Bagel Barn had been closed, she wouldn't have told this man so. Looking at him up close was definitely a thrill at first sight, and then and there she dismissed from her mind the other nine Alaskan men who should rightfully be hers.

"N-no," she stammered. "I haven't closed yet. What would you like?"

"What have you got?" he asked, looking over as much of her as he could see. The counter at the front of the booth came to above her waist, and she wore the perky red checkered apron that Sidney had insisted upon and in which she felt less than radiantly chic.

"I have bagels," she said, and she reeled off the different kinds. She also told him what kind of drinks they had, and he ordered a bagel with cream cheese and lox and a Classic Coca-Cola. This was a good sign. Martha had long ago decided that her lips would never touch those of any man who drank new-formula Coke. Or who smoked. A quick glance told her that there was no telltale rectangle of a cigarette package in his chest pocket. Two points in his favor. But did he like chocolate-chip cookies?

While she was preparing his bagel, she felt as though she had six thumbs on each hand. Furthermore, the man didn't go and sit on one of the nearby benches but leaned on the counter, his flannel-clad elbow blocking her access to the toaster oven. She had to ask him to remove it, which made him raise his eyebrows and step backward to give her more room, but he still didn't sit on the bench.

She handed him his bagel and his drink, and he *still* didn't go sit on a bench. He didn't say anything, either, and Martha felt awkward. He was so close she felt as though she ought to talk with him, and yet he didn't look as though he cared if she talked to him or not. So Martha merely pretended to go on cleaning the ledge where the toaster oven rested, even though she'd cleaned it once before.

She watched from underneath her lashes as he ate the last of the bagel and wiped his hands with a napkin.

"Pretty good," he allowed.

"I'm glad you liked it," she said uncertainly. She was ready to pull in the top half of the simulated barn door that comprised the front wall of the booth, but he was in the way, his elbow resting on the counter again.

"Only one way it could be better," he told her.

"How?" she asked.

"You should be using Alaskan fish instead of what you're selling."

"It's the very best lox," she said, a bit too defensively. "My boss orders it from Los Angeles."

"Yeah, I know, I know. But it's not really salmon. It comes from the Atlantic Ocean near Nova Scotia or Newfoundland, and biologically it's trout, like all its Atlantic relatives known as salmon. Real salmon comes from the Pacific."

"Oh," Martha said, surprised. She had never been big on biology. She didn't see what difference it made whether she served salmon or trout as long as it tasted good.

"You're catering to tourists here, right?"

She nodded, captivated by the gleam in his brown eyes. They weren't only brown; closer inspection revealed them to be swimming with little golden flecks.

"And do you know what tourists order in Alaska? Salmon. They take it home in cans. They order smoked salmon to be sent back to them in the Lower Forty-eight. They even pay hundreds of dollars to charter planes and boats and guides so they can fish Alaskan streams to catch Alaskan salmon. And you're selling lox from Los Angeles. That's a shame."

Martha considered this. The man had a good point. However, Sidney ordered the lox; she was too new at her job to know if she would be allowed to stock Alaskan salmon.

"We have smoked salmon that would taste great on your bagels. It's smoked with alder wood. You can't beat the flavor."

"I'm sure it's very good. It's just that I have my orders as to what I should sell here, and I can't take matters into my own hands yet. Maybe later. Where would I buy this salmon?"

"Oh, there's a little shop down the street. Just go in and they'll show you what they have."

She flashed him a smile. "I'll do that—someday."

"Someday," he agreed, and with one last grin he hurried off along the boardwalk toward the docks.

He was an attractive man, and she wished she'd made some kind of impression on him. She didn't think she had, however. He'd obviously been more interested in talking her into using Alaskan salmon on her bagels than in anything about her. Perhaps he was one of the local fishermen; he looked rugged and individualistic, the way Martha imagined a fisherman should look. He was only trying to drum up some business, and she couldn't blame him. She'd probably have done the same thing herself.

Martha slowly made her way to the car, stepping over lots of puddles. By the time she got back to her apartment, she had conjured up a scenario where he came back to buy a bagel the next day and the next and then they cruised off together into the sunset in his boat as she gazed into his brown eyes.

Which was utterly ridiculous, and she knew it. He was probably only being polite when he said he liked the bagel. And if he was gazing into her eyes as he piloted the boat, they'd capsize or worse.

The trouble was that on her second day here, Martha was very lonely. She'd never been in a town where she didn't know one single person. She'd never had to start from scratch in building a social life. Come to think of it, she wondered if there was any social life around here.

That was something she'd find out tomorrow. There had to be something to do besides stand around in the rain and wish that weathered, rugged-looking men would carry her off into the sunset.

Anyway, he probably hated chocolate-chip cookies.

Chapter Three

Not long after he said goodbye to Martha at the dock, Nick Novak stomped the mud off his feet on the wide wooden porch of his snug cabin on Mooseleg Bay outside the town of Ketchikan.

The cabin was called Williwaw Lodge; his father's fishing boat had been driven ashore at this point on the ragged coastline of the bay during a furious williwaw, the name Alaskans gave to the often violent winds that roared over steep mountains, striking the water close by the shore. When the storm cleared to reveal a far-flung landscape of exaggerated grandeur, Nick's father knew that this horseshoe-shaped cove was the place where he wanted to raise his family. The Novaks became homesteaders. Nick had lived here all of his thirty-two years.

"Nick! Nick!" called a small voice, and a dark-haired boy catapulted around the woodpile stacked at the side of the house and latched on to one of Nick's legs.

"Hold it, hold it," he said, but then he swung the boy up and around, hoping that he would laugh. The boy never laughed.

"How are you, Davey?" he said, smoothing the boy's hair tenderly.

"Okay," said Davey.

"What does Hallie plan to feed us for dinner?"

Davey buried his face in Nick's neck.

Nick patted Davey on the back and strode, still carrying him, through the door into the house. The screen door slammed behind them.

"Hallie?"

"I'm back here," called his housekeeper. Nick saw her chunky figure through the kitchen window. She was bending over to pick strawberries.

Nick shifted Davey to his free arm and lifted the lid of the iron pot on the stove. Inside was fish stew, Hallie's own special concoction of fish and tomatoes, onions and peppers, and it smelled good.

Hallie huffed and puffed her heavy frame up the back steps. She carried a basket she had woven herself from marsh grass and seal gut, and it was filled with plump, juicy strawberries.

"I'm going to whip up a cobbler for dessert," she said breathlessly. "Davey helped me pick some of these, didn't you, Davey?"

Davey's eyes lit up with pride, but still he didn't speak.

"That's wonderful, Davey," Nick said.

"It'll be an hour or so before dinner's ready," Hallie said. "There's plenty of time for you and Davey to do something together if you like." She had recovered from her exertion on the stairs, and began to hull strawberries over the sink. *Poor Hallie,* thought Nick. It was a lot to ask of her to keep up with a lively little boy every day.

Nick knew it was hard for Hallie, sociable soul that she was, to live here with Davey day in and day out when Davey hardly ever spoke a word. Hallie would prefer to live closer to her fellow Tlingits in the town of Ketchikan, which is what she had been planning to do three years ago when he'd suddenly, with no prior warning whatsoever, brought Davey home to stay.

"I see I can't leave you with an infant on your hands," Hallie had said on that long-ago day.

"If you could just stay until I get someone else," Nick suggested, not knowing at the time how hard it would be to find another housekeeper who was willing to live in the wilderness on the edge of the bay. Now, three years later, Hallie still lived here, and she was tired of the rigors of the Alaskan bush.

These days it seemed less likely than ever that Hallie would feel free to leave anytime soon. Of course, there was nothing holding her here—Nick had made it clear that if she absolutely wanted to, he would not make it difficult for her to go. No, there was nothing holding Hallie—nothing except a sweet little boy who hardly ever talked.

Nick carried Davey out to the wide, grassy front slope that led down to the dock where both his boat and his floatplane were moored. Davey ran to get a rubber ball, and they tossed it back and forth; Nick's quick eye discerned that Davey's motor development was equal to that of any of the children his age whom Nick had observed playing in the park at Ketchikan. Davey would be four years old tomorrow, and there seemed to be nothing wrong with him physically. He was just slow in learning to talk, that was all.

Later, after dinner and after he had tucked Davey into the bottom bunk bed in the boy's room, Nick and Hallie sat out on the front porch, fighting the monster mosquitoes that stormed out of the woods on summer nights. Nick sat on a wide wooden settee with cushions covered in wool plaid, and Hallie rocked in a capacious rocking chair. Hallie burned an odoriferous bug bomb that held the insects at bay for a while, and even though Nick would have rather been inside reading a good book, he didn't excuse himself. Hallie had so few people to talk to.

"I spoke with Cheryl on the shortwave radio today," Hallie said. "She's baking the cake for Davey's birthday celebration tomorrow evening."

"Chocolate, I hope," Nick said with a chuckle. Davey loved chocolate, and Cheryl, who was Nick's sister-in-law, baked the best chocolate cakes Nick had ever tasted.

"Of course it'll be chocolate. I'm going to fry a few chickens and mash some potatoes for dinner, and Davey and the other kids can drop clothespins in bottles and pop balloons after we eat."

"Are the adults expected to join in?"

Hallie laughed. "I guess it depends on how good you are at dropping clothespins into bottles."

"Not too good, as I recall. I only went to one birthday party during my childhood because we always lived way out here."

Hallie's smile faded. "That's too bad. A kid should live near other kids, I've always thought."

"I had other kids. My brothers Dan and Fred. And my friend Hank." Hank had grown up on the bay with the three Novak boys; his family had homesteaded a parcel of land on the other side.

"Davey has no one. Maybe you should think about moving

into town. Davey might talk more if he had children his own age to play with."

Nick's father had fished Alaskan waters all his adult life from this homestead on the bay. Nick couldn't imagine living in town after all these years. He said, "Mmm. I've been thinking about it. I can't picture leaving the old home place, though."

"For Davey's sake you could leave," Hallie pointed out.

"It depends on how well the store does this summer," Nick hedged.

"How's business so far?" Hallie wanted to know.

"It's off and running. These tourists can't get enough Alaskan salmon. I'm glad now that I opened the store, and I wonder why I waited so long."

"Are you going to close it this winter?"

"I haven't decided. There won't be so many tourists then, but maybe we'll do a brisk local business."

"I doubt it. So many of the locals catch their own fish or know somebody who does. They won't want to buy smoked fish out of a store when they can get free fish and smoke it themselves."

Nick sighed. "That's true." He wondered idly about the Cheechako woman he'd met today at the new Bagel Barn down by the dock. Surely she wasn't planning on keeping that little snack shack open in the winter. He wished he'd been able to talk her into serving Alaskan salmon on her bagels. She might want to try sablefish, too. He'd mention it to her next time he saw her.

"I heard there's a new snack place in town," said Hallie as though she could read his mind.

"Yeah, I know. I ate there today."

"What do they sell? Wanda told me it was some kind of doughnut." Wanda was Hallie's sister; they talked every day on the shortwave radio, which was the only way to communicate from Nick's cabin with anyone in town.

"It's not doughnuts. It's bagels."

"I've never had a bagel."

"I'll bring you one sometime."

"Maybe I'll stop by there next time I go to town. Wanda says the lady who runs the bagel place is real pretty. Maybe she'd make you a good wife. If you had a wife, I could go live in town with Wanda and her grandkids.''

Nick shifted uncomfortably on the settee. "You can go live with Wanda anytime you really want to," he said.

"Hummph. I won't really want to as long as Davey needs me. You know that, Nick.''

"Yeah. I know that." Suddenly Nick stood up. "I can't handle the mosquitoes any longer," he said. "I think I'll turn in." He wheeled and walked abruptly inside.

"Good night," Hallie called after him, but he didn't reply. Well, Nick was always a little moody. Like Hallie said, Nick needed a wife.

Hallie lingered for a while on the front porch, creaking back and forth placidly in her rocking chair and staring out over the slick black water of Mooseleg Bay. Out on the bay, rearranging the reflected patterns of stars on the surface of the black water, she saw a slow-moving troller. She heard the engine juddering along toward the other shore and wondered who it was. It was a lonely job, fishing. She was glad Nick didn't fish anymore. He had plenty to do with running Novak and Sons Cold Storage and Cannery and now the new store selling fish to tourists.

Of course, Nick had been a highliner, as the best fishermen were called, for a long time, and he was still in partnership with his brothers Dan and Fred, who were the ones who oversaw the Novak and Sons fishing-boat operation now. But Nick seldom went out on the boats these days because Davey needed him at home.

Hallie wished she knew the full story about where Davey came from and whose child he really was. Even with all the gossip passed on by her sister Wanda, Hallie had never cleared up the mysterious circumstances surrounding Davey's arrival in Nick Novak's home. First it had been just Hallie and Nick in the cabin after Nick's father, old man Novak, died. And then Hallie had decided to move to town to live with her sister Wanda, who was raising five grandchildren and needed Hallie's help. But one day shortly thereafter Nick had shown up with Davey. The fat baby boy's black button eyes had peered fearfully at Hallie from amid the folds of the fluffy white blanket, and Nick had curtly announced that Davey was henceforth going to live with him.

No one knew how or why the baby came to live with Nick, even though the rumors around Ketchikan had flown fast as fur in a cat fight. Pretty soon the gossip had died down to a speculative glance at Nick now and then, usually whenever someone would forget and say, "I wonder why that handsome Nick Novak has never married." Then someone else would reply in a hushed tone, "Well, he has that little boy, and there's something not quite right about the kid."

Hallie had learned to field questions about Nick or Davey with no more than a shrug and a smile, as if to say that the peculiarities of the situation were beyond her. But still, Hallie wondered, too. As far as she knew, Nick had never explained anything about the boy to anyone. If he had, the story would have been all over town. Ketchikan, with its fourteen thousand people, was like a small town anyplace. Everyone knew everyone else's personal business.

Except for Nick Novak's personal business, that is.

Hallie slapped at a mosquito and extinguished the bug bomb. Time to go in and get to bed. Nick and Davey rose early in the morning, and thus so did she.

The door to Nick's room was closed, and no light shone from under it. Once again Hallie wondered, *Isn't he lonely?*

But it was something she'd wondered many times before, and so she didn't spend a lot of time on the thought now. She figured if Nick Novak was lonely, he knew what to do. And for all she knew, maybe he did.

NICK ALWAYS ATE a big breakfast, and ordinary breakfast food annoyed him.

"Give me a steak in the morning," he always said. "Don't give me anything sugary. And for heaven's sake, no waffles." In Nick Novak's opinion, waffles were for namby-pambies.

Part of it was that Nick had grown up hauling nets and rigging outriggers, which was what he was supposed to do as the son of a fisherman. It was cold, damp work that could sap a man's energy; therefore it was best that energy be at a high level when a man left the house in the morning. Survival on the treacherous sea wasn't easy. You never knew when you'd be swept overboard into waters too cold for survival. If that happened, you'd need to draw on all the remaining strength in your body just to stay alive.

So Hallie understood about breakfast. She cheerfully prepared steaks and salmon and hearty stews, all of which Nick ate in the morning. She drew the line at feeding Davey the same diet, however.

"A kid should have oatmeal," she told Nick. "A kid should know what Cream of Wheat tastes like. And Davey likes scrambled eggs."

"But no waffles," said Nick. He didn't know where he'd acquired this prejudice; he just had it.

"No waffles," Hallie had agreed.

And so this morning, after all the "happy birthdays" had been said to a solemn and unresponsive Davey, Nick and Davey sat down to eat, and Nick ate salmon steaks and Davey ate oatmeal.

Nick paused in the act of lifting a forkful of salmon to his mouth when he noticed that Davey was pointing at it.

"Yes?" he encouraged Davey.

Davey just pointed.

Nick knew that Davey knew what the morsel on his fork was; they ate a lot of salmon in this house. He hoped that Davey would say the word. But Davey's vocabulary seemed sadly limited to Nick's name, Hallie's name and "okay." It was fortunate, as Hallie pointed out, that Davey's only word other than their names was "okay." It could so easily have been "no," which would have made things a lot harder on all of them.

"This is salmon, Davey," Nick said. "Would you like some?"

Davey nodded.

With a clatter, Hallie slid a plate across the table and Nick transferred a good-sized piece of salmon to it before setting the plate in front of Davey.

"There," Nick said. "That looks good. Go ahead and eat it, Davey."

Davey's eyes lit up, and he dug into the salmon. It was alder-smoked; Nick hadn't brought it from the big smokers at Novak and Sons but had smoked it himself with alder wood cut from the trees in the forest surrounding the cabin, the way his father had taught him.

Suddenly Nick thought of something.

"Hallie, will you please put some of that salmon in a plastic bag?"

"Sure," Hallie said as she complied. This was nothing new. Nick often took a bit of breakfast along and ate it at his office in the cannery when he thought he might not have time for a lunch break.

Nick stood up and dropped a kiss on top of Davey's shiny black hair. "I'll see you tonight," he told him. "Make sure you save room for plenty of that chocolate birthday cake." He looked at Hallie standing behind the boy. She, with her Tlingit features, might have been the boy's grandmother, they looked so much alike. But, of course, Hallie was not related to Davey in any way.

"Bye, Davey," Nick said, waiting as he always did for the boy to answer. As usual, the boy said nothing, merely staring up at him with huge dark eyes—eyes to break your heart.

Down at the dock, Nick cast a practiced glance at the gray clouds dragging their petticoats on the mountaintops before he donned his yellow slicker, and then he cast his father's old troller, the *Tabor*, off from the dock. The only way into Ketchikan from Mooseleg Bay was by water or air. Like one out of six Alaskans, Nick was a licensed pilot and owned a floatplane, but when he wasn't in a hurry he preferred the water to the air.

Still a fisherman at heart, Nick had never been able to bring himself to sell his father's old boat; it was reliable transportation from the cabin on Mooseleg Bay to the Ketchikan dock and back. Nick felt at home at the helm, probably because he had grown up there. Nick had always been able to reach a certain clarity of thought on the water; the motion of rolling waves had a soothing effect. There was nothing to interrupt his train of thought when he was in his captain's chair except the sight of other boats far away in the mist and the forlorn piping of gulls overhead. Nick thought about Davey this morning as he rested his big hands on the ship's wheel.

For a long time it had been easy to fool himself into believing that everything was going to be all right with Davey, but he was unable to tell himself that anymore. This birthday was a milestone in that regard. A four-year-old should be jabbering away, laughing, teasing, telling jokes. Davey did none of that.

Nick was sure that Davey was a bright child. Intelligence fairly shone from the boy's dark eyes. Also, it was obvious that Davey heard everything that he and Hallie said to him, so it couldn't be a hearing problem. Furthermore, the words that Davey did use were always clear and well articulated; Davey's failure to talk wasn't a speech problem. And Hallie was wonderful with him; she talked to him a lot, since she was a talkative person anyway.

"So what is it?" he whispered softly to himself as he drew the boat alongside the dock. "Why wouldn't a smart kid like Davey talk like other kids?"

Take those three kids up on the dock, the two boys and a girl clustered around the new Bagel Barn. They looked as though they belonged to a harried young couple who were evidently tourists out for an early-morning walk. They must have stopped to buy breakfast on the run.

Anyway, the kids were pushing and shoving, complaining about one another and petitioning their parents most volubly for the kind of bagels they wanted. None of them was over, say, the age of six.

Then Nick remembered the smoked salmon he had shoved deep down in the pocket of his slicker. He pulled it out and, still wearing the yellow rain slicker, stopped at the Bagel Barn just as the noisy family was settling themselves on a nearby bench.

"Hi," he said to Martha.

Her eyes opened wide as she recognized him. Her lips curved into a smile and her eyes crinkled at the outer edges. It was amazing how her smile brightened those eyes, and he was surprisingly gratified to think that he was the one who had sparked such an enthusiastic response from her.

"Well, hello," she said cheerfully.

"I brought you some alder-smoked salmon. Why don't you try it on a bagel?"

She grinned. "How'd you know I never got down to that store you recommended?"

"I figured that 'someday' hadn't arrived yet. I also figured that you're going to love the taste of this salmon." His eyes teased hers; they held a challenge that might mean he wanted her to try more than smoked Alaskan salmon.

Martha's mind raced. Here he was again, and he had sought her out on purpose, and she had no idea how to keep him here. She didn't even know his name.

"If you decide you want some more of this salmon for your customers, here's my card. You could call me." He handed her a white rectangle, and Martha glanced down at it. Her lashes were long and dark; they lay smoothly against her cheek like tiny feathers.

"Nick Novak," she read out loud. "Novak and Sons." To Martha, this encounter seemed like an opportunity sent from heaven. She lifted her head and held out her hand. "I'm Martha Rose," she said. His hand was big and warm, and his touch raised the hairs on her arm, surprising her so much that she withdrew her hand from his a microsecond too rapidly for good manners.

Confused by the way she snatched her fingers from his, Nick swallowed so that the muscular contour of his throat moved in a most mesmerizing way. She stared at his throat, fascinated. He thought she was being brashly forward staring at him like that, and suddenly he noticed the slim-skirted linen dress she wore underneath the silly red checkered apron. This woman wore high heels and gold bracelets that jingled, and the heady scent of her expensive perfume filled his head. On the dock in Ketchikan, she looked exotic and out of place. For all he knew, she might be laughing at him and his fellow townspeople for their simple rustic ways.

"Let me know how you like the salmon," he blurted, all his confidence evaporating in the face of Martha's glossy sophistication. And then he was gone, striding off along the dock with his yellow slicker flying behind him in the wind off Tongass Narrows.

The hair on her arms settled down, and so did Martha's heartbeat. "Nick Novak," Martha mumbled. "His name's Nick Novak." She was completely unaware that her sophistication intimidated him, and she wished he hadn't left so abruptly.

"I beg your pardon?" said Randy.

"Oh, nothing," was Martha's quick reply, and then she laughed. Here she was practically drooling over a man and she had no one to tell about him. She felt a pang of homesickness for Polly and decided to phone her soon. What good was it to meet Mr. Wonderful Plus—and to have no one to tell?

Today cruise ships clustered in the harbor to disgorge more than their usual number of passengers, and Martha was busy serving her customers until after noon.

"Well, Randy," she said finally, prepared to take a breather when the line of customers had dwindled, "I think I'll eat lunch."

"Here's a bagel," he said. Randy was in charge of toasting bagels this morning; Martha was in charge of toppings.

She spread her toasted bagel with cream cheese and realized that she had never tried Nick's salmon. She found the little plastic bag where she had put it in the refrigerator and arranged the salmon on top of the cream cheese.

"I'm going for a stroll, Randy," she told her helper. "You can take your lunch break when I come back."

It felt good to get away from the confinement of the Bagel Barn. Tourists chattered as they left the Chamber of Commerce information booth; a group of beautiful dark-eyed Tlingit girls giggled as they thumbed through a teenage magazine.

Martha, bagel in hand, sauntered down the wooden boardwalk along the waterfront. Boats, both for business and pleasure, bobbed at their moorings on the dock, and although a stiff breeze blew in from the Narrows, the clouds overhead shone with the pearly light of the sun behind them.

Martha sat down on a bench and watched a man with a ladder carefully climb it to water the hanging flower baskets on each lamppost. Watering the plants was an awkward task because the man had to carry a large watering can up the ladder.

Nick saw her gawking openmouthed at the man on the ladder and paused to smile. She still wore the linen dress; it was a pale pink that brought out the translucence of her skin. From the way she was gawking, he'd never have guessed that she was the same self-possessed woman he'd talked with this morning. Suddenly he considered the possibility that her sophistication was just an act. Surprising himself, he sauntered over to her.

"He's pretty good at that balancing act of his, isn't he?" said a familiar voice over her shoulder, and Martha looked up into Nick Novak's gorgeous face.

"I was just about to try your salmon," she said, self-consciously waving her bagel in the air.

"Go ahead," he said. He came around the bench, propped one boot up on the seat beside her and leaned forward expectantly. With him looking down at her in that appealing way, Martha doubted that she would be able to swallow. It was all she could do not to emit a deep sigh of pleasure.

"Well?" he prompted. Now *she* was the one who appeared uncomfortable in *his* presence. He wondered why. He decided to stick around to see what happened.

She took a breath, took a bite and tried to concentrate on the taste for Nick's sake. The salmon had a distinct flavor, smoky but not too smoky. Salty but not too salty. She chewed thoughtfully, fully aware that Nick Novak was assessing her. She wondered how she looked when she chewed. She felt a wave of gratitude to her mother, who had insisted long ago that Martha learn to chew with her mouth closed. If she hadn't she'd have looked like a cement mixer, and no doubt Nick Novak would take off at a run. As it was, it looked as though he meant to stay right where he was, a fact for which Martha was supremely thankful.

Martha swallowed. "It's mild and moist," she told him. "And the flavor is superb."

"You see? I told you."

"How do you get that distinctive flavor?" She hoped that the smoking of the salmon was a long and involved process and that Nick would tell her every detail, bar none.

"First I go out into the woods and I find an alder tree," began Nick, but then she was concentrating on his hands, which were big enough to hold a couple of split bagels each, and his chin, which had an interesting scar on the right side, and his eyes, which were the most interesting thing about his whole face. His face looked like a face chiseled from Mount Rushmore and scaled to human size, and naturally it had a liveliness that a face of stone wouldn't have.

There was more of him that she found interesting, but he finished telling her about smoking salmon before she could concentrate on each individual feature in rapt appreciation. She hadn't, for instance, had time to spend marveling at his broad shoulders or his ears, which weren't from Mount Rushmore at all. They reminded her more of the ears on one of the Seven Dwarfs at Disneyland. The cute one, Dopey.

But there wasn't anything dopey about Nick. He exhibited a keen intelligence that Martha wanted to explore. How to explore it, though?

She wanted to keep his interest as long as possible. Long enough to impress him in some way. Long enough to become his friend. She did miss all her friends, though there had been no one like Nick in Kokomo.

"We sure didn't have anything like him in Kokomo," she whispered, half to herself, missing Polly and Sigmund's instant laughter.

"In Kokomo? Is that your home?"

"Why don't you sit down?" she suggested suddenly.

He hesitated a moment, and Martha thought, *Maybe he doesn't want to spend time with me,* but then Nick sat, stretched his boots out in front of him and lifted his face into a ray of sun that had managed to penetrate the clouds.

And so then she told him about managing the boutique in Kokomo, and how she had moved to San Francisco on an impulse, and how she had ended up in Alaska on another impulse.

Nick smiled at her. Now that he knew she had worked at one of those trendy little boutiques, he understood the shimmery eye shadow, the well-cut linen dress and the high heels. She was making what he believed was known as a fashion statement. He wondered what she was really like, and he was impressed with her enterprising spirit.

"You know, I haven't done this in a long time," he confessed, scarcely believing that he was actually relaxing in her company. Since Davey had come to live with him, he'd seldom sought the company of women. They sought him, and whatever urges he needed fulfilled were usually fulfilled quickly and urgently, after which Nick would again be alone. The competition in Alaska was keen for women; with ten males to every female, there weren't enough women to go around. Add to that Nick's high standards, and women—or at least a steady relationship with one—didn't seem worth the trouble.

"What *is* there to do in Ketchikan? For single people, I mean?" A glance at Nick's ring finger had revealed no wedding band. He could still be spoken for, however. She held her breath, waiting to see if he'd give her an indication.

"The usual," he said. "I'm not into the singles scene much."

She surmised from this vague statement that he was single. She wanted to laugh out loud in relief, but she only said, "I haven't been here long, but I wonder if it'll be difficult to meet people. I had a lot of friends where I came from, and I was hoping it would be easy to find people I like here, but..." She let her voice trail off self-consciously. If he had half a brain, he'd see that she was practically handing him an opening to ask her out.

"An attractive woman like you shouldn't have any trouble," he said lightly, looking up at the mountains across the water.

Momentarily discouraged, Martha plunged on. "I put in long hours at the Bagel Barn," she said. "I guess you must know what it's like to work long hours, too."

He opened one eye at her, then opened the other. "I do. And I guess I'd better get back to my office. Let me know if you want to order any of that salmon. You might like sablefish on your bagels, too. I'll bring you some and let you try it. I could drop it off at the Bagel Barn today after I leave work." He pulled in his feet, stretched and stood up.

She smiled her most engaging smile. "That would be fine. We could go somewhere and have a drink together afterward if you like," she said, as naturally as she could manage. She didn't remember ever suggesting such a thing before in her life, but in this case she was desperate to let Nick Novak know that she was interested.

Her heart plunged to her toes when Nick looked distinctly uncomfortable.

"I can't tonight," he said, his expression clouding. He had to be there for Davey's birthday party. He owed it to Davey to be there. And he owed it to his brothers and their wives and children, all of whom were making a special effort to make the long boat ride from town to the cabin at night so that they could all be together.

Martha knew that she didn't dare let Nick see how disappointed she was. Or how humiliated.

"I understand," she said evenly.

"Maybe some other time," he told her.

"Sure," she said. She forced a smile. "Thanks for the salmon."

"I'll drop the sablefish off at the Bagel Barn later," he assured her. She was magnificently controlled, but he saw the hurt in her eyes. He wished he could have taken her up on her invitation, but tonight it was impossible. He couldn't tell her about Davey. To do that might raise more questions than he was prepared to answer. He was well aware that the boy's presence in his life was a mystery that half of Ketchikan longed to solve. Embarrassed, he scuffed at a leaf that had blown against the toe of his boot. Then he wheeled and headed toward Novak and Sons.

Martha couldn't eat the rest of her bagel. She didn't know what had upset her more—making a fool of herself or being turned down.

When Nick showed up at the Bagel Barn later to give her the sample of sablefish, Randy told him that Martha had already left for the day. Nick stuffed the plastic bag of fish deep in the pocket of his slicker and took off down the dock before Randy could suggest that he leave the fish with him. Nick didn't want to leave the fish with anyone but Martha. He had counted on her being there, and now that she wasn't he was angry with himself for thinking she would be. After all, he had turned down her offer to have a drink with him. Nice as she was, she'd probably found someone else who could be more accommodating.

Nick unlashed the *Tabor* from her mooring and headed for home, feeling oddly deflated. He pictured Martha's bright eyes and smiling face in his head, and he wished he was sitting across from her, nursing a drink, asking her to go to dinner with him afterward. Now that might never happen, and it was all his fault. All his fault, and nothing he could do about it, and that made him feel rotten. Even a spectacular sunset that turned the waters of Mooseleg Bay to molten gold failed to raise his spirits.

Chapter Four

Whatever there was to do in Ketchikan, she hadn't found it yet. That was Martha's discouraged reflection four days after Nick turned down her invitation.

She wasn't used to not knowing anyone. In Kokomo she'd been a part of the elaborate social rituals that exist among people who know each other. She waved to the traffic cop at the school-children's street crossing every morning on her way to work; he waved back. She was greeted and bidden farewell by her co-workers at the boutique every day. Martha had never realized before how those automatic little courtesies made her feel connected to people.

Here there was none of that, and she felt adrift without it. That was in addition to her loneliness and lack of anyone to talk to. She missed having someone to ask her if she'd had a hard day; her roommate back in Kokomo had always been available for commiseration or, more often, having fun. So had Polly in San Francisco.

But in Ketchikan Martha had met no one except the few customers who returned to the Bagel Barn, and they always arrived at the busiest times, when there was no chance to expand upon their acquaintance. Nick Novak hadn't been back. She hadn't seen him around the dock, even though she had surreptitiously kept an eye out for him every day.

So now, four days after the Debacle of the Refused Invitation, as Martha now thought of her disappointment with Nick, Martha was struggling with the apartment's difficult electric can opener trying to open a can of soup for dinner when the doorbell rang.

She peeked out the window to see a wiry, rugged-looking woman standing there with a steaming pot held in both hands. Of course, Martha opened the door.

"Hi," said the woman, marching in full speed ahead and setting the hot pot on Martha's stove. She turned around to face the disconcerted Martha.

"I'm Faye Murphy. I live in the apartment in back of this one. Sorry I wasn't here to welcome you when you got to Ketchikan, but I was out in the bush working. More about that later. What's your name?"

"Martha. Martha Rose," Martha said. The woman appeared to be in her late fifties, and she wore a black eyepatch.

"No, I'm not a pirate, dear. I got clawed by a lynx over on Chichagof Island a long time ago. I like the drama of black, don't you? I figure this patch gives me a reckless air. Have you had dinner yet? I brought you some chicken soup."

Martha wouldn't have cared whether Faye had brought a pot of glue, she was so happy to see a friendly face. And chicken soup was the best medicine Martha could imagine, even though she wasn't sick. Chicken soup reminded Martha of her mother.

"Thanks," she said, beaming at Faye. She lifted the lid. "It doesn't look as though it needs heating."

"I shouldn't think so. It's been simmering all afternoon. Do you have some bowls? I hope you don't mind my inviting myself for dinner, but I just got back from a week in the wilderness, and I needed to see a friendly face."

Martha filled big stoneware soup bowls with steaming hot soup, and Faye produced a box of crackers from the front pocket of her hooded sweatshirt. They sat down at Martha's little table.

"So tell me about yourself, dear," Faye said briskly. "What brings you to Ketchikan? The men?"

"Men?" Whoever this Faye Murphy was, Martha decided, she was definitely unconventional.

"Ten men to every woman in Alaska. Surely you knew that."

"Well, um, I'd heard about it. But no, that wasn't a factor in my decision," Martha said. "What brought me to Ketchikan was purely business." And she went on to tell Faye about Sidney and the Bagel Barns and how she would eventually share in the profits.

"Sounds good to me," Faye told her. "Most of the women

we get—well, they're thinking about the lonely guys who come here to fish for a living or work at the cannery or the lumber mill. *They*—the men, I mean—come to make a killing financially. They can work for a high salary at the mill or the cannery for a few months, live cheaply and sock it all away and go back to Seattle or Vancouver to loaf for the rest of the year. That's not for me. I like to keep busy all the time.''

''What do you do?'' asked Martha.

''I'm a nurse, dear. Came up here in the fifties looking for adventure, and I found it, all right. I accompany Dr. Andy Sharf when he flies out to take care of people who live too far from town to see a doctor. Would you like to hear about the lynx attack?''

Martha nodded. She'd wanted to ask, but thought it might be a topic Faye would prefer to avoid. By this time, however, Martha had an idea that Faye didn't avoid any topic.

''We made an emergency landing in Dr. Andy's plane on Chichagof Island—this was back in sixty-some, I've forgotten exactly when. There was an old hunter's shack still standing, so Dr. Andy and I prepared to spend the night. We'd emergency-landed before a couple of times when we had engine trouble, and we figured somebody'd find us by morning. So Dr. Andy says, 'Faye, go get some of that dry grass outside so I can start a fire in the fireplace.' There was plenty of wood stacked up inside, you see, but there wasn't any tinder. So I stepped outside and walked smack into a mother lynx protecting her young. I screamed and ran inside, but not before she slapped me with her paw. I managed to slam the door on her whiskers, but by that time my eye was a goner. Glad I have one left, though, I'll tell you.''

Martha was shaken by Faye's story and the matter-of-fact way in which it was told.

''Oh, you don't need to worry,'' Faye assured her. ''You won't run into a lynx in Ketchikan unless you go outside the town. Anyway, bears are much more common.''

''Bears? I've always been afraid of bears. I didn't even want a teddy bear when I was a kid!''

''Stay inside town and you'll seldom see a bear. A live one, anyway. There might be a few teddy bears wandering around.''

''Good grief!'' muttered Martha, whose irrational dislike of bears was real and based on having been frightened by them as a child when she visited the zoo. To hide her agitation, she got up and brought out the chocolate-chip cookies she'd brought from San Francisco.

"My, these are good," exclaimed Faye as she nibbled at the last one.

"Can you recommend a place where I can buy fresh-baked cookies?" Martha asked anxiously as she watched the cookie disappear into Faye's mouth. "I think I've developed a full-blown addiction."

"Sorry, but I don't know of any local bakery that bakes cookies as good as these, and as for shipping in freshly baked cookies, freight takes a week to get here by sea from Seattle, so by the time they got here they'd no longer be fresh unless they're shipped by air, which is expensive. I have a recipe for chocolate-chip cookies, though. It's a good one; it was my mother's. I'm not much good at cooking or baking, I'm sorry to say. Still, if you'd like it, I'll bring the recipe over. You could bake them if you decide you need a quick fix."

Martha laughed. "I'm afraid I will by tomorrow. I haven't gone a day without chocolate-chip cookies since I arrived in San Francisco."

"Do you miss it? San Francisco, I mean?"

"I miss my friend Polly. You're the first person I've met socially since I've been here."

"We'll have to remedy that. I know lots of people. I'm single and I love to have fun. Maybe I should throw a party to introduce you around. Would you like that?"

"Why, that would be nice." Martha was touched that Faye would do that for her. The length of their acquaintance seemed to make little difference to Faye, however. She warmed to the party idea by the second; Martha could almost watch the wheels spin in Faye's mind.

"How about a party next weekend? After I get back from heaven-knows-where? Dr. Andy and I will be leaving Tuesday, flying back in on Friday. How about a gathering of some sort on Saturday night? You could meet some of my married and single pals."

"I'd love it," Martha said warmly. She could have hugged

this little woman; it was clear that the two of them were going to be friends.

Faye rose to leave. "You keep the rest of the soup and crackers," she said. "I'll bring the chocolate-chip cookie recipe over before I leave town, and maybe you could make some for the party."

"I'd be glad to bake cookies," said Martha in relief. She hadn't known what to offer. Chocolate-chip cookies sounded easy enough, and baking them would give her something to fill the time.

Faye made a quick mental checklist. "We'll cook salmon steaks on the grill. We'll set up tables outside—my apartment is as small as yours. Paper plates and plastic forks, if you don't mind. This isn't going to be one of those grand affairs where there's so much silver on the table that you could perform an operation—preferably a lobotomy—on a too-boring dinner partner. No, I like people to mingle."

"What if it rains?"

Faye raised her eyebrows. Her eyepatch tilted rakishly. "Rain never stops anything in Ketchikan. We'll set up the tables under the house. I've done it lots of times. Oh, it'll be fun."

After Faye left, Martha threw a sweater over her shoulders, went out on the front steps and peered through the cracks between them to look beneath the duplex. Sure enough, because the house was built on stilts, there was room underneath for tables. The ground looked dry and trampled hard. Someone had strung outdoor Christmas lights from nails driven into the house's supports. Garden flowers bordered the area; although she couldn't have imagined a party held underneath a house, it was really quite pleasant.

"We sure didn't have anything like this in Kokomo," she murmured to herself as she shivered her way back inside her apartment, and for the umpteenth time she missed Polly's ready laugh. She even missed Sigmund's.

MARTHA SAW Nick Novak leaning against a post beneath the house after the party had been in full swing for about an hour. He had a certain way of leaning against things, a relaxed spine and an alert incline of his head, that made his figure unmistakable. He also had a kind of dignity that kept him aloof from others, though not in a way anyone noticed without studying him.

"I'd like you to meet someone," Faye said, appearing suddenly and propelling her forward. Martha's mouth became the Sahara Desert. She wiped her hands against her slacks. She should have guessed he'd be here. Faye had said she knew every eligible male in Ketchikan.

"This is Nick Novak, Martha," Faye said. "He—"

Martha was so nervous at seeing him again that she interrupted Faye without realizing that she was doing it until it was too late.

"We've met," she said.

Nothing about his expression changed. No grin, no twitch of eyebrow or widening of eyes, so that Martha was afraid that Nick Novak wasn't going to acknowledge her at all. But then he smiled and slowly extended his hand, and his fingers curved around hers.

If she hadn't known better, Martha would have thought he was wired for electricity. She felt a definite tingle at his touch. Nothing like it had ever happened to her before; maybe it had something to do with the dampness of her hand and the fact that Alaska was close to magnetic north. Or maybe, if she was to believe in love songs, it had something to do with the way his eyes lit up along with his smile.

"Are you serving your bagels with Alaskan salmon yet?" he asked.

"I'm afraid not," Martha said. Usually a party brought out the wit and sparkle in her, but none of that wit and sparkle surfaced now when she really needed it. She couldn't think of anything to say.

"You liked the salmon, though, didn't you?"

"Oh, yes," she said. *And you,* she wanted to add. Among the thoughts reeling through her head was the important realization that Nick had known that this party was being given in her honor. He must have wanted to come, then. Immediately a hope that she had thought long dead, the hope that Nick Novak might find her interesting, resurrected itself. How could the flare of attraction, which was so obvious to her, go unnoticed by Nick?

Nick studied her for a moment, taking no pains to conceal his thorough inspection. Tonight Martha was dressed more casually than he'd ever seen her. She wasn't wearing a dress, for one thing, but a sweater with an angora swan on the front and a pair of gray wool pants that did a lot for her legs. Nick Novak liked to see women in slacks. In his opinion, dresses did little for most women. They exposed the veins in their legs and other imperfections, while slacks or blue jeans showed off the curves of hips and thighs. There was certainly nothing wrong with those parts of Martha Rose's anatomy.

While Nick was taking his time looking her over, conversation escaped Martha. But Faye, pleased that her guest of honor was getting along so swimmingly with the other guests, bustled off in search of Dr. Andy, who had volunteered to cook the salmon steaks. This left Martha alone with Nick, which might have been a pleasant situation if her knees hadn't suddenly turned to spaghetti.

"I haven't seen you around the docks lately," she said, and then she wished she hadn't said it. It made her sound as though she'd been looking for him. She had, but it wasn't necessary for him to know that.

"I've had business out of town," he said, slowly and soberly. "I hadn't expected to go just now, but—" He let the sentence hang in midair.

"I guess your business takes you away from Ketchikan often?" she asked.

"It wasn't that kind of business," he said with unexpected gruffness, which left her confused.

"Oh," she said, and with that simple syllable the conversation ground creakingly into neutral. Martha was wondering how she could possibly shift gears when Faye jumped up on a chair and banged on an aluminum pie plate before calling, "All right, everybody. The food's ready. Nick, why don't you show our guest of honor the ropes? Dr. Andy, bring that platter of salmon over here. That's right, set it on the buffet table. Now, you all must try the chocolate-chip cookies. They're my mother's own recipe, but Martha has improved upon it."

"Looks like we're dinner partners," Nick said, smiling down at her. The grin surprised Martha. He had looked so serious only a moment ago.

Nick had evidently been to one of Faye's cookouts before.

He showed her how there were two lines to the buffet table. The portable picnic tables were covered with plaid cloths. Faye had lit the string of colored lights; they cozied up the unconventional picnic area considerably. A light rain curtained the party from passing cars on the street, and smoke from Dr. Andy's charcoal grill spiraled away at the back of the house. The guests were dressed warmly in jeans and light wool coats, and everyone wore waterproof boots except Martha, who wore a pair of hastily bought sneakers.

"You need to buy yourself a pair of Southeastern sandals," Nick said, holding out one of his red rubber boots for her inspection. They reached three-quarters of the way to his knee.

"Is that what you call those? I've noticed lots of people wearing them."

"Unless you happen to have webbed feet, they're a good idea. You can wear them anywhere in Ketchikan, even to weddings." Martha smiled at this and was unnerved when Nick seemed to be serious. Back in Kokomo—but she wasn't in Kokomo anymore. She was in Ketchikan, Alaska, where people held parties under houses and wore red rubber boots to weddings. The people she was with wore plaid lumberjack shirts; her own high-fashion hand-knit sweater seemed out of place. Her hair curled annoyingly around her face, but somehow she didn't mind. The important thing was that Nick Novak stood beside her, and that in itself seemed peculiar. Always before, the important thing had been how she looked and the impression her appearance made on others.

When they had filled their plates with charcoal-broiled salmon, baked potatoes, salad and creamed corn, Martha sat self-consciously across from Nick at a corner table. Next to them sat Nick's brother Dan and his wife, Cheryl. Cheryl was bright and pleasant company, and Dan was stolid and calm. Nick's oldest brother Fred and his wife, Andrea, stopped by to say hello, but moved on to a less crowded table.

"Nick, I haven't seen you since you came back from your trip," Cheryl said.

"I've had a lot to do," he told her, taking a large bite of baked potato.

"Well, when you get a chance, stop by our house. I've got

some toys that my kids have outgrown. They'd be just about right for Davey, though. You can have them.''

"Thanks, Cheryl. I'll come over soon.''

"This Nick,'' Cheryl said playfully to Martha. "He's always saying that. But we don't seen him very often. Him or Davey.''

Martha, listening to this familial exchange, wanted to ask who Davey was. But there was no chance, because Faye, who clearly enjoyed being a hostess, stopped by the table.

"Anything you want to know about Ketchikan's social life,'' she said teasingly, "you just ask Nick Novak.''

Martha could have sworn that Nick actually blushed, but here in the corner, where two strands of multicolored lights blended their colors so brilliantly, it was hard to tell.

"I don't know that much about the social life,'' he objected, but Faye fluttered away to laugh at a joke told by another of her friends. Martha wondered how much of Nick's protest was real and how much was due to self-consciousness.

After dinner, Cheryl and Dan left. "Have to get back to the kids. We left them alone tonight. I guess our daughter at thirteen is old enough to keep the six-year-old in line, but I don't like to leave them alone too long.''

"Do your kids like cookies?'' Martha asked on impulse.

"My Wendy is the original cookie monster,'' Cheryl told her.

Martha wrapped some of her chocolate-chip cookies in a strip of aluminum foil. "Here, take them these. There are plenty for the other guests.''

"Why, thanks. They're delicious cookies, Martha,'' Cheryl said.

"I've baked a lot of them for the party. I even have a couple of extra tins of cookies in my apartment,'' Martha said with a laugh.

When Cheryl and Dan were gone, Nick turned to her curiously. "Do you really have more cookies in your apartment? There are trays of cookies already here.''

"I've been baking batch after batch, perfecting Faye's mother's recipe for this party. Not that the cookies weren't wonderful to begin with, but there was this place in San Francisco where I used to buy the best fresh-baked cookies every day. I brought a big supply with me, but I ran out and now I'm trying to duplicate that flavor. Anyway, I don't have anything else to do after work, so I like baking the cookies to occupy my time."

"If you don't have anything to do after work," Nick said slowly, fighting his own embarrassment, "maybe we could get together for that drink sometime."

Her startled gray eyes flashed astonishment at this unexpected invitation.

"Maybe we could," she said when she had recovered.

"Maybe," he said, even more slowly, trying to get to the bottom of the confusion in her eyes, "maybe we wouldn't have to wait until after work. We could get together sooner if you like."

"When?" she said, unaware that she was almost whispering, but overwhelmingly aware that he was standing closer to her than he had all evening and that the hair on her arms was standing on end. Certainly no man had ever had this effect on her.

"Would you like to go somewhere tonight after the party? I don't have to be home early." He held his breath. He was certain that, because he had once turned her down, she would want to get even with him by refusing his impromptu invitation.

"I'm the guest of honor. My obligations—"

He caught one of her hands between his and held it still. "I've always been sorry I couldn't take you up on your invitation to meet you after work that day. My previous engagement was important or I wouldn't have said no. Now I want to make up for it. Is it too late?" His eyes darkened. She would have died before she'd have disappointed him. She would have died before she'd have disappointed herself.

Convinced that he could hear her answer pounding in her blood and singing in her heart before she even gave it, she paused for a respectable moment and said, "Yes! I'd love to go somewhere with you!" all in a rush. Then, embarrassed, she laughed up at him, and he saw the happiness gleaming in the depths of her eyes.

Nick was so relieved that she'd accepted that he had the almost uncontrollable urge to call her "darling" and then to go on to tell her how happy he was. But the word *darling* was not one that had ever sprung to his lips before, and he did not say it now. In fact, he was totally astounded to find such a word rattling around in his brain in the presence of a woman whom he barely knew. He had called women "dearie" from time to time, meaning nothing in particular. He had occasionally addressed his high school sweetheart as "sweetie," but that was because that was what she called him. But—"darling"?

As she looked up at him, her cheeks rosy, her eyes sparkling, her irises the exact shade of Mooseleg Bay on a day when the sun was on the verge of peeping through the clouds, Martha Rose did bring the endearment "darling" to mind. Thank goodness he hadn't said it. Thank goodness he wasn't that open with women when he was beginning to get to know them. No telling what a woman like Martha would infer from being called "darling." Why, she might take it too seriously! She might think it meant more than it did. All it meant, his wanting to call her that, was that she looked, to his eyes, darling at this moment.

So all he said was, "Later we'll figure out where and when Tomorrow's Sunday. Do you have to work?"

"No," she said.

"We can go out late then tonight, if the party ends late?"

"I suppose so," she said, not at all reluctantly.

"Unless you'd rather wait until tomorrow night," he amended, hoping that she wouldn't prefer that.

"*No!*" Martha exclaimed.

"You're already telling Nick Novak no, and you've only been here for a couple of hours? Nick, I do believe you've met your match in this young woman," Faye said.

Nick was glad he'd already completed his arrangements with Martha. If the truth were told, he'd always been shy. Faye was so straightforward that she sometimes embarrassed him.

"Now, Nick," Faye went on, "you've been monopolizing Martha all evening, and I want her to meet some other people That's why I'm having this party, after all, so people can mingle Mingle, mingle! You just go over and chat with Lenore Parham She wants to tell you all about her trip to the Lower Forty-eight Go on, Nick." She gave him a little shove in the direction of a round-shouldered, lackluster loner who looked like a misfit in this congenial group.

"I hope you don't mind," Faye whispered. "Lenore's so depressing that hardly anyone wants to talk to her. I'm afraid it was Nick's turn to be bored next. Aren't you lucky, Martha, that you don't have that problem? Everyone here just loves you to pieces already. Here's Perry Thompson. Perry, this is Martha.'' And Faye left her to talk with Perry, who played up to her unashamedly even though her attention kept wandering to Nick, who was gallantly doing his best to hold up his end of the conversation with Lenore.

Martha didn't get a chance to see Nick throughout the rest of the party. It wasn't, however, for lack of trying. In between mingling, she kept working her way to the fringes of the group, easing her way around little clumps of people, excusing herself occasionally to freshen a drink that she never really refilled. She kept hoping that Nick would join her, but the opportunity never presented itself. He was tied up with Lenore until a watchful Faye intervened with her cry of ''Mingle! Mingle!'' Then Dr. Andy occupied the whole group's attention by telling about the time he'd won a twenty-day-long sled-dog race on the Iditarod Trail from Anchorage to Nome.

Although Martha was fascinated by Dr. Andy's story, which was highlighted by his hair-raising accounts of crossing mountains, speeding down Yukon River ice and skirting the Bering Sea, she kept watching Nick to see if he was observing her. When he caught her at it she looked away quickly, but she smiled, and out of the corner of her eye she saw that he smiled too. *How silly,* she thought. It had always struck her as funny that when a man and a woman wanted to get together they had to go through a ritual of eyeing each other first.

After Dr. Andy refused to entertain with any more stories, the party grew more raucous, but then the rain began to fall more heavily and the temperature became colder, so many guests decided to head for home and a warm fireplace. Perry unexpectedly offered to give Lenore a lift to her apartment, Faye began to pick up paper plates and cups and stuff them into plastic garbage bags, and Martha worked with Dr. Andy to wrap the leftover food.

When he had helped fold and stack the picnic tables against a support post, Nick said to Martha, ''I'll help you carry the cookies upstairs.'' Then Faye said, ''My age is finally beginning to catch up with me. I'm going to call it a night,'' and Dr. Andy bade them a quick farewell before driving off in his Jeep.

Nick and Martha were suddenly alone.

"Somebody should pull the plug on all those colored lights," he said.

"I think the plug's over here," Martha said, and when she pulled the plug out of its socket the surroundings went suddenly and blindingly dark, the blackness punctuated by the patter of softly falling rain.

"You'll have to send out radar signals," said Nick, who was holding two trays of cookies. "I can't see a thing."

"I'm over here," Martha said.

"I wonder if I'll be able to find the stairs," he said.

"Follow me."

"Keep talking so I'll know where you are," he said.

"It's as black as the inside of a cow," Martha replied, a giggle catching in her throat.

"Have you ever been inside one?"

"No, but I have a good imagination. Watch your step; these stairs are damp."

He followed her inside her apartment, looking around curiously to see if the apartment was decorated in the same glitzy way Martha dressed. He was relieved to see that it was a typical rental efficiency, nothing special, nothing fancy. She had tried to brighten the ho-hum decor with assorted handwoven baskets and a bouquet of fresh flowers on the coffee table.

While Martha dumped the cookies into a tin, Nick stood at the window, looking out at the rain.

"Where would you like to go tonight?" he asked her suddenly, wheeling around.

She shoved the container of cookies into a cabinet and joined him at the window. "I don't know many places in Ketchikan," she said. She was beginning to feel nervous at being alone with him. This jitteriness hadn't happened to her in years. Usually she felt in control when she was with a man. Now she didn't feel in control at all. Nick was such an unknown quantity.

"There's a nice little pub near the shopping mall on the west of town."

"That sounds fine. Only—"

He turned and looked at her. There were question marks in his eyes. Why was she suddenly reluctant?

"It's raining so hard," she said in explanation. She laughed a little, and she knew she sounded jumpy. "I guess I'm just not accustomed to rain like a native—Ketchikaner?"

He laughed. "I think the proper term is Ketchikanite. And I can understand your distaste for the rain. Our liquid sunshine takes some getting used to." He paused for a moment. "You know," he said more intimately, "we wouldn't have to go out. We could stay right here. I'm not trying to invite myself, and I promise I won't wear out my welcome. But if you'd be more comfortable—"

She thought about it, a lightning-flash kind of thought. She certainly didn't want him to think he was invited to spend the night, but she didn't read that expectation into either his words or his expression. She sensed that he wanted her to feel more at ease than she obviously was. She could have been embarrassed that he understood her so readily, but she wasn't.

"Let's stay here, then," she said. "No crowds to battle, no rain, no interruptions." She smiled at him and sat down on the couch. She patted the cushion beside her. Now that she was sure of her ground, in her own territory, she knew how to act. Making the other person feel at home was something she instinctively knew how to do.

"I've told you about myself and how I happened to be in Ketchikan," she said as he sat beside her. "Why don't you tell me about Nick Novak?"

He relaxed. It was easy now to do so with Martha gazing at him so warmly. The rain outside the window seemed far distant; her smile was bright and glowing. He grinned at her. "I'm really just a fisherman," he said. "That's how I think of myself, anyway. I grew up just outside Ketchikan. My father homesteaded our place on Mooseleg Bay, and he married my mother, who was the daughter of a gold miner who settled in Ketchikan after he failed to strike it as rich as he would have liked in the Klondike. Papa fished for a living, and my brothers and I followed along."

"What kind of fish?"

"Salmon, halibut, herring. We had a fleet of boats and part ownership of the cannery by the time my dad died. I'm still a full partner in my brothers' fishing fleet. We bought out the other partner in the cannery a few years ago. We needed a little place to store the fish that are being shipped out of Ketchikan; that's why I added Novak Cold Storage to the cannery. And the store—well, that's just an offshoot of all the rest.''

Martha had seen the store. It swarmed with tourists.

"The store looks as though it does well. And the cannery and cold storage firm seemed prosperous, too.'' As a business-woman, such things interested her.

"We're doing very well. In fact, it's all I could have hoped for when I took over the management from Papa. My brothers leave the business end of everything to me; they have their hands full with the fishing fleet. I mind being away from home more than they do, and fishing with the fleet means months and weeks away from home at a time. Dan and Fred don't mind that, so it works out fine.''

That seemed odd to Martha. "Dan and Cheryl have children, don't they? And Fred and Andrea do, too?''

"Two each.''

"I should think you'd be more free to leave home than they would,'' she said slowly. Her eyes met his, only to realize that he had retreated somehow. "Of course, it's none of my business,'' she said, making her own fast retreat.

He was silent for a few seconds, seeming to weigh his thoughts. When he spoke, it was quietly.

"I'm responsible for a child,'' he said. "Davey. He lives with me.''

"Oh,'' Martha said, taken aback. She had not expected the conversation to take this turn, although now she recalled that Cheryl had mentioned someone named Davey at dinner.

"Davey is four years old. Just turned four, in fact.''

"That's a nice age, I think,'' Martha responded, determined not to let the conversation die. "At four they're out of the baby stage, and the terrible twos are finally behind them, and they can walk and talk and begin to be good company.'' Her last roommate had had a four-year-old daughter, and Martha still considered herself the child's honorary aunt.

Nick looked at her strangely for a moment. "Davey hardly talks,'' he said abruptly.

"I—uh,'' Martha said. From the cautious tone of Nick's voice, she sensed that he didn't want to talk about Davey. But the expression in his eyes made her think that he did.

"Would you like to tell me about Davey?'' she asked softly,

deciding to go with the expression on his face rather than the tone of his voice. Martha had an impulse to reach over and cradle his big hand in hers, but that was one impulse she managed to resist. Instead she composed herself and gave him all her attention.

Nick stared at the floor for a moment, trying to figure out if he wanted to talk about Davey or not. He hadn't ever wanted to before. He had managed to keep mum about Davey ever since the boy came to live with him. Even his family really didn't know the whole story, and he didn't intend to tell them, either. But recently he had become so worried about Davey. He felt completely at a loss when it came to figuring out how to help the boy.

"It's not something I want to discuss with everyone," Nick said at last. "Davey is special to me."

"Don't talk about it if you don't want to," Martha said softly, although she felt a great need to draw Nick out of himself and to find out why he was so concerned about Davey. She tried to convey her interest in her attitude and in the warmth of her expression. Finally she yielded to her impulse to take his hand and wrapped her fingers gently around his. Her touch generated instant emotional electricity, intimate in nature but not sexual.

The expression in her eyes was one of total absorption, and instead of wanting to back off as he usually did, Nick found himself feeling profound relief that he'd finally happened upon someone who cared.

"But I do want to," he said, slowly and with surprise. "I want to very much."

And because this was true, and because it seemed like the most marvelous thing in the world to have met someone whom he could trust instinctively, and because he somehow sensed without a doubt that Martha was the thoughtful and loyal friend he hadn't had since his friend Hank died, Nick began to talk about Davey.

Chapter Five

Nick must have talked for over an hour, telling Martha how frustrating it was to live with a little boy who would not talk. The ready sympathy in her eyes made him reveal his feelings more than he had intended, but he felt much better after he had expressed his frustration over Davey in words.

"And Hallie—does she have any idea what's wrong with Davey?" Martha asked.

Nick shrugged. "Hallie's a fine woman, and she's been around kids a lot. She's cared for her sister's grandchildren from time to time, but Hallie doesn't have any more idea what could be wrong with Davey than I do."

"If Davey is as bright as you believe he is, he ought to be talking by now," Martha said. She was thinking of Tiffany, her former roommate's little girl. Tiffany was a nonstop chatterer.

"That's what I think, too," Nick said.

"Have you taken Davey to a doctor?"

"Dr. Andy has taken care of Davey since he was a baby. He seems to think that Davey will talk when he gets ready. I used to believe that, too. Now I've changed my mind. Something is wrong with Davey, and I don't know what it is."

"My mother is a kindergarten teacher. She had a kid in one of her classes years ago who wouldn't talk. I've forgotten what the reason was. I'll ask Mother about it next time I talk to her on the phone."

"Would you?"

"Nick, of course I will."

Nick leaned back on the couch cushions. "It's hard rearing a child alone," he said, almost as if to himself. "Mothers have a network. They tend to confide in each other and pool their knowledge about child-rearing. But men don't do that. I don't know any single fathers. My brothers leave the upbringing of their kids to their wives. Sometimes I feel as though—" Nick stopped, suddenly aware that he'd been rambling.

"You feel as though what, Nick?" Martha prompted gently.

"Like I'm the only man in the world with a kid who has a problem. It's such an isolated—and isolat*ing*—feeling."

"I wish I knew how to help," she said.

He turned his gaze on her, and in his eyes she noted an intensity that she had never seen there before.

"You have helped," he said. "I don't feel so isolated anymore," he went on. His voice was low, and its uncharacteristic roughness exposed his vulnerability; she hadn't thought of him as vulnerable before. She was aware of a wave of warmth emanating from him, and she suddenly found it difficult to breathe.

She had known she was sexually attracted to him from the first time she'd seen him, but for over an hour that attraction had been suspended, or perhaps sublimated, to another kind of stimulation. For a while she had been privy to the real concerns of Nick Novak. They had done away with pretense, with trying to impress each other, with banalities. Compared to what she usually experienced with men in the early stages of a relationship, this honest communication was refreshingly different.

"And now," he said lightly, more lightly than he felt, "I've taken up too much of your time telling you all my troubles. I ought to go."

What should she say? She certainly wasn't ready for him to leave, and yet she feared that any suggestion that he stay would be misconstrued. A bond had begun to form between them when he disclosed his fears about Davey, but the bond wasn't solidly forged yet. The bond wouldn't be really strong until he knew more about her. She realized that, and yet she still didn't know what to tell him about herself. Especially when he seemed so ready to leave.

"Would you like something to eat or drink before you go?" she said, because it was the only thing she could think of to keep him there.

He stood up and grinned. She stood up, too. He slid an arm companionably around her shoulders.

"How about some of your delicious chocolate-chip cookies?" he asked with a twinkle in his eye, and that was when Martha knew for sure that she had found a kindred spirit.

NICK DROVE BACK to the cannery, where he had a cot set up in his office for nights when he needed to stay in town. It was still raining, and the gentle swish of the windshield wipers of his company car was rhythmic and comforting.

It had been so easy to talk to Martha. That was the most surprising thing. Usually he couldn't talk to women. They didn't want to listen. Or if they did listen, they were just waiting for a chance to say what they wanted to say. And if he tried to change the subject back to a topic of importance to him, he was likely to be accused of being uncaring and uncommunicative.

Communication! If there was a buzzword of the 1980s, *communication* must be it. Everyone was always exhorting everyone else to communicate. Communication took two people, however. One to send the signals and one to receive. The sender and receiver should switch places once in a while. That, to him, was what communication was all about.

Well, Martha had been a wonderful listener tonight. Her sea-gray eyes had revealed interest and intelligence, and her attitude had been helpful and nonjudgmental. He'd never considered confiding in a woman before, although now that he'd done it, it made sense. His best friend Hank had died tragically in an accident, and now that Nick had Davey it seemed that he didn't have any close men friends anymore. Most of them couldn't identify with Nick at all.

Nick hadn't told Martha the whole story about Davey, but then he'd never told anyone that. He'd talked out his anguish about Davey's problem, though, and somehow he could think about it more clearly now that he'd put it into words. He needed to find a specialist for Davey. Dr. Andy was good, and his heart was in the right place, but his knowledge wasn't sufficient to help Davey now.

Nick supposed that the logical place to start was to find a pediatric speech-and-hearing specialist in Juneau, the nearest big city. He'd make an appointment for Davey as soon as possible, and then he'd take Davey there. He'd tell Martha about this plan next time he saw her.

And next time he saw her he'd be the listener and let her do most of the talking. He'd like to know more about her. Who was she, really? All he knew was that she was a visitor from the Lower Forty-eight who would be leaving at the end of the summer. Like a lot of the other women who came here, she'd tire of the rain and the isolation on Revilla Island, which he and some of the other natives called The Rock. He'd seen it happen before. Maybe the rain and the dampness and the lack of interesting things to do would depress her. That happened often enough to people from the Outside. She might need someone to talk to.

If Martha was leaving at the end of the summer, that didn't give him much time to get to know her. The thought shot an unexpected pang of sadness through him, much more than the situation warranted. He had become attached to her in a ridiculously short time, and he wasn't used to becoming attached to anyone.

He hadn't even made a date to see her again. Why hadn't he? He'd merely eaten the cookies she'd offered, sipped at the tea she'd brewed and wandered off into the rain as though he hadn't appreciated the warmth and pleasure of her company at all.

She had gazed up at him before he left, and he knew that it was more than loneliness he saw in her face. He knew she'd been lonely here; she'd told him so. It would have been easy to take advantage of that loneliness, and pleasurable, too. Yet he felt that they had both held loneliness at bay tonight, and they had established an emotional connection on which they could build.

That was why he hadn't even considered kissing Martha. It was much too early for that. It wasn't that he didn't want to—he had been jolted by the sexual intensity of those final moments in her apartment as much as she had. She was beautiful, with her great, glowing eyes and her dark, glossy hair, and he had felt a sensual stirring tonight that he hadn't felt in a long, long time. She was the kind of woman a man had fantasies about, the kind of dreams that kept you awake at night.

He was sure she would have welcomed his kiss and maybe

even more, but he'd never offend Martha Rose in any way. He didn't want her to assume that he thought she was easy.

Considering their mutual attraction, why hadn't he made a date to see her again? He didn't even have her telephone number. He wasn't used to asking for a woman's telephone number; there was no telephone at the cabin on Mooseleg Bay, only the shortwave radio. But there was a telephone at the cannery, and he knew when he drove up at the outside door to his office that he would use that telephone to call Martha Rose.

He had to ask Information to get her number. It was a new number, and therefore not listed in the directory. As late as it was, he knew that Martha couldn't have fallen asleep in the short time it had taken for him to drive from her apartment to the cannery.

She answered on the second ring, sounding slightly apprehensive.

"It's me, Nick," he said.

"Oh, Nick. When the phone rang, all I could think of is a disaster of some sort because it's so late. Is everything all right?"

He'd been away from her for only twenty minutes, and just the sound of her voice almost made him forget what he wanted to say.

"Everything is fine," he said, "especially if you're free to go somewhere with me tomorrow."

"Tomorrow?" she said, with a little catch in her throat.

For a moment he thought that she might be busy. But hadn't she told him that she didn't have enough to do to fill her free time? She'd said that was why she'd baked so many chocolate-chip cookies.

She said, "Why, tomorrow would be fine, Nick," but the hint of disbelief filtering through her words made him wonder if she was angry about his calling so late.

"I'm sorry about calling so late," he apologized.

"That's perfectly okay," she said, and in his relief he knew from the agreeable sound of her voice that she was smiling.

"What would you like to do? We could take in some sightseeing if you haven't had time for it yet, or we could eat lunch, or we could climb Deer Mountain—or possibly we could do all three."

Martha laughed. He loved the sound of her laughter; it reminded him of birdsong, but not from any bird he knew. Her laugh was the trill of an imaginary bird, bright and golden and sleekly feathered.

"I'll let you decide on the entertainment," she said.

"What time shall I pick you up? Is nine in the morning too early?"

"Why—I suppose not," she said, though she wasn't used to seeing men so early in the day. Maybe morning dates were a local custom; she didn't know.

"Are you sure nine o'clock is all right? I'm not pushing you, am I?"

He sounded every bit as eager to see her as she was to see him.

"I'll be ready at nine," she said firmly.

Had he made a fool of himself for suggesting a morning date? Well, it was too late for regrets. He had none, and it didn't sound as though Martha did, either.

"I'll pick you up at nine, then," he said, and then he replaced the receiver in its cradle and sank down on the narrow cot in his office.

If he picked Martha up at nine, would that mean he had to spend the whole day with her? What if things didn't go well tomorrow and he wanted out? Could he reasonably leave her at, say, noon? No. She'd expect more than that. Anyway, why wouldn't things go well? Everything had been very natural between them tonight. Why shouldn't it be that way again tomorrow?

Of course it would be. But what if it *wasn't*? What had he gotten himself into, anyway?

He should go straight home to Williwaw Lodge tomorrow morning and spend his Sunday with Davey, but it was too late for that now. He was committed to spending the day with Martha Rose.

He unbuttoned his shirt and lay down on the cool, damp sheets, picturing her lovely gray eyes in his mind, and thought about how much he hated sleeping alone.

WHEN HE ARRIVED at her apartment promptly at nine in the morning to pick her up, she was decked out in something called harem pants and a filmy but regrettably nontransparent blouse. He had to explain to her that what was appropriate dress in San Francisco was not appropriate for strolling in downtown Ketchikan in wind-driven rain.

"But I don't *have* anything suitable," Martha said, thinking of her closetful of useless fluttery skirts, silk dresses and open-toed shoes. "I know," she said quickly after seeing the resigned look on his face, "I'll borrow something from Faye."

She ran next door and came back wearing a sensible plaid shirt, faded jeans and a pair of red rubber boots that were known as Southeast sandals. She pulled a yellow crewneck sweater over her head.

"That's better," he said with a grin.

With an answering grin, Martha dragged her umbrella out from behind the door and said, "Shall we go?" Nick knew then that he'd found a woman who knew how to adapt. She couldn't possibly have known how happy that made him.

"There are three driving tours," he informed her as they drove away from her house in his company car. "There's the route to the north end of the road, the route to the south end of the road, and if you're feeling truly adventurous we can hazard the dirt road east to the lake."

"But I thought we were going to take a look at the historic district. Faye says it's charming."

"But to do that we'd have to walk in the rain," he objected.

"That's what I'd like," she insisted.

"It's also very windy," he said dubiously. On the inevitable day that Martha became disgusted with Ketchikan's ubiquitous wind and rain, he'd rather she wasn't with him, although he couldn't quite imagine Martha being disgusted with anything.

She only said happily, "I know, but don't you love the way the rain looks sweeping over the Narrows?" and when he parked the car on Front Street she tumbled out into the puddles with an eagerness that surprised him. His doubts about spending the whole day with her evaporated then and there. He raised her umbrella, and they had to walk very close together in order not to get wet.

They strolled past the closed and shuttered Bagel Barn, and Martha told him how Sidney was going to cut her in on the profits eventually. Nick had already decided that it was Martha's turn to talk today. He prodded her now and then with interested questions, impressed by how much she knew about running a business.

Running a business was something they had in common. He'd only managed to get two years of college under his belt before he'd come home to help his brothers run the fishing fleet when their father became ill. Martha, with her degree in business administration, impressed him as a shrewd businesswoman. He didn't mind mining her for information, which she was pleased to give.

Martha thought that his accountant was giving him unsound advice, and she suggested getting the opinion of another accountant. She told him she thought he needed to set up a computer record system for Novak and Sons, which was something he'd been thinking about but had never quite gotten around to doing. It turned out that she had helped set up such a system for the owner of a chain of boutiques in Indiana. They had plenty to talk about; *she* had plenty to talk about. They only lapsed into silliness when they reached the bridge spanning Ketchikan Creek in the historic district with its wooden sidewalk and rustic wooden buildings.

"This," he told her expansively, "is the notorious former red-light district of Ketchikan. Back in the olden days when loggers and fishermen hung out here, they used to say that this was the only spot in Alaska where both fishermen and fish went upstream to spawn."

She laughed the way she was supposed to, and he glanced over at her. Her hair was misted by tiny bright droplets, and the warm pink coloring of her cheeks was sheened with moisture. Little ringlets, which he had never noticed before, curled over her forehead. He looked away, thinking that no one had ever been so beautiful.

Leaning on the wet railing on the Ketchikan Creek bridge beside Nick Novak, Martha knew that their gears had finally meshed. She wasn't sure why she thought of their relationship in terms of gears; Martha was not a particularly mechanical person. It was simply, she knew in retrospect, that the wheels of their romance had started turning way back when she'd seen him propping himself against the lamppost near the Bagel Barn.

When he took her hand today after they stepped out of his car into a rain blowing sideways in a southeasterly wind, she knew that he knew that they both knew they were more than just friends.

"What's the worst thing about you?" he asked suddenly.

"The worst thing?" She had to think for a minute. It wasn't eating chocolate-chip cookies in bed at night and getting crumbs all over the sheets. It wasn't forgetting to water her houseplants until they were gasping their last.

"Well," she said finally, "something happens to my hands when I get nervous. They fly around like frightened bats, or I crack my knuckles. I chew on the skin at the sides of my fingernails. It used to drive my friend Polly crazy."

He looked down at one of her nicely manicured nails. Sure enough, the skin on the sides looked slightly gnawed. "Why don't you just bite your fingernails like everyone else? Why do you chew on the skin?"

She shrugged. His rain poncho nearly slid from her shoulders; he had to grab it to keep it from falling in the creek. He left his arm there, and she wasn't about to object.

"I can't bite my fingernails. It would ruin a perfectly good coat of nail polish," she said.

"In Ketchikan you won't have to wear nail polish. And you may want to keep your fingernails short for the outdoor life. Speaking of which, are you tired of walking in the rain yet?"

"No," she said. She'd always liked rain, and walking in it with someone special seemed fitting and right. It also kept the hair on her arms slicked down. She still hadn't figured out why it stood on end whenever he was around.

"Aren't you glad you changed clothes?" he asked her.

"I'd forgotten how comfortable sweaters and jeans can be. And thank goodness I can wear boots here instead of three-inch heels. Any woman who says she likes wearing those little instruments of torture ought to have her head examined." She'd always felt this way; why then had she become so enamored of high-heeled shoes? At the moment, she couldn't imagine.

By this time it was close to noon, and they had been rambling around in the rain for a couple of hours. He said as much.

"As long as we keep moving, mold won't grow on us," she said solemnly.

"We can walk between the drops," he said.

"The rain washes down my umbrella," she said. "You'd be surprised how dusty my umbrella gets when it sits behind the door for a day or two."

"You mean on days when it doesn't rain? I don't remember any."

"I remember one. I think it was one of the first days I was here. The sun came out, decided there must be someplace better to go and hurried back where it came from."

"Martha, I do believe you're the first Cheechako I've ever heard joke about our weather."

"Cheechako? What's that?"

"Someone who hasn't been in Alaska for a year yet."

"I'm going to fool people into thinking I'm a real Alaskan by getting my own pair of Southeast sandals," she said.

"You do that and I'll take you on a hike. We have some of the most beautiful scenery around here, and I want to be the one to show it to you."

She beamed up at him. "And I'd like you to be."

"For now, though," he said thoughtfully, "maybe you'd like to take a look at Novak and Sons' cannery." It wasn't anything he would have suggested to just anyone, because a cannery operation was messy. He had an idea, however, that Martha would be interested.

And she was.

The cannery hunkered on the edge of Revilla Island, not far from the boat basin. It was an awkward arrangement of white painted buildings. Rain ran in streams off corrugated metal roofs. A pier jutted out into the water, its pilings thick with barnacles.

They went inside the office building through the outer door of Nick's office. Martha sent him an inquiring look when she saw the cot folded up in a corner.

"I slept in my office last night," he said. "I often do that when the weather is too bad for me to go home to Mooseleg Bay."

He led her through other offices and past a time clock and a bulletin board. They climbed metal stairs to a catwalk suspended above huge bins of halibut. Workers below slapped fish onto conveyor belts from which the fish were swallowed up by big machines, only to emerge as cans of food at the end of the complicated process. After that, the cans were steam-processed. It was noisy and smelly, but Martha watched avidly. She glanced once at Nick. He looked as if he enjoyed this.

"Come on," he said finally, as though just recalling that she was there.

He took her to the section where the cans of fish were stacked in cartons. She had to jump out of the way of a speedy forklift carrying a load of sealed boxes to a loading dock.

"I'm surprised that so many people are working on Sunday," she shouted over the clang and the clamor.

"Fresh fish don't stay fresh for long," he shouted back. "Seiners bring their catch in by Saturday, because usually they don't work on weekends. By the time the quitting whistle blows tonight, we'll have this batch of fish put away. Monday's our slack day. We call it Sockeye Sunday, and it's traditional to rest on that day." He motioned for her to follow him. They went back through the plant, and Martha noticed that several of the workers ogled her with curiosity. Nick ignored them, however.

Back in his office, with several doors shut between them and the din, he turned and grinned. "Well?" he said.

"I had no idea the cannery was such a big operation," she said.

"It wasn't until a few years ago. I built it up. My brothers always hated the cannery—the smells, the problems with the workers who get in fights because they have to live together in the company bunkhouse. I installed a shower off my office so I don't reek of fish when I leave here, and I keep my workers happy with high wages and fringe benefits. I like what I do."

They went outside, and Martha inhaled a breath of fresh, salt-scented air. The rain had stopped sweeping off the Narrows, and a fog was rolling in.

Nick took her hand. "How about a bowl of chili?" he offered. "There's a café at Stedman and Creek Streets that makes the best in town."

They went to the café and sat together at a little table. The air was steamy with the smell of wet wool, and the floor was damp with tracked-in water. He watched the way Martha studied the menu, the way she smiled at the waitress, the way her spirits seemed not to have been dampened by a day in the rain or the smells of the cannery.

And he knew that he had reached a turning point in his life. Whoever and whatever he had been before he met her was on the verge of becoming something different. Something more. That she was here with him now, blissfully spooning up chili, amazed him. He had spent all his life until this point without her, unaware that she even existed. Now it seemed impossible that Martha could have been somewhere in the world without his knowing it. The fact that she had appeared so suddenly on this cold, damp island in Alaska seemed like a miracle.

Martha looked up from her chili to find that Nick was watching her. His ruddy skin looked paler than normal, and at first she thought that perhaps he didn't feel well. In spite of his paler-than-normal skin, however, he was smiling at her.

"Is anything wrong?" she asked, though by this time she knew there wasn't. With a sudden flip of her heart, she knew he was in love with her.

"My dear Cheechako," he said gently, coining an endearment uniquely hers. "Nothing is wrong. In fact, everything seems perfectly right."

"Rightly perfect," Martha whispered.

After that, neither of them could finish eating.

Chapter Six

It was the third week in June, and the sun, which was making a rare appearance, seemed blindingly bright. The day had invited Nick and Martha outside and beckoned them to Deer Mountain. Ketchikanites joked that Deer Mountain was the world's tallest barometer: if you couldn't see the top of Deer Mountain, it was raining. If you could, it was going to rain. Today it was going to rain, because all of the mountain was visible. They both hoped that the rain would hold off until they got back to civilization.

The view from their private spot on the mountainside was breathtaking; below them, the town spread alongside the glittering water of the Narrows, with Pennock and Gravina Islands beyond. Birds in the Sitka spruce trees surrounding them nattered querulously at this invasion by two humans.

Martha leaned back against a fallen log and let the sun bake her face. She propped her feet, which, like Nick's, were handsomely clad in a pair of brown leather hiking boots, on a tree stump. "What a nice day," she said lazily.

"Rain or shine, any day is nicer when we spend it together," Nick said. He picked up her hand; she had dispensed with the rose-colored nail polish, and her fingernails were short and squared off.

"Mmm-hmm," she agreed.

"Hungry?" he asked her.

"I didn't bring any bagels, if that's what you're wondering," she said, opening one eye and squinting at him.

"No matter," he said. He reached into a pocket and pulled out a small packet.

"What's that?" Martha said.

"Gorp. Want some?"

She opened both eyes. "With a name like that, it doesn't sound like anything I'd want to eat. Are you sure it's not some awful Alaskan insect you dug out from under a rock?"

"Gorp is made up of granola, dried fruits and nuts, and it is considered very nutritious by backpackers." He tossed a raisin into his mouth, watching her.

Martha opened her mouth, too, like a hungry baby bird. Nick very gently placed a raisin on her tongue and closed her mouth with a kiss. He would have continued kissing her if she hadn't pulled away.

"I can't chew when you're kissing me," she explained.

"Stop chewing, then."

She did. He kissed her again, this time more thoroughly. He tasted of sunshine and raisins, which was unusual. She'd become accustomed to rain-flavored kisses.

"If I'd known that hiking was this much fun, I'd have taken it up long ago," she murmured into the long lean line of his jaw.

He rubbed his cheek against her chin and wrapped his arms around her so that he could hear her heartbeat. It sped up in response to his. He kissed her again and eased her down into the sweet-smelling grass.

She smiled up at him, her dark hair fanning out in a shining frame for her face. She traced the lines at the outer corners of his eyes with the fingers of both hands, and let her hands continue across the ridgelike cheekbones and around his head until she could pull his lips down to meet hers.

Martha had been kissing Nick a lot lately, but she would never get enough of it. Not much more than kissing had happened, but she liked it that way. She'd watched a whirlwind romance developing between Polly and Sigmund before her very eyes, and such a beginning seemed hasty and insincere to her now that she knew Nick.

She had learned a lot about Nick in the past weeks. By this time she knew that he could turn moody, abrupt or remote in an instant. She had also discovered that he could laugh and be serious and that he adored her. Their sexual attraction was right up there, "...a top attraction," Nick had said, "but not *the* top attraction."

The top attraction between them, they had decided seriously on the Sunday when he had taken her to see Novak and Sons' cannery, was the real person inside each of them.

"Too often I've seen people fall in love with the person they *thought* the other one was. They create the perfect mate in the one they love and then they're disappointed when the other one doesn't live up to it."

"I thought that was the way it had to be," Martha said.

"It doesn't," Nick said firmly.

"But it's normal to put the best foot forward when you're interested in someone."

"Sure it is. But most people do more than that. They get caught up in pretending to be what the other person wants. And the other person perpetuates it by having the wrong expectations. Let's not do that."

"We won't," Martha had agreed solemnly. And they had kissed on it, their first real kiss.

Consequently they had stood back and watched their love grow and blossom in a most natural way. Here on Revilla Island, where nature played such a big part in their lives, it seemed only right that they learn all the different facets of each other, a kind of extension of nature study, as Martha termed it. Like most people in love, they were caught up in themselves.

For Martha, this discovery of Nick was marred only by the knowledge that she would be leaving after Labor Day to return to San Francisco. Right now, September and San Francisco seemed far away, but they lingered in the back of her mind like two yellow lights signaling *caution*. She had fallen in love with Nick Novak, but she would eventually have to leave him. It would be hard for her to leave an established relationship; she knew that much about herself. It would hurt to say goodbye— it would hurt so much that she could hardly stand to think about it.

She had no idea if Nick had thought about how he would feel about parting at the end of the summer. Now Nick lay back on the grass beside her, content. She was content, too. She was much too content to think about future sorrows.

"All the rainy days make me appreciate the sunny days so

much more," Martha said dreamily. Above them, a bald eagle inscribed lazy circles on a brilliant blue sky. A breeze ruffled a field of wildflowers sloping down the side of the mountain.

"Don't you think there's something beautiful about the rain, though? For instance, I've grown to enjoy kissing you in the rain very much." He reached for her hand and meshed his fingers with hers as the rugged lines of his face softened into an expression of pure happiness.

Martha answered with a smile. She had learned a lot about adapting their kisses to the moment. A quick peck on the cheek to speed them on their separate ways. A spur-of-the-moment kiss when they were walking together in the park and something made them laugh. A lingering kiss on her porch, their cheeks misted by a dewy rain.

Her serenity lapsed into nostalgia. "I've always loved the rain, even back in Greenleaf, Indiana, where I grew up. When I was a little girl, on rainy days I liked to bundle up in a warm afghan and sit at the big window where I could listen to it rushing through the downspout right outside. My mother would bake cookies for me and my two sisters, and the fragrance would waft all through the house...."

"Chocolate-chip cookies?"

"Yes, although I'd forgotten until just now that those were the kind. I'd better ask her for her recipe. Maybe I could combine it with Faye's and get that special flavor I'm looking for."

"Did you ever ask your mother about the child in her kindergarten class who didn't talk?"

"This week, when Mother and I talked on the phone, I mentioned it. She says she kept some of her notes from her conferences with the child's parents, and she's going to look for them and mail me copies. But she did say that the child finally started to talk."

"Did he?" Nick sat up, fully alert at this news.

"Mother said it took time. How's Davey doing? Any better?"

Nick shook his head. "This morning when I left he said my name, but that's not unusual. I wish you could see his eyes, Martha. They're what really gets to me. I feel as though there are words locked inside him, a whole universe of feeling and thinking and—well, you'd have to see him to know what I mean." Now that he had found someone with whom he felt comfortable communicating his own feelings, he was doubly anxious for Davey to do the same thing. It seemed to him that Davey was locking himself inside his own heart, perpetuating a loneliness that needn't exist. If only he, Nick, could find the key to unlocking Davey's heart, to setting the little boy free from the cage in which he imprisoned himself!

Nick touched a hand to her cheek. "Martha, I think it's time for you to meet Davey. Will you?"

"I'd like that, Nick," she said.

He kissed her on the lips. "Will you come out to Williwaw Lodge next weekend? You could spend Sunday with us. With Hallie and Davey and me, I mean."

Martha nodded and smiled. She loved him so much, and now he was prepared to share this aspect of his life with her.

"I can hardly wait," she said.

"MARTHA—" Faye said with a worried look, but then she stopped.

"Go ahead," Martha said. She and Faye were walking along the winding trails through the park across the street from their duplex. Last week, Faye and Dr. Andy had flown to a remote outpost on an isolated peninsula, where Faye had spent the whole week cooped up in a tiny community center inoculating children against common childhood diseases. She could not stand staying in her apartment one more minute, Faye had said when she'd appeared at the door of Martha's apartment shortly after Martha had returned from work at the Bagel Barn, and she'd dragged Martha along on a walk.

"Martha, about Nick and that little boy," she said.

"I know, Faye," Martha said. "Davey is four years old and he doesn't talk."

"Nick told you?"

Martha nodded.

"What else did Nick tell you?" Faye asked sharply.

"What do you mean?" Martha said. She darted a look in Faye's direction. Faye appeared to be weighing something in her mind.

"I'm fond of Nick and his whole family, you know that," Faye said.

"Of course." Martha stepped over a fallen branch in the path and turned to stare at Faye. "Faye, are you trying to tell me something?"

Faye sighed. "I'd rather not, but you don't know too many people in this town, and if I don't tell you, you will surely hear it on the mukluk grapevine."

"Mukluk grapevine?" Martha said, looking at Faye as though she must have a screw loose somewhere.

"Mukluks are soft Eskimo boots made of caribou skin. A mukluk grapevine is one of our quaint Alaskan expressions, meaning that gossip creeps quietly on foot. By the time you hear about Nick and Davey, it might be too late."

"Too late for what?"

"Too late to put a lock on your heart," Faye muttered grimly.

Martha stopped walking. "A lock on my heart," she repeated faintly. It was already too late for that.

"There's something you don't know about Nick," Faye said.

"I think maybe I'd rather not know," Martha said. She sank down on a park bench beside a rock-lined pool and drew her windbreaker more closely around her.

"When you know, you still won't know," Faye said, but there was more worry in her expression than mystery.

Martha looked Faye straight in the eye. She was getting tired of all this beating around the bush. "Why don't you just come out and say what you want to say?" she said, knowing that was what Faye would do anyway.

"Nobody knows whose little boy Davey is," Faye blurted.

"He's Nick's child. Isn't he?"

"No one knows," repeated Faye.

"I thought Nick must have been married before," Martha said with increasing bewilderment. "I thought that Davey was his child from his first marriage."

"Nick's never been married to my knowledge," Faye said.

"Then whose child is Davey?" Martha asked. A puzzled frown pleated her forehead.

The bright gaze from Faye's one eye cut into her. "That's right," she said bluntly. "Everyone in Ketchikan would like to know the same thing."

Sudden tears sprang to Martha's eyes. She blinked rapidly, then looked up at the blue-green branches of the Sitka spruce overhead and drew a deep breath. The sharp evergreen fragrance stung her nostrils.

"Whose child do you think he is?" she asked at last.

"I'm not sure," Faye said slowly. "I've certainly wondered about it, but Nick Novak isn't the type to provide any explanation. He simply showed up with Davey one day, and that's all anyone knows about it. You wouldn't know this because you've never seen the boy, but Davey is obviously part Indian. Tlingit, I suspect."

"Does he belong to Hallie or one of her relatives?" Martha asked, trying to think of all the possibilities.

Faye shook her head. "I doubt it, although Hallie is a wonderful caretaker for him. No, it's Nick who considers himself primarily responsible for Davey. If Davey were Hallie's responsibility, Nick wouldn't take his duties toward Davey so seriously."

"I wonder if Nick will tell me," Martha said.

"Nick clearly trusts you. Whatever the mystery about Davey is, perhaps he'll enlighten you. Are you going to ask him?"

Agitated, Martha jumped up from the park bench. She was far down the path and proceeding at a fast clip before Faye caught up with her.

"Are you going to ask him?" Faye repeated.

"I don't know, Faye. I just don't know," Martha said.

ON SUNDAY, the day she was finally to meet Davey, Martha met Nick at the floatplane dock. He had told her earlier that they would fly to Williwaw Lodge in his Cessna 210 floatplane if the weather was clear. He was eager for her to get an aerial view of the mountains, forest and town.

He greeted her with a kiss, unaware of the questions running through her mind. He fastened her seat belt for her, and in a few minutes they were trailing a white wake behind them as Nick taxied along the surface of the water preparatory to takeoff.

Nick's plane seemed dwarfed by the towering, snowcapped mountain peaks surrounding them. As they spiraled upward from the city of Ketchikan, Martha was again impressed with how small the little cluster of buildings was in comparison with its surroundings, and how confined by them.

The wilderness, which included both the sixteen-million-acre Tongass National Forest and the two-million-acre Misty Fjords National Monument wilderness area, seemed to press in upon Ketchikan, threatening to crowd it into the chilly depths of the Narrows. Here and there the blue-gray water of outlying bays and fjords was dotted with sand-bordered islands, all deeply forested. The scenery, the scope and depth of it, was majestic, a sight to make Martha's soul soar in appreciation of its beauty. She was also mindful of the determination it took to live in such a place, separated from the rest of the world by the natural barriers of mountains, forest, water and weather.

Because of the noise and vibration of the plane, Nick and Martha barely talked during the short flight. Of course, after Faye's startling revelation earlier in the week, Martha was full of questions about Davey, but she felt ambivalent about asking them. Maybe she'd feel more sure of her ground once she met Davey face-to-face. Surely there would be some clue to this parentage in the child's looks.

When she first saw Nick's cabin at the edge of a clearing on Mooseleg Bay, it was no more than a gray speck on the edge of the water. Then the plane circled, and Nick set them down gently before taxiing toward a floating dock that rose and fell with the tides.

He helped her down the ladder steps affixed to the plane's struts. He held her hand as she stepped from the pontoon over the dark, narrow strip of water and onto the dock. It rocked gently under their weight, and overhead a screeching gull wheeled close, then soared away across the bay, leaving them standing in a silence so deep and so overwhelming that Martha scarcely dared breathe for fear of disturbing it.

"Welcome to Williwaw Lodge," Nick said, resting his hands on her waist. "I've imagined bringing you here hundreds of times, and now you're really here."

Whatever else he might have said was interrupted when a tiny lone figure began to advance slowly down the slope of grass from the cabin.

"There's Davey," Nick said. He kept one arm around Martha's waist, and they went to meet the boy.

Davey walked slowly and cautiously, as though he didn't trust what he saw.

"He's not used to my bringing anyone home with me," Nick said in an undertone. "He wonders who you are."

I wonder who Davey is, too, Martha said silently to herself.

Nick, however, remained unaware of Martha's curiosity. "Davey," called Nick. He and Martha walked forward, off the dock and onto the grass. "Here's a friend I'd like you to meet."

Davey stopped where he was.

Martha's first impression was of a four-year-old who seemed unnaturally wary. He was a chubby little boy with dark, straight hair worn a little too long in front, so that his eyes appeared to be peeping out from under a thatched overhang. His almond-shaped eyes were big, bright and extremely anxious. Though Martha scrutinized Davey's face carefully, his appearance gave her no clue as to whether he was Nick's son or someone else's.

"Nick?" Davey said, shifting awkwardly from one foot to the other. His voice was barely a whisper.

"I've brought Martha to see you. Martha lives in Ketchikan."

Davey shook his head doggedly back and forth in active denial of her presence. Shutters seemed to click down over his eyes, shutters to block Martha from his sight. Nick had been right about Davey's eyes; they were bottomless pools of sadness. "Nick," Davey demanded more loudly.

Nick removed his hand from Martha's waist and strode forward, picking the boy up in his arms. He walked slowly back to where Martha stood.

"Martha, this is Davey."

"Hello, Davey," Martha said, quietly and gently. She smiled. "I'm very happy that Nick brought me to see you." She longed for this meeting with Davey to go well because it seemed to mean so much to Nick. She wanted to reach out and touch the boy, but from the way he shrank away from her she knew that this would be the wrong thing to do.

Davey stuck his face in the opening between the collar of Nick's shirt and his neck. He refused to raise his head.

"Come on," Nick said, his eyes warning Martha to be cautious and not to make a fuss over Davey right now. "Let's go inside and meet Hallie."

Martha pointed to her canvas tote bag, where she carried two dozen of her latest batch of chocolate-chip cookies. She'd brought them in hopes that they'd win Davey over, and she raised her eyebrows now in a silent question, but Nick shook his head.

"Wait," he mouthed silently to her, and just as silently Martha nodded her understanding. Presenting cookies to Davey at this point might create more of a problem than it solved. He clearly wasn't ready to admit Martha's presence here. Martha had the idea that if Davey were able to talk, he'd say without hesitation, "Go away."

They had barely reached the wide front porch when Hallie stepped outside, smiling broadly. "I'm so glad to meet you," Hallie said, taking Martha's hand and wringing it.

"Nick's told me so many good things about you," Martha said.

Hallie laughed. "I should be the one telling you good things about Nick," she replied with a meaningful look in his direction. "I've often told him he needs a—girlfriend." Hallie had been about to say that Nick needed a wife, but she'd changed her mind at the last minute. This Martha Rose might not have marriage in mind. The way she looked at Davey, and the way Davey refused to look at Martha—well, there was no telling how that would go. Nick had never brought a woman here before.

Martha, trying to dismiss Davey's behavior and take heart from Hallie's, turned her attention to Nick's cabin. He'd told her about it and how his father had built it of logs he had cut himself from the surrounding forest. Nick had knocked out the original small windows and replaced them with larger ones with a spectacular view of Mooseleg Bay. He'd also extended the cabin by adding on two bedrooms and a bathroom for himself and Davey after the boy came to live with him. Hallie's room and bath were at the other end of the house, along with a small guest room for visitors. A stone chimney surmounted the shingled roof; a huge stack of firewood cut in three sizes leaned against one of the side walls.

Inside, Martha found Nick's cabin both homey and comfortable. Because Nick was quietly trying without success to convince Davey to lift his head, Hallie took it upon herself to show Martha around.

A big living area was centered around a cavernous stone fireplace. Behind that was a kitchen, where all meals were eaten. Martha was quick to notice the feminine touches of fresh flowers, an embroidered Bless This House sign over the mantel and needlepoint throw pillows on the couch. Another framed cross-stitch motto said, Old Sailors Never Die, They Just Get a Little Dinghy, which made Martha smile.

Hallie saw her admiring these touches. "I made the sign and the pillows," she said with a hint of pride. "When Mr. Novak was alive and all the boys were home, this place needed a woman's touch. It was my job to make a home for them, so I did. Mr. Novak and the boys couldn't have cared less how the place looked. All they wanted was meals on time."

"You've done a good job," she said. Hallie seemed nervous and eager that Martha like what she saw.

"These are some photos that Nick and his friend Hank took," Hallie said, gesturing toward several framed pictures of Alaskan wildlife that hung on the wall closest to the kitchen. There was also a picture of a dramatic orange sun setting behind a stand of trees, a few solemn-eyed pictures of Davey in various stages of growth from infant to toddler and a female nude silhouetted against an unusual rock formation. Martha turned her eyes resolutely away from the nude. It only reminded her that there had been other loves in Nick's life before her, and that there would be others after her, too.

"Hallie, I'm going to take Martha out and show her around," Nick said. He still cradled Davey in his arms, and now he spoke softly to the boy. "Davey, would you like to go with us? I'm going to show Martha the paths and the strawberry patch and Hallie's garden."

Davey dug his head farther down in Nick's collar, as though he was certain that it was the route to China, which Martha figured was where Davey would probably rather be.

"Now, now," Nick said gently. He set Davey on the floor and prized Davey's fingers from around his neck. Davey immediately ran into one of the bedrooms and slammed the door so hard that the pictures clattered against the walls.

"I'll see that he's all right," Hallie promised. "You two go ahead."

With an inquiring look at Nick, Martha followed him outside.

A dirt path led around the woodpile and behind the house. To the left was Hallie's big garden planted with onions and carrots. The garden's prize feature was row after row of huge purple heads of cabbage. Beyond the garden was the forest, a dense and aromatic stand of birch, spruce and alder.

"Don't worry, Martha," Nick said when they were out of hearing distance of the cabin. "Davey hasn't taken an instant dislike to you. He's always like that with strangers." Nick enclosed Martha's hand in his and twined his fingers through hers as though everything were fine.

If everything was fine, Martha wondered tenaciously as they headed toward the woods, why didn't she have the gumption to jump right into this situation up to her earlobes and say, "Where did you get Davey, Nick?"

Usually Martha's well-honed problem-solving instincts enabled her to ferret out answers on her own, but she was stumped by Nick's silence on the matter of Davey, by Faye's disclosures about the boy's origins and by Davey himself. Also, was the communication all that great between Nick and herself if she couldn't bring herself to ask him an honest question and expect an honest answer?

Vacillation wasn't Martha's style. She usually jumped right into things. For better or worse, she was a creature of impulse.

"Nick," she began, thinking to broach the subject of Davey and her uncertainty about his role in Nick's life, but at that precise moment Nick whispered, "Look! There's that mountain chickadee I've been trying to get on film! I'll be right back!" He took off at a run for the cabin and returned almost immediately with his Minolta. Of course, silence was called for as Nick fiddled with the long-distance lens. When he finally snapped the lens cap on after several clicks of the shutter, it was with an exuberant cry of satisfaction. By this time, the chickadee had spread its wings and flown away.

"I've been trying to get that chickadee on film since I first saw it. I think it's building a nest nearby. I've been keeping track of this particular bird because I want Davey to see it."

"Does Davey respond to the things you show him?" she said, retreating once more from asking the specifics of Davey's origins. *I'm a coward,* she told herself.

"Davey's eyes brighten in response to things he likes, and he can become avidly interested in some things. He just doesn't talk about it."

"I spoke to my mother on the phone again yesterday," Martha said slowly. "She found the material she kept about her former student who had the same problem as Davey. She told me a little bit about it."

They were walking on a descending path through the woods now. Nick let the camera swing from its strap around his neck. He held her elbow as they negotiated a turn in the path.

"Did she shed any light on what might be going on with Davey?"

"She said that the child she was teaching finally went to a psychologist, who figured out that he had been terribly frightened when the family's house burned down when he was a baby. It was so traumatic that the boy's verbal development was arrested at that point and he never learned to talk."

Nick was silent for a long time as they walked. His grip on her elbow grew tighter, and Martha felt an indefinable tension in the air almost like the times when Nick became abrupt or aloof and withdrawn.

"And what happened to the boy?" he asked after a while.

"He made a full recovery. He needed counseling and love, Mother says."

"I've told you I'm going to take Davey to a pediatric speech-and-hearing specialist in Juneau," he said.

"Yes."

"We're going next week. I have reservations on a commercial flight out of Ketchikan; we'll spend a couple of days in Juneau."

"Oh," Martha said, wondering how even the anticipation of her separation from Nick could cause her heartache. She felt a little knife-sharp pain in her chest when she thought of Nick going away without her. She chided herself for being silly. She'd always known that there wasn't a future in their love. After all, wasn't she going to leave Alaska at the end of the summer?

While she was striving to be philosophical about this prospect, she heard the sound of rushing water. The forest path descended into a damp green glade. Ferns sprang up under their footsteps, and Martha smelled moss and wet rocks.

"Our waterfall," Nick said, standing aside so that she could see it. It wasn't a spectacular waterfall, but it was high, and water gushed over the rock to a wide pool that tumbled into the underbrush.

"You didn't tell me you had a waterfall," she said accusingly.

He hadn't told her some other things, either, but as much as they were on her mind, she knew this wasn't the time to bring them up.

"Why don't you stand over there on that rock and I'll snap your picture in front of it?"

"Oh, Nick," she protested.

"Your mother went to some trouble getting that information she's sending me about her former student, so the least I can do for her is send her a picture of her daughter deep in the wilds of Alaska, right?"

Laughing, Martha climbed up on the rock. Her mother would never believe that her fashion-conscious daughter could be so happy wearing jeans and a cotton turtleneck with a red plaid flannel shirt knotted around her waist. Maybe a photo was a good idea. She'd get her mother to show it around to all her friends in Greenleaf, Indiana, who would wonder what in the world Martha had gotten herself into now. But vanity made her hide her short, unvarnished fingernails behind her back.

"Let's have the hands out front where everyone can see," chided Nick as he advanced the film for another shot.

"I thought I could get away with hiding them," Martha said in chagrin, but for the next shot she let her hands dangle at her sides.

She had completely given up trying to govern her unruly hair in this damp climate; nowadays she let it do what it wanted to. Nick professed to like her new unstyled look. When he finished taking her picture, he sauntered over to the rock, ran his fingers through her hair until it stood up in curls all over her head, and stepped back to take another picture.

"Nick!"

"Sorry, but this is the way I like you. Natural. Not made up."

Martha waited self-consciously for him to snap another photo, then jumped down from the rock.

"It was a compliment," he assured her.

"I know. I'm even getting used to the more casual way of life here. Yesterday I forgot to put on mascara before I went to work. And then I was glad because I didn't have to worry about it running in the rain. Once upon a time I would have hurried home and put some on. I wouldn't go out of the house if my eyes weren't completely made up."

"The question is," Nick said as they strolled back up the path, "is this woman in jeans and no lipstick the real Martha, or is the former boutique-styled and mascara-ed Martha the real Martha?"

"Good question," she agreed.

"It's a serious question. It follows along with what we discussed before," Nick said.

"You mean about people putting on a show for each other when they first start to date?"

"Exactly."

Martha sighed. "I feel very natural like this. Very *me*. I really enjoy not gunking my hair up with hairspray. I *like* it getting wet. I don't mind that it gets too curly when it rains. I don't know, Nick, maybe this is the real me. Maybe the real Martha Rose got buried under the mascara and makeup base a few years ago and just now burrowed out."

"Got washed out." Nick grinned. "By a Ketchikan rain."

She laughed, and her laughter echoed back from the treetops.

They headed back toward the cabin. They stopped to admire the huge cabbages in Hallie's bounteous vegetable garden, and Martha sampled the sweet strawberries from the strawberry patch. She prolonged the time alone with Nick as long as she could. She wanted to go on savoring his slow smiles and his awareness of her, which she was sure would evaporate as soon as he was around Davey again.

When she went back inside, she'd have to jump right in and resume the task of trying to win Davey over. She knew how much Nick worried about him, and she wanted to help. It seemed so important to him that Martha and Davey like each other.

She already liked Davey. It was well within the limits of her generous nature to like children—almost all children, except for the ones who kicked and bit and whom nobody could love except their mothers. Her experience with children had been extensive for a nonmother, what with several nieces and nephews and leading park nature walks when she was a teenager and having Tiffany as an honorary niece.

But Davey was an entirely different kind of child from the ones Martha had known. Martha had an idea that making him like her was going to be a very difficult task indeed. Now that she had met him, she could see that it was definitely going to take more than a few chocolate-chip cookies to win him over.

She reminded herself to be patient. But being patient was difficult for a creature of impulse.

Chapter Seven

The next week, Nick and Davey went to Juneau for their appointment with the pediatric speech-and-hearing specialist.

Martha hated being the object of Randy's sympathy, but there was no throwing him off the track. Just because she kept dropping things and because her mind kept wandering off, as he said, "like a lovesick moose," Randy kept offering to perform tasks at the Bagel Barn that Martha usually did. He even went to the bank for more change without being asked, which was unusual, because Randy liked to stay in the Bagel Barn where he could wait on customers.

"Why don't you have a sablefish special and take a break?" Randy suggested solicitously when Martha made the wrong change for the fifth time that morning.

"That won't fix what's wrong with me," she retorted with uncharacteristic crossness, but she accepted the bagel Randy handed her and set off walking along the dock, staring up into the rare blue sky from whence Nick and Davey's commercial flight would descend on its arrival from Juneau later that day.

She nibbled at the bagel, and she had to admit it tasted pretty good. However, she just wasn't hungry. She hadn't been able to eat much since Nick had left. Casting a guilty glance back at Randy, she shoved the bagel into the nearest trash can. She simply couldn't eat when she was so concerned about Nick.

"It's only for five days," he had told her before he left. He had kissed her tenderly the night before his departure and had promised to telephone her regularly, which was something he couldn't even do when he was at his cabin on Mooseleg Bay.

Still, for Martha the five days had dragged. She hated being away from Nick, and she worried about Davey.

"The pediatrician here in Juneau says that there's absolutely nothing wrong with Davey's hearing or speech apparatus," Nick had reported enthusiastically the first night when he telephoned.

The pediatrician had suggested that Davey see Dr. Whitmer, who was a noted child psychiatrist. It had taken Nick a day of wheedling in order to get the psychiatrist's receptionist to schedule an appointment before he and Davey had to leave Juneau, and that was where they were today. Martha was on pins and needles, because she suspected that Davey's problem was a psychological one, especially after she read the packet of materials her mother had sent.

Nick and Davey had already left for Juneau by the time the information had arrived, and Martha had called her mother immediately to discuss it.

"As I recall," Martha's mother said, "the little boy in my class was highly intelligent. They'd tried everything to get him to talk, but nothing worked. He seemed like a very sad little boy, and it took us a while to get to the bottom of it. But who would think that a house fire when the boy was a baby was responsible for his not saying a word until he got professional help!"

"Your description of your student sounds a lot like Davey," Martha said. "Davey's a sad little boy, too."

"Your friend Nick—doesn't he have any idea what's wrong with Davey?"

"Unfortunately, no," said Martha. "That's why he's taken Davey to Juneau for an expert opinion."

"Has Davey been subjected to any traumatic experiences? Any serious family problems or anything like that?"

"I'm not sure," Martha said. No one would know that except Nick, and if Nick knew, he wasn't telling.

"I know it's not a laughing matter, Martha, but your sister Roxie brought both kids over to the house today, and we couldn't help wishing for some peace and quiet! How those children can carry on!" And then Mrs. Rose proceeded to brag about her darling grandchildren, which only made Martha despair more. Hearing about other children's noisy exploits only made her more aware of Davey's problem.

She had made absolutely no headway in getting to know Davey. Nick had brought him over to her house one day, and although Davey had finally eaten the peanut butter and jelly sandwich Martha offered, and although he had settled down agreeably in front of her television set to watch a children's special, he had barely acknowledged that Martha was there. He had seemed well aware of his surroundings, brightening considerably when Martha and Nick took him to the park. He had played alongside other kids and had even responded enthusiastically to a game of tag. But Martha felt no closer to Davey than she had when she first met him, and she knew this was starting to upset Nick.

"You've been so nice to Davey," Nick said, cuddling her close on the night before he left. "Davey couldn't ask for any more consideration."

Indeed. On that particular day, Martha had set aside what she was doing, had put off filling out orders for supplies from Sidney because Davey and Nick were there, had forgone baking a new batch of chocolate-chip cookies in which she planned to increase the amount of brown sugar and decrease the amount of vanilla flavoring. She'd even made a quick trip to the grocery store in the rain so she'd have peanut butter for Davey because he liked it. She'd given one hundred percent and had received no response from Davey. Not that she expected anything, knowing how Davey was. But it would have been nice to have some encouragement from the child after all.

Sometimes she wanted to hold him in her arms, and a couple of times she had. At those times Davey had only sagged against her unresponsively, as though he hadn't even known she was there. Finally Martha reached a new understanding of Nick's frustration. She had felt the same hopelessness over Davey herself.

Right now it felt good to be away from the Bagel Barn, even for a few minutes. The breeze off the Narrows freshened, bringing with it the scent of brine. Formerly a landlocked midwesterner, Martha had developed a firm affection for the sea; she loved its fragrance, its wildlife, its scenery and its mercurial nature. The sea was impulsive, as she was. She couldn't imagine living inland again. Fortunately, she wouldn't have to. San Francisco would soon be her permanent home.

This thought reminded her that she hadn't yet sent off the weekly supply order to Sidney. She'd do it later, dropping it off at the post office when she left work. She wondered if Sidney would notice that she was ordering the same number of bagels this week but less lox.

Martha was ordering less lox because the Alaskan salmon, which she now bought in quantity from Nick's store, was so popular. It wasn't unusual, even with her well-fed cruise-ship passengers, for customers to try one bagel heaped high with alder-smoked Alaska salmon and then return for another. Sales were brisk, in part because Martha had taken the responsibility for serving bagels with Alaska salmon but also because Randy was such a good salesman.

She never regretted hiring Randy. He had a likable, outgoing personality, and he was always urging customers to try this or that for the first time. He was so jolly and pleasant that the customers usually tried what he recommended. Sometimes they'd return with a friend or a fellow passenger and say, "He wants one of those bagels with the Alaskan salmon, too."

It was Randy who had started offering a daily special priced twenty percent off the regular price. Randy had discovered that cruise-ship passengers, after paying top dollar to sail on a luxury liner such as the *Trondheim*, loved the idea of finding a bargain in Alaska, which was generally considered an expensive place to visit. Most Alaskan prices reflected the expense of shipping all supplies in by sea or air. Today's sablefish special had been Randy's idea, and as with all their specials he had lettered a neat but noticeable sign and tacked it on the side of the Bagel Barn so that tourists coming up the ramp of the dock would know right away that the Bagel Barn offered a bargain.

At the moment, Randy was toasting and serving bagels as well as brewing tea, pouring soft drinks and handling money. A line formed to the right of the Bagel Barn. Martha had better stop shirking her duties and give poor Randy the help he needed.

She glanced at her watch. It was three o'clock. Only two more hours before Nick and Davey returned from Juneau.

Her spirits lifting, Martha hurried back to the Bagel Barn, where she put on the silly red-and-white apron required by Sidney and attacked her work with renewed vigor. Two hours wasn't long to wait; two hours was nothing compared to the five days that Nick had already been away.

MARTHA WENT TO MEET Nick and Davey at the ferry terminal, where she spent an anxious hour pacing the floor because their scheduled airline flight had been late.

Nick, carrying Davey with one arm and with a small suitcase in the other hand, hove into sight immediately after the ferry docked. He wore a felt outback hat, which made him look dashing, and he towered over the other passengers. Martha's heart swelled at the sight of him; she had missed him so much.

Nick set Davey down and swept Martha into his arms. "Dear Cheechako," he said, the words coming easily to his lips. He had noticed happy tears glistening on her eyelashes in the moment before he embraced her, and the sight of them had so overwhelmed him with emotion that he felt a bit teary himself. He hadn't believed how much he had missed her quick humor and her pleasant disposition all the time he'd been away.

She pulled slightly apart from him. Her gray eyes sparkled; her lips were slightly parted and moist. He wanted to kiss her again, but Davey was silently and insistently tugging at the bottom of his coat.

"I have food at my place," Martha offered quickly.

"Davey and I are invited to Dan and Cheryl's for dinner," Nick said.

Martha didn't reply, but she looked crestfallen.

"I'm sure you'd be invited too, if they knew you'd like to come."

She had hoped to have Nick to herself. Nick and Davey, that is.

"I don't know," she said doubtfully.

Nick realized then that Martha had planned for his return, that she probably had a complete dinner waiting. He should have told her earlier that he and Davey were invited to eat with his brother and his family tonight. He simply wasn't used to including Martha automatically in the day-to-day details of his life yet.

"Hey," he said, tipping her chin up so he could look into her troubled eyes. "I'll call Cheryl and beg off. Okay?"

"I don't want to interfere with family plans," Martha said.

"Don't be silly," Nick said. "Cheryl told me she wasn't planning anything special. She was having a big chicken casserole and Davey and I were invited to eat it if we could make it. And our plane was an hour late; they've probably started eating already."

Martha smiled. Suddenly everything was all right again. "My car's over there," she said, and Nick took Davey by the hand and followed her.

"I'm glad we can have some time together," Nick said on the way to Martha's apartment. "I have a lot to tell you. Later." He shot a meaningful look over the back of the front seat at Davey.

Martha served a mouth-watering meal of king crab legs and wild rice, fresh broccoli and carrots. Davey ate well and then sat down to work an easy puzzle that Martha had bought for him in a local variety store. Martha and Nick sat down on the couch to catch up.

"The psychiatrist, Dr. Whitmer, tested Davey," Nick told her, keeping his voice low so Davey couldn't hear. "But he wants to give him more tests in two weeks. We'll be going back to Juneau then."

"I missed you," she said, her heart in her throat. "I wish you didn't have to go away again so soon."

Nick's face was momentarily clouded with sadness. "I missed you, too. It certainly wasn't fun being apart. But this was something I had to do. You understand, don't you?" His brown eyes, swimming with flecks of gold, swept her face.

"I do understand," she said slowly.

At the table where he was working the puzzle, oblivious to their conversation, Davey yawned and scrubbed at his eyes with both fists.

"He's tired," Nick said. "Aren't you, Davey?"

Davey nodded. His eyes were heavy and thick-lidded.

"Why don't you let him lie down on my bed?" Martha suggested.

"Good idea," Nick replied, and he lifted the unprotesting Davey in his arms and carried him into Martha's bedroom, where Martha peeled back the bedspread so that Nick could put Davey down on top of the blankets. She brought a warm comforter from the closet and together they billowed it up and over the boy, tucking it in on both sides.

Davey closed his eyes immediately. His thick black eyelashes curved against plump cheeks; his chest rose and fell evenly with each breath. He was such a beautiful little boy, Martha thought. He looked so healthy. Looking at him now, no one would ever guess that he was a child with a problem.

Nick bent over and brushed Davey's forehead with his lips. In the dim light from the hall, Martha saw the crease of worry in Nick's forehead. Her heart went out to him. Nick was so conscientious. He tried so hard. He desperately wanted Davey to be normal, and he was afraid that Davey never would be.

"Come on," she said, folding her hand in his, and together they went out of the room and closed the door.

"I brought you something," Nick said suddenly when they were back in her living room. He produced a small square package.

Martha hadn't expected a gift. She pulled the gilt wrapping off and opened the box. Inside was a wide carved ivory bracelet. The series of carvings on the curved sides of the bracelet depicted animal motifs that she had learned to associate with Alaskan Native art. A polar bear stood on its hind legs. An Eskimo paddled a kayak. A caribou picked its way through a landscape of wildflowers.

"The bracelet's made of walrus ivory by a Native Alaskan," Nick said. "New England whalers who came here long ago passed along the art of scrimshaw carving to Alaskan craftsmen. I thought you'd like it."

"It's so pretty, Nick," Martha said, captivated by the pictures.

"Let me do the honors," Nick said, slipping the bracelet on her arm and raising her hand to kiss her fingers. He wrapped his arms around her from behind, then nuzzled her cheek.

"It'll be something to remind me of Alaska once I've gone home," she said. Her voice quavered, and Nick's embrace loosened in surprise. Martha couldn't believe she had startled him with her statement about going home. She had never led him to think that she planned to stay in Ketchikan. Going back to the Lower Forty-eight was inevitable.

"Martha," he began uneasily.

She turned in his arms until she faced him. "Shhh," she whispered against his cheek. "Some things are better left unsaid."

He folded her in his arms, but she sensed the tension in his muscles. It was too soon, she thought with regret. Why had she brought up a subject that was better off ignored? It must be that their unavoidable separation was on her mind more than ever now that she knew how much she hated being apart from him. She rested her head against his chest, drawing comfort from the strong, steady sound of his heartbeat.

After a moment he said, "Let's sit down. We need to talk about this. We'll have to face it sooner or later." He led her to the couch and pulled her down beside him. He held both her hands fast in his as he turned toward her.

"I've never made any secret of the fact that I'm going back to San Francisco in September," she began haltingly.

"And I haven't made any secret of the fact that I'm crazy in love with you." His voice remained quiet, but there was something commanding in his tone. He released one hand and cupped her cheek in his palm. "In love with you," he repeated, in case there was some remote chance that she hadn't comprehended.

"I have an agreement with Sidney," Martha said, fighting to regain her composure. "He's going to cut me in on the profits. I'll be vice president in charge of setting up Bagel Barns all over the United States. It's the chance of a lifetime to get in on the bottom floor of a business."

"I can appreciate that," Nick said slowly.

"Can you?" Martha asked, her eyes searching his. "You were able to expand an existing family business in order to get where you are today. I didn't have that opportunity, although I might have if things had been different."

"What do you mean, 'different'?"

"Oh, Nick, I don't know that it's important to tell you about it."

He could tell from the restrained tone of her voice that she was becoming agitated, from that and the way her fingertips twitched within the clasp of his hands, but he wanted her to go on talking. He wanted to be a good listener for her, just as she had been for him.

"Of course it's important," he said seriously. "Everything

about you is important to me." It went without saying; didn't she know that?

"I made up my mind a long time ago that I was going to succeed in some facet of business," she said with a steely glint in her eye that he had never noticed before. "It has a lot to do with my father and the way I was brought up."

She looked so stiff and uncomfortable, so patently unlike herself, that he knew this was a sensitive subject. He decided to make it easier for her.

"Your father wanted a son, but had three daughters," Nick guessed. "He wanted a son to take over the business."

Martha blinked. "How did you know?" she said.

"I must have seen a movie like that once. Let me tell you the rest of the plot. You were the one he was counting on to take over the business. And you knew he was counting on you. Am I right so far?"

Her eyes, which had looked so somber, showed a hint of sparkle. "So far, yes."

"And so you worked very hard in school and in college and—"

"And?"

"And why don't you finish the story? There must be some reason why you didn't take over the business as scheduled."

Martha bit her lip. "Yes, there was," she said quietly. "Dad died, and then there wasn't any business anymore." She shrugged lightly as if to deny the pain, and her fingers jerked convulsively in his.

"I'm sorry, Martha," he said. "I didn't mean to make light of it."

Martha inhaled a deep breath. "It's all right. I've pulled through it. But when Dad died at the beginning of my junior year in college, I thought it was the end of the world. I had just declared a business major, and I'd spent the summer working with Dad at the retail clothing store he owned in Greenleaf. It was a pretty-good-sized operation; he sold both men's and women's clothes."

"You must have liked the work," Nick said.

"Oh, I loved it from the beginning, even from the time when Dad would take me to the store with him on Saturday mornings and feed me Reed peppermints from his bottom desk drawer.

When I was older, Dad was thrilled that I took an interest in the store because my sisters Roxie and Carolyn never had, except to work there during the summers while they were in high school. Dad and I both looked forward to the day when I'd be able to take over some of the responsibility from him so he could get some well-deserved rest. But after Dad died and we found out how deeply in debt he was, there was nothing to do but sell the store.''

''Wasn't there anything else you could do?''

Martha shook her head. ''It's very risky, running a business of your own. You have to tie up a lot of money in inventory. There's no one to fall back on if you have a couple of bad years. I saw it happen with Dad, and that's why I wouldn't start my own business. That's why I was happy when Sidney made it possible for me to be part of his. I won't turn my back on this opportunity. I can't.''

''Is it the money, Martha?''

''Not the money, especially, although that's nice. It's the feeling of accomplishment. It's knowing that I'll be responsible for making important decisions. For building a business practically from the ground up.''

''You could do that anywhere,'' Nick stubbornly pointed out.

''There are very few companies where I'll have the chance I have with Sidney Pollov Enterprises,'' Martha said. ''No risk for me, and every opportunity. I can't go wrong.''

''You can't go, period. I don't want you to leave at the end of the summer, Martha.''

''Nick, I can't continue selling bagels on the dock in the winter. Unless it were frozen bagels, and I don't think that's what Sidney has in mind.''

She wasn't going to give an inch, at least not during this go-round. Nick sighed and pulled her into his arms. He would have liked to shake some sense into her, but he knew it would be futile. Anyway, he'd rather kiss her, and he did.

She forgot everything when he took her in his arms and began to rain little kisses on her ear, on the softly curving line of her jaw. His delicately teasing kisses made her hungry for more, and she pulled his lips down to hers. All the loneliness of the past five days faded away, and Martha felt herself opening to him, unfolding in the heat of his pleasure. His shoulder muscles hardened beneath her gentle fingertips, and she tasted and explored him with unrestrained joy and wonder.

"My dear Cheechako," he murmured against her lips, and his hands moved up her back, then drifted along her rib cage until they encircled her breasts. His touch was gentle yet sure, awakening nerves and hypnotizing her with pleasure.

They slid downward on the couch, and the emotion in Martha's sea-gray eyes drowned him in its sheer intensity. She loved him; he could see that. And he loved her. It was time for their relationship to progress to the next step, the merging of their bodies and minds in the most beautiful form of communication ever known.

Despite her acquiescence up to this point, Martha apparently had other ideas.

"Nick," she said. "Stop."

At the sound of her words, Martha struggled her way out of a lovely romantic daze, and at first she wasn't sure Nick even heard her.

But then he pulled back.

"Something's wrong?"

"I'm not comfortable with what was happening between us. Oh, I know, I know. We love each other, and we're both getting tired of only hugs and kisses. But I'm going away at the end of the summer, and maybe we don't want to get involved." Her hands fluttered, a sign of nervousness. Nick captured them with his and kissed her lightly on the lips.

"*I* want to get involved," he assured her.

"It's different for a man," Martha said.

"I don't think so. Not when the man loves the woman as much as I love you. I do love you, Martha. You know that, don't you?"

"Yes," she whispered, looking even more troubled.

"And I want to be with the woman I love," he finished. When she looked into his face, she couldn't doubt his sincerity.

He was the dearest man; he was masculine, considerate, thoughtful and kind. He was emotionally self-sufficient. He was wonderful with children. Martha had seen that in the way he took care of Davey.

But how could she tie herself to a man she would leave in a few short months? Polly would have said it was better to have loved Nick completely than only to have loved him halfway. Polly, of course, would have been referring to the physical side of their relationship. Martha knew herself well enough to understand that if she loved Nick that way she might never be able to leave him. She doubted that there could ever be a future for her in Ketchikan.

"I guess I'm just not ready," she said lamely, searching for understanding in Nick's expression.

It was one of the things she loved about him most. She could always count on him to understand the way she felt, even when she provided only minimal explanation. He might have absorbed her emotions by osmosis or ether waves; there seemed to be no logical explanation for his instant comprehension.

"Well, Martha," he said, touching his lips to her fingertips with something that looked like laughter in his eyes, "just remember this. I'm ready whenever you are."

At that he really did laugh, a loud, booming sound that woke Davey, but before Davey could come into the living room he kissed Martha with a thoroughness that completely proved his point.

During the next few days, Martha delighted in her reunion with Nick. Their five-day separation made every moment even more precious to her, especially because she knew she would not stay past Labor Day.

Nick met her at the Bagel Barn every day and together they ate lunch, sometimes in Nick's company car if the weather was bad, sometimes in the café where they always ordered steaming-hot bowls of chili in honor of that first Sunday they had spent together, sometimes overlooking the Narrows with the boats sailing in and out past the big cruise ships anchored offshore.

And they laughed. They laughed at everything. They laughed at people and the tourists and themselves. They laughed at silly jokes. Most importantly, they laughed at the same things. Over and over Martha was taken with their compatibility.

Occasionally Martha felt that this part of her life was taking place in a happy dream. They were both so absorbed in one another that they each developed an urgent, insatiable need for the other's presence. No matter how cloudy the day, no matter how cold the drizzle, they created their own sunshine and warmth when they were together.

Those were emotional days, but there were no more emotional nights. Martha knew that Nick was purposely giving her the space she needed. She was grateful to him for that even when every fiber of her being longed to be with him through the long, cool nights, warmth against warmth.

But although he kissed her and told her he loved her each day, he did nothing to pressure her into a physical relationship. And that told her he really loved her more than anything else.

She *thought* he loved her, anyway. Until one morning when she called his office to find out if their previously agreed-upon time for lunch still stood and was told by his secretary that Mr. Novak was out of town.

"Out of town? Are you sure?" Martha said, staring hard at the buttons of the pay phone on the dock.

"He left early this morning," was the short reply.

"When will he be back?" Martha asked.

"He'll be gone indefinitely. We don't know when Mr. Novak will return."

"Did he leave a message for me?"

"No. No message."

The click on the other end of the line preceded the loud buzz of the dial tone.

"Indefinitely?" Martha whispered unbelievingly as she replaced the receiver on its hook.

She simply couldn't believe that Nick would leave Ketchikan without a word to her.

Chapter Eight

What had happened?

Martha asked herself this anguished question over and over each day that Nick didn't come home. Had she said something to drive him away? She went over every word they'd said since he'd returned from Juneau. They had been so happy together. Why would he leave suddenly without telling her?

She thought of asking Hallie, but Hallie was at Williwaw Lodge, and there was no way to contact her except by shortwave radio. Martha didn't have access to shortwave, although she knew there was one at the office of Novak and Sons. After being so summarily turned away by Nick's secretary, however, she wouldn't ask to use it.

Faye was away in the bush ministering to the sick, and so Martha had no one to talk to. Randy was kind and sympathetic, but Martha hadn't enlightened him about the reason for her distraction. She thought Randy was very clever, therefore, when he asked her abruptly one day, "What's the matter? Has Nick gone away again?"

She nodded quietly and busied herself with counting the money from the cash register. She had to keep a tight hold on the bills; for a week a brisk wind had swept in off the Narrows, and it showed no sign of letting up.

Randy waited until she was finished counting the money before he said, "Nick's always traveling someplace or another. I'd get used to it if I were you."

This surprised her. "I thought Nick preferred to stay home," she said. "Because of Davey, you know."

"That may be true, but Nick's his own person. He takes off from time to time, and he never tells anyone where he's going. He doesn't take Davey, either. The only time he's ever taken Davey with him is when they went to Juneau."

"I didn't know you knew Nick that well."

Randy shrugged. "I don't. My mother is Hallie's sister Wanda's closest friend. So I hear a lot of things about Nick."

Sometimes Martha forgot what a small town Ketchikan really was. Randy's disclosure didn't help her. It only worried her more. She couldn't understand why Nick would tell her he didn't like to work on the family fishing fleet because he wanted to stay home with Davey and then take off for days at a time for some unknown destination.

Could it have something to do with her refusal to make love the night he came back from Juneau? Martha turned that thought over in her mind and weighed it carefully. Maybe he knew someone else, another woman, one who didn't live in Ketchikan. And yet, if he did, she felt as though she'd know. She didn't think that Nick could have been so open and trusting and loving with her if he had another woman stashed away in the wilderness somewhere. He didn't strike her as a two-timer.

And yet he had gone away without a warning.

Alone in her apartment, she cried because she didn't understand. At the Bagel Barn, she kept up a cheerful front so that Randy and the rest of Ketchikan wouldn't know how Nick had disappointed her.

She would wait until Nick came home. He would explain everything then.

THE TELEPHONE WOKE HER in the middle of the night. She reached for it blindly, jangled into confusion by the insistent ring.

"Martha?"

"Nick?" She blinked eyes gritty with sleep.

"Yes. How *are* you?"

Martha squinted at her alarm clock. It was after midnight.

"I—I'm all right. It's one o'clock in the morning, Nick. Where are you?"

"In Petersburg. I was hoping you'd still be awake."

"Well, I am now," she said. She knew that the town of Petersburg was over a hundred miles to the north. What was he doing there?

"I love you, Martha. I'll be home tomorrow."

"That's good," Martha said, lamely, but she felt a surge of anger. How did he expect her to react when he'd disappeared for four whole days without a word?

"I'd like to see you tomorrow night."

"Well, I—"

"I've missed you so much. You can't imagine."

Martha wasn't ready to give him a piece of her mind, but she could and did reply tartly, "I can't imagine, all right. I can't imagine why you disappeared without a trace for four days, especially when we had a prearranged date for lunch."

"Didn't you get my note?"

"What note?"

"The note I stuck under your door. I left on the first plane out of Ketchikan in the morning, and I didn't want to wake you up. I stuck it under your door on my way to the airport."

"I never saw any note."

"Martha, I— Oh, hell." He sounded disgusted, either with her or with himself. A long silence ensued, a silence during which Martha gazed up at the ceiling and clamped her mouth shut so that she wouldn't say something she'd later regret.

When she didn't speak, he said in a resigned tone, "I'll see you tomorrow night. Goodbye, Martha," whereupon he hung up, leaving Martha holding a dead line and with a feeling of utter incredulity.

She could not for the life of her imagine what he was doing in Petersburg, nor could she understand how, if he loved her as he claimed he did, he could leave for four days without a word.

"THAT'S NICK NOVAK for you," Faye said philosophically. She took a bite out of a doughnut and dunked the remains into her coffee.

"No, it's not Nick Novak for *me*," Martha said miserably. "For somebody else, maybe, but not for me."

"You can't say I didn't warn you," Faye said.

"You warned me about Davey. You warned me that no one

knows whose child he is. But you didn't warn me that Nick Novak was going to disappear for days at a time."

"Face it, Martha. He's a secretive guy. You could know Nick for years and still not really know him."

"I thought I knew him. We've talked for hours; I know his thoughts, his longings, his ambitions, his secrets—"

Faye leveled her doughnut at Martha like a wagging finger. "But not *all* his secrets," she said.

"Don't remind me," Martha said. She was late for work already, but she had heard Faye's laundry thumping in the dryer in their shared laundry room and peeked in to find Faye and a box of fresh doughnuts. Now she was pouring her heart out to Faye, hoping that Faye would understand. She wasn't sure that Faye did understand. Instead of a shoulder to cry on, Faye offered nothing but flippant remarks.

"Oh, Martha," Faye said, suddenly setting her doughnut down. "Don't take it so hard. Wait and see what Nick says. Maybe he did really leave you a note. Where did he say he left it?"

"He said he put it under my door."

"Well, perhaps he did. If it's been as windy here as it's been in the bush all week, that note could have blown clear to the Klondike before you woke up."

That idea was something of a comfort. She would see Nick tonight and find out what had really happened.

HE GREETED HER at her door with a kiss, although she was less than enthusiastic. One look at her told him that she was angry; the naked pain in her eyes was eloquent testimony of her disappointment in him. He was instantly caught up in a riptide of regret. On the morning when he left, he should have awakened her and told her personally that he was leaving Ketchikan for a few days; slipping the note under her door had not, in retrospect, been a good idea. He admitted to himself that in a way he was a coward. He hadn't wanted to face her questions.

But now, it seemed, he must face her anger.

"Let's go out and get dinner someplace," he said.

"I don't think I could eat," she said.

"Please? I'm hungry because I had to skip lunch to catch up

on things at the plant.'' Besides, he'd much rather sit across a table from her for the quiz session she had in mind. He had an idea that being out in public would decrease the tension between them. He'd had no experience with Martha's anger before, but in case she turned out to be the type who yelled and threw things, a restaurant seemed like a good idea. He knew she'd never make a scene in public.

Martha considered the restaurant idea for a moment. ''All right,'' she conceded. She disappeared into the bedroom to get a jacket.

Nick had the nightmarish premonition that Martha's icy anger was going to last for weeks. They drove to the restaurant, a place on Front Street where he could order a big steak. On the way, she sat immobile on her side of the car, the hurt radiating from her in waves. The trouble was that the two of them didn't have weeks for Martha to indulge her anger. They had a little over two months left to be together at all. It seemed ridiculous to him for them to quarrel and spoil everything.

Over cocktails, after the dining-room waiter had taken their order, Nick said carefully, ''I *did* leave you a note before I left. I'm surprised you didn't find it.'' He always thought it was better to take the offensive rather than to be placed on the defensive. He saw a darting flash of pain in her eyes, like a strike of lightning.

''I never found the note,'' she said.

''I did finally telephone,'' he pointed out.

''By the time you phoned you had already been gone four days.''

''In my note I mentioned that I'd call you as soon as I knew when I'd be home. I didn't know for sure until last night,'' he said, feeling a little desperate. Obviously she was not going to relax and accept his apology.

''Why didn't you know? Where were you the rest of the time?'' Martha asked in a determined voice.

''I was—on business.''

''Business?''

''Yes.''

She shifted uneasily in her chair. She looked like an icicle, ready to drop and shatter at any minute. He knew that she didn't believe him, and he longed to reassure her. But he didn't know how.

"Something's wrong," she said. "Isn't it?"

"The only thing that's wrong is that you don't believe me when I say I was away on business. Do you?"

Martha bit her lip. "I'm not sure," she said, watching his face.

He sighed and leaned back in his chair. The silence stretched between them, tight as a haul line on a trolling rig. He'd missed her terribly, and he'd hated the fact that this most recent separation had come so soon after his trip to Juneau with Davey. Still, there hadn't been anything he could do. He'd had to go.

Martha leaned forward in her chair, and a muscle twitched in her left eyelid. "Nick," she said quietly, "this isn't like us. I have the feeling that you're not leveling with me. You're not *talking* to me, Nick, and I feel left out and lonely. I feel abandoned. And I'm furious because we had plans and then you disappeared into thin air. I got what sounded very much like a brush-off from your secretary, and I've been miserable for days. If you'd tell me where you've been and what you've been doing—"

"I can't tell you," he said, more curtly than he'd intended.

"You can't tell me," she repeated slowly in disbelief.

"No."

"Then what am I supposed to think?" Martha shot back. Her face paled and her eyes filled with tears.

He put his hand over her fist, which was clenched on top of the table. "Dear Cheechako, think that I love you and that I'm telling the truth."

His use of the endearment he had coined for her almost melted her cold detachment. She paused for a few seconds to blink the tears from her eyes. "I'll only believe you if you tell me where you were and what you were doing," she said.

"There are parts of my life that I can't talk about," he said, giving her a look that would have drawn blood from a stone.

"That's not good enough," she said. A hard, cold knot was growing where her heart had been.

"I'm afraid it will have to be." Nick hated what he was doing to her, and he hated what he was doing to them as a couple. He began to feel as though their relationship was veering out of control and there was nothing he could do to stop it.

"Nick, under the circumstances it's hard for me to believe that you care about me at all," she said.

"I care," he said slowly. "I love you."

"What does that mean to you?" Her eyes were like chips of flint, sharp and cold.

"That I—that I—" He found it difficult to put his feelings for her into words when confronted by her anger.

"I'll tell you what love means to me," Martha said. "It means that we trust one another. It means sharing, Nick—sharing our joys and our sorrows. Our *feelings*."

"I've shared my feelings," he said evenly.

"Something happened to make you leave town suddenly, and it was important enough so that you'd leave me and our supposed relationship behind. You came back and tell me we can't talk about where you went or what you were doing. This is not communication, Nick."

He knew she was right, but he also knew that he could do nothing about it. "I know it's a lot to ask," he said desperately. "Please, try to understand."

She stood up. Her eyes were the gray of thunderclouds.

"Martha!"

"I can't eat anything," she said, tossing her napkin down. "I'm sorry." And she walked out.

HE RAN AFTER HER, but by the time he had paid for their drinks she was nowhere in sight. He couldn't figure out where she had gone; a few couples, probably tourists, roamed the streets, and a car full of rowdy young men lurched past, but there was no sign of Martha. He stood for a moment on the cold, dark, rain-wet street, his collar turned up to protect his neck from the fierce and biting wind. Then he drove to his office.

He sat in the chair at his desk and punched out her telephone number, letting the phone ring until she answered.

"I wanted to make sure you're safely home," he said gruffly.

"Faye was in the bar having a drink with friends. They were getting ready to leave, and they drove me home."

"I want to see you soon," he said.

"I need time to calm down. Time to think it over."

"Martha, it goes entirely against my grain not to tell you everything. But there are things you cannot know. Not now, not ever. I'm asking you to trust me enough not to ask me about them."

"That's a lot to ask, Nick."

"Maybe. But I'm asking it anyway. I love you, Martha. I'll call you soon." With that he hung up and pushed his desk chair back until he could prop his feet on top of the desk. From the cannery came the clatter of the machines, the shouts of the employees. For Nick they didn't exist. He was thinking of the past four days and the ordeal that he was honor-bound not to discuss with anyone.

THE CALL HAD COME to his office early in the morning five days ago, and Nick, who had slept there overnight because of a dense fog between Ketchikan and Mooseleg Bay, answered it.

"Nick Novak?"

He recognized the voice and his heart sank. When he heard that gravelly voice, it usually meant trouble.

"This is Billy Long. Granny's bad again."

"How bad?"

"In the hospital. This time they don't think she'll last."

Nick sighed. He knew what Billy wanted—money. And Nick's presence.

"Can you come? She's been asking for you. And for Dolores."

"Well—"

"She's real bad, Nick. You know as well as I do that Granny's money is all gone, and I don't have much. Also, my kids have been needing things like clothes and a car for Billy Jr., and Gloria had to have an operation on her foot last month."

"I'll be there, Billy. I'll get there as soon as I can."

Nick hung up, threw the few changes of clothes he kept at the office into a small suitcase and rushed to the airport to grab the first flight out. On the way, in the thin gray light of dawn, he stopped by Martha's apartment and stuck a hastily written note under her door. At the airport he arrived just in time to hop on the plane to Petersburg, which gave him time to plan what he'd do when he got there.

Billy, highly nervous, met Nick at the airport. Nick had known he would. Billy was dependable in that way, at least.

"How is she?" Nick asked.

"The Med-Evac helicopter had to come and get her. She started coughing and choking in the middle of the night, and Gloria sat up with her and gave her her medicine, but it didn't do any good. That's when we knew we had to get help. They put her in an oxygen tent in the hospital, and the doctors say she has pneumonia."

The hospital and its smells and uniforms were familiar to Nick by now, and so was the wizened little Tlingit Indian woman with sunken cheeks and skin the color of a walnut who barely mounded the bed covers in the high hospital bed.

"Elsa?" Nick said gently when she opened her eyes and stared at him hostilely from beneath the oxygen tent.

"Who are you?" Her voice was high and thin. She was a querulous old woman.

"I take care of Davey. Remember?"

"Oh, yes, Davey. Where's Dolores?"

Nick's forehead knitted in a frown. He glanced at Billy.

"Dolores is dead, Granny. You remember that."

Elsa let her wrinkled eyelids drift shut, and Nick thought that she was asleep, but in a moment they shot open again. She regarded him balefully.

"You took Dolores," she said accusingly to Nick.

"No, Granny," Billy said. "Nick didn't take Dolores. Dolores loved Hank, and they went out on the boat together. Remember?"

Elsa Long mumbled something unintelligible.

"Granny? Granny?" Billy said anxiously, but the old woman didn't reply. Nick and Billy sat beside her bed, watching her struggle for life until a nurse padded in and asked them to leave.

"Well?" Billy said once they had shut the door to the hospital room behind them. "Granny is going to die this time. I am sure of it. She's very old and very tired. The thing is, Nick, how long are you going to stay?"

Nick thought of Martha waiting for him back in Ketchikan. Always before on such missions, he'd only had Davey to think about, but now he had Martha and he desperately longed to be with her. Standing here in this cold and antiseptic hospital corridor, Martha with her bright gray eyes and her soft dark hair seemed an inviting vision indeed, but Nick resolutely pushed her image from his mind.

"I'll stay a few days," he promised Billy, and then they went to check Nick into a local motel where the walls were damp and where the sheets smelled of Clorox. Nick didn't complain. He had stayed there many times on similar visits, and he was used to it by this time.

But, surprising everyone, Elsa Long did not die. Instead she rallied, and the doctors said she could go home on the third day of Nick's visit. On the fourth day, after paying Elsa's considerable hospital bill, Nick arranged for a private helicopter flight from Petersburg to the isolated house on Bilgewater Creek where Billy Long and his family lived during the summers.

He was touched by the Longs' eagerness to please, but he was all too aware of their lack of creature comforts, so Nick declined Billy's wife Gloria's offer of overnight hospitality. After he had made sure that Elsa was installed in the hospital bed that he, Nick, had provided for her on a previous occasion, and that she was comfortable, he returned to Petersburg on the helicopter in the dead of night.

Once back in his lonely, Clorox-scented motel room, Nick called Martha for reassurance and love and to tell her that he would return tomorrow. He was both surprised and taken aback when she was angry. He was chagrined when he learned the reason.

Yet he knew that he could never tell Martha the reason that departing for Petersburg so precipitously was important to him. Elsa Long's health was precarious at best, and although he was sure that her grandson Billy and his wife Gloria meant well, he knew they couldn't afford expensive doctors and health care. That was why he had chosen to become so involved with them. He wanted Elsa Long to have proper health care and enough money in her declining years.

In his mind, she deserved no less. After all, Elsa Long was Davey's grandmother.

"HE'S INVITED ME to spend the day with him and Davey tomorrow at Williwaw Lodge," Martha said. It was Saturday; she was taking the day off and Faye was visiting.

"So go," Faye said. She measured out brown sugar for the cookie recipe, which she claimed had become a full-time hobby for Martha. Martha was always fiddling with the amounts of the ingredients, trying to capture the indefinable flavor of those cookies from the kiosk in San Francisco. Privately Faye wondered if Martha was chasing the impossible dream, but she didn't say so. Martha needed something to do, especially if she and Nick were going to break up, which was what Faye figured would finally happen.

"I don't want to go," Martha said. She slid a tray of cookies in the oven, closed the door and began to stir the brown sugar into the batch that would go in the oven next.

"So don't go," Faye said.

"I wish you'd make up your mind," Martha said. "First you say 'go,' then you say 'don't go.'"

"Martha, you and you alone can make up your mind," Faye said firmly.

"I miss him. I hate not seeing him every day. Only—"

"Only what?" Faye asked, stealing a chocolate chip from the bag.

"I wonder where he was and what he was doing. Do you realize, Faye, that I don't know if he's involved in something illegal or worse? I don't know if it's another woman or a family he has hidden somewhere in the woods or—"

"My," Faye said admiringly, "your imagination has really run the gamut, hasn't it?"

"I suppose it has," sighed Martha.

"I doubt very much that Nick is involved with anything illegal, so you can put it out of your mind. As far as another woman, somebody in Ketchikan would have heard a rumor if that were so. There have been cases before when everybody had an idea that a married man had a little hanky-panky going on the side, but with Nick that's more or less ridiculous. He's a bachelor. He wouldn't have to hide a woman away in the woods. No, whatever Nick is up to, I'm sure it's both moral and legal."

"I wish I could be so sure," Martha muttered.

"One thing I know is that you'll never find out if you don't

give Nick a chance. At this point, he's not going to tell you
what he's up to; he's made that perfectly clear. He might tell
you, though, once he trusts you more. That can never happen if
you cut the romance off now.''

"That's a good point. How'd you get to be so wise, Faye?"
Martha asked, her spirits lifting.

Faye laughed. "Lots of men, honey," she said. "Lots of
men." And she stole a few more chocolate chips while Martha
went to call Nick's office to leave a message that she would
visit him and Davey at the cabin the next day.

Chapter Nine

One surprise on Sunday morning, when Nick's Cessna taxied up to the dock in Ketchikan where Martha waited, was that as soon as the propeller stopped whirling Hallie clambered out of the plane.

"I'm going to visit my sister Wanda while you're at Williwaw Lodge," Hallie said, beaming. "I'll fly back with Nick after he returns you to town this evening. I've cooked some food for your dinner. Nick says he can heat it up." Hallie waved at Davey, who had accompanied them, and hurried off to meet her sister.

Davey eyed Martha solemnly. "Hello, Davey," she said as she always did, even though he never replied. She climbed into the plane where she sat beside Nick, with Davey in the back seat.

She watched Nick covertly as he ran through his pretakeoff checklist, searching for some sign that he felt guilty for leaving last week. She saw none. He was his normal self, friendly and likable. She felt herself yearning for him as though nothing had ever happened. She had almost forgotten her anger in her happiness at being with him, near him, again.

Was such happiness logical—or even normal—under the circumstances? She didn't know. She looked away from his sinewy hands, so capable as they moved along the instrument panel flicking switches and pushing buttons. It wasn't hard to act natural around him, at least not as hard as she'd thought it would be. Maybe that was because he was helping by being ordinary.

By being the real Nick, the one she'd come to know in the firs
place.

They took off in a plume of spray that they left behind onc
they were in the air. Davey obviously enjoyed flying. He leane
forward in his seat, eagerly peering out the window as the build
ings of Ketchikan grew smaller and smaller below.

Before taking them to the cabin, Nick flew over part of Mist
Fjords National Monument. Martha thought that he did it t
break the ice between them. Whatever his reason, she was gla
for the opportunity to see it.

"Misty Fjords is one of the largest wilderness preserves i
the world," Nick shouted over the roar of the airplane engine
"It was carved by glaciers and rain, and it's only accessible b
boat or floatplane."

Martha lost herself in appreciation of the panoramic landscap
below. Vertical granite cliff walls rose three thousand feet abov
the many fingerlike fjords thrusting between them. The moun
tains were capped with snow, and lush forests carpeted th
slopes from the tree line to the salt water.

Nick pointed to a wild river tumbling through a valley. "Th
water is that peculiar greenish-gray color because there's wha
we call 'rock flour' from the surrounding glaciers suspended i
it," he said, his mouth close to her ear so that she could hea
him.

Nick decreased their altitude and followed the river. To Mar
tha's amazement, salmon struggling upstream to spawn were s
thick that they seemed to pattern the surface of the water wit
silver. Bald eagles pounced from the shallows of what, to a
eagle, must have been the equivalent of a take-out window a
McDonald's.

"Look, I see a bear!" cried Martha. She supposed that if sh
had to see a bear, the best way to do it was from a safe plac
in the sky.

Nick swooped the Cessna low over a grass flat where a brow
bear was in the process of raking a big fish from the water. Th
bear raised his head when the plane passed over, then single
mindedly returned his attention to the fish, which was now flop
ping on the ground.

Nick banked over dense spruce and aspen, and soon Moosele
Bay appeared.

"That's Williwaw Lodge," Nick said, pointing to a speck in a grassy clearing bordering the water. He soon brought the float-plane in for a perfect landing.

Nick had no sooner docked the plane than Davey scrambled down and ran up the slope and behind the cabin to play.

"Davey seems more at ease with me today, I think," observed Martha, who had caught the glimpse of a tentative smile before the boy had taken off at a run.

"He's used to you now," Nick said with an approving grin. He would have slid his arm around her shoulders, but she moved away too quickly.

So that's how it is, Nick thought unhappily, but he decided to bear with her. He was trying hard to see things from her point of view. But he also thought she should consider his track record. He'd never lied to her before. She should have known that he wouldn't start now.

Martha walked briskly to the back of the cabin, where Davey was digging among Hallie's carrots, onions and cabbages with a small trowel. Martha knelt down beside him. On the damp ground beside him were two earthworms, which he apparently had dug up.

"Worms, huh?" she said.

Davey widened his eyes. Finally, cautiously, he nodded, *yes*.

"I suppose there are lots of worms in Hallie's garden," Martha observed. Careless of her clean blue jeans, she sat down next to Davey and picked up a stick. She poked the ground with it a few times and pulled out a worm. "See? Here's another one."

Davey looked at it. He picked up his two earthworms and put them on the ground beside Martha's.

"Now we have three worms. Let's find more."

Nick had silently joined them and sat on a rock watching bemusedly. He wasn't about to interrupt. It pleased him that the two were communicating. Or at least Martha was communicating. He wasn't sure about Davey; the boy didn't communicate much.

"I know another word for earthworms," Martha said. She spared a sidelong glance to see if Davey was listening. "They're called night crawlers. Isn't that a neat name?"

Davey rested the dirty tip of his trowel on the ground and

stared at her. Martha pretended not to notice; she merely went on talking.

"In some parts of the world, earthworms get to be about eleven feet long," she said. "That's about as far as the distance from you to Nick. I certainly hope we don't find one as big as that!"

She laughed, suddenly aware of Nick's eyes upon her. He smiled, but she looked away quickly.

Soon Martha and Davey had seven or eight earthworms writhing in all directions on the ground between them. Davey tried without success to keep them in a straight line.

"Let's get a glass jar," Martha suggested. "We'll put dirt in it and you can keep your worms in the jar and watch them. They'll dig tunnels next to the glass and you can see them. That'll be fun, won't it?"

"Okay," Davey said.

The word was so unexpected that Martha gaped at him. That was the first word he'd ever spoken directly to her. She glanced at Nick. His expression, astonished at first, turned to one of triumph.

"I'll get the jar," Nick said, heading toward the house. He felt as though he could perform handsprings all the way to the back stoop. He couldn't recall Davey's speaking directly to anyone except Hallie and him—not his cousins, his aunts or uncles or any of Hallie's numerous family members, including Wanda's five grandchildren, whom Davey occasionally visited. But now Davey had spoken one word of his limited three-word vocabulary to Martha—this was indeed a sign of progress.

Nick returned with a clean pickle jar he'd found under the sink, and with Davey's avid participation they shoveled dirt into it and set the earthworms on top of the dirt. Then they took the jar into the kitchen and covered it with wax paper held fast by a rubber band. They set the jar on a kitchen windowsill and Davey sat entranced, watching the worms wriggle their way below the surface of the dirt.

"Hallie will be delighted, I'm sure, to see her new terrarium," Martha said wryly.

Nick only laughed. "Hallie won't mind," he said.

They washed their hands at the kitchen sink, and when they

had finished Nick peeked into the refrigerator to take stock of the meal Hallie had left.

"We'll eat around six," Nick said, glancing out the window. "I'll want to get you back to Ketchikan before eight. The weather service is reporting a squall line out to sea, and I won't be able to fly when it comes into the area."

"When will it arrive?" Martha asked.

"You can never count on what the weather's going to do, but I checked earlier, and the weather service was forecasting good weather until after ten o'clock tonight. Come on, I want to show you those photographs of the mountain chickadee that I took the first day you visited here."

They sat side by side on the couch, and Nick pulled an album out of a trunk. He opened it to a page displaying the chickadee photos and some others he'd taken.

"When did you get interested in photography?"

"I guess it was when I was a teenager. My friend Hank bought a camera, and I borrowed it. When I was out on the boat working with my father or brothers we'd see whales and sea otters, all kinds of wildlife. I finally bought my own camera to help me while away the time on long wheel watches. I've been a photography buff ever since."

Martha's eyes flew involuntarily to the picture on the wall, the one of the nude woman silhouetted against a rock, and it occurred to her to make a wisecrack about the amazing diversity of Alaskan wildlife, but as she was opening her mouth to say it they heard a crash in the kitchen and Davey called, "Nick! Nick!" Nick immediately pushed the album into Martha's lap and rushed to find out what was wrong, which Martha figured was just as well. Sarcastic remarks probably wouldn't help their relationship at this point.

Evidently Davey had spilled something when he was pouring it, and Nick stayed in the kitchen to clean it up. While he was gone, Martha idly flipped through the pages of the photograph album. She saw many family pictures that Nick had taken of his father and his two brothers. She hoped to find a picture of Nick's mother, who had died when he was a boy.

She turned another page, and the loose color photograph of a woman fell out of the book, landing facedown on the rug. Martha bent to pick it up, then held it up to the light from the window to study it further.

The woman was obviously pregnant. Her abdomen was big and round beneath the shapeless garment she wore, and she was laughing into the camera lens as though she hadn't a care in the world. But this woman could not be Nick's mother. This woman was an Indian.

She was beautiful. She sat on the bow of a boat, and spread out behind her were a sky fleeced with clouds and a sea of silvery blue. Her teeth were white and straight, and there was something familiar in the way her high cheekbones rounded into the planes of her face and in the way her thick hair tumbled over her forehead.

This was Davey's mother. There was no doubt in Martha's mind about that. From the kitchen came the reassuring sounds Nick made to Davey as he cleaned up the mess Davey had made. Martha felt a blank, numb chill stealing over her as she continued to look at the picture. She swallowed and blinked away sudden stinging tears. To her way of thinking, there could be only one reason Nick Novak would have a picture of this pregnant woman in his photo album.

She shut the album quickly, blindly. She didn't want to look at the photo any longer. The woman's happy, smiling face, her look of total well-being, was imprinted on Martha's brain forever.

There was nowhere Martha could go to think this over. She couldn't run away as she had in the restaurant. She'd have to tough it out for the rest of the day, because she couldn't leave until Nick flew her home in the plane. At present she was in an emotional ferment; she didn't know what to think. She loved Nick, and despite his disappearance last week she wanted to believe that double-dealing and deception were not part of his character.

But as Faye had said, how would Martha find out the true story if she called an end to her relationship with Nick now?

Her mind raced, trying to form a conclusion that would enable her to get through the rest of the day somehow. Martha could confront Nick with the picture, point out the woman's marked resemblance to Davey and ask him point-blank what his relationship with her was. She was sure she knew what response this would elicit in Nick. He would clamp his mouth tightly shut and refuse to answer the question. He would repeat that she must not ask questions about certain parts of his life. She knew that was what would happen. She knew Nick Novak.

Or she could curb her impulse to ask, stay here and play the part of the Martha who knew nothing, who suspected nothing. She could continue to give Nick the impression that she was recovering from their quarrel last week, and in that way perhaps she could get him to open up, to tell her something about Davey and his mysterious origins. She already knew in her heart that Davey and this woman in the photograph were mother and son.

"Martha?" Nick stood at the door to the kitchen, holding a damp towel in his hand and leaning against the doorjamb. He wore a red and black lumberjack shirt, and his bronze hair barely brushed the collar. Her heart jumped at the sight of him, and she felt the instant attraction that had bowled her over the first morning she'd seen him leaning against the lamppost, drinking coffee from a Styrofoam cup. Compared to falling in love with Nick Novak, the experience of being struck by lightning would have been relatively mild.

And so she only looked up innocently, concealing her true feelings. Then she went to help him heat up Hallie's pot roast. They all ate in the big kitchen, Davey kicking the legs of his chair until Nick told him to stop, Martha feigning bright conversation, and together they all cleaned up the kitchen when they had finished the meal.

How many ways human beings find not to communicate with one another, mused Martha. In order to get along with others we pretend we're something we're not, or we pretend we're not something we are. We retreat within ourselves, become defensive and aloof, anything to keep a distance. We even use noncommunication as a tool to foster eventual communication, which she realized was what she was doing. Did any of it make sense? Maybe not. Time would tell.

Later, as they flew back to Ketchikan early in order to beat the squall line that was advancing in the form of a pewter-colored glaze on the horizon, Nick congratulated himself on how well the day had gone. Martha and Davey seemed to have achieved a rapport at last, and Martha had apparently recovered from her fit of pique over his disappearance last week.

Everything was all right. And it would stay all right, he supposed, unless Elsa Long got sick again.

"DUMP HIM," Polly said.

"That's easy for you to say," Martha said with feeling. She had called Polly as soon as she'd gotten home from her visit at Nick's.

"What do you mean?"

"Polly, you've got Sigmund, who lives in your house. You're madly in love and he's practically eating out of your hand. Why, his favorite crystal sits in the middle of your coffee table. He's not going anywhere. But I've hardly had a chance to get to know Nick."

"I'd say you know enough about him right now. He's unreliable, and there's no telling what he's doing when he goes off somewhere."

"He drinks Classic Coke. He likes chocolate-chip cookies and he doesn't smoke."

"He keeps a picture of a pregnant woman who is obviously Davey's mother in his photo album. I'd say get out right now, before you get hurt any worse."

"I'll be leaving after Labor Day anyway," Martha said unhappily. She bit down into one of the latest batch of cookies. It tasted pretty good, almost as good as the ones she used to buy in San Francisco.

"Right. According to statistics, there are nine other men in Alaska looking for you. I'm sure that some of them drink Classic Coke, like chocolate-chip cookies and don't smoke. Why hang out with a loser, Martha?"

"Nick isn't a loser," protested Martha after swallowing quickly. "He's built up his family business, and he's very smart. He's also wonderful with Davey; he takes his responsibility for Davey quite seriously. Anyway, he makes the hair on my arms stand on end. That must mean something."

"It must mean you're shivering in an icy blast from the North Pole," sighed Polly. "Martha, you're not making good sense. You're obviously seriously confused by the whole mess. What you need to comfort you is some of those cookies from that kiosk where you used to buy them. Want me to send you some?

Maybe a few chocolate chips will straighten out your thinking. I could even throw in a jar of Dippety Do. To keep the hair on your arms in place, you know.''

By this time, Martha was paying no attention to Polly. Martha was regarding the cookie she held in her hand with growing excitement. The texture was perfect—firm and yet moist—and the flavor was ideal. Finally she had hit on the exact flavor-and-texture combination she'd been trying hard to achieve.

''You won't need to send cookies,'' she said. ''Instead, I'll send you some of the latest batch I've made. They're good—in fact, I think they might even be better than the ones I used to buy there!''

''No kidding! Now that's an accomplishment!''

Martha studiously and appraisingly ate the rest of the cookie, not caring in the least that she was paying long-distance rates for Polly to listen to her munch.

''It even *sounds* like the ones you used to buy here,'' Polly said dryly.

Martha swallowed. ''No, really, I'm delighted that I've finally found the right combination. I'll send you a batch of these cookies tomorrow, okay? And don't let Sigmund eat all of them. I'm interested in your opinion.''

''Why? You didn't think much of my opinion about what to do about Nick Novak.''

Martha reached for another cookie. ''I love him,'' she said again. ''I love him and I want to find out what the real story is.''

''And if you don't like the answers you get?''

''Well,'' Martha said thoughtfully, ''I guess that's just the way the cookie crumbles.''

HOPING AGAINST HOPE that she would win his confidence, Martha continued to see Nick every day. It was a time of rebuilding a relationship that had turned out to be weaker than Martha had thought. She knew Nick had the ability to be open, tender and intimate. She waited for him to be that way again. Superficially, everything went on the way it had before between them; to the casual observer, everything seemed fine. They never spoke of

Nick's unexplained absence. Deep down, though, Martha still wondered, *Why?*

About a week after her phone conversation with Polly, Martha took several dozen chocolate-chip cookies down to the Bagel Barn and tried them on Randy. He loved them. Later, she and Nick ate chocolate-chip cookies for dessert after their lunch of bagels with cream cheese and salmon. She anxiously awaited Nick's opinion.

"You know," he said appreciatively, "this is the best chocolate-chip cookie you've baked yet. The flavor is superb."

"Do you really think so?"

"It's great. Not too crisp; it doesn't fall apart when I bite into it. And you've finally figured out the perfect proportion of vanilla. I can barely taste it, and yet I know it's there."

Martha beamed. "You and Randy have been my main test pilots. And you both think this cookie is ready to fly."

"Fly?"

"Sure. I'm going to package two very large cookies in cellophane, and I'm going to try selling them to the customers at the Bagel Barn. Chocolate-chip cookies are going to be Randy's special during the week after next."

"You'll have to call it the Bagel and Cookie Barn if you don't watch out," teased Nick. He loved to see Martha so enthusiastic about things; her eagerness made her light up with a special brilliance that was all her own.

"If I start calling it the Bagel and Cookie Barn, Sidney Pollov will have a stroke." Martha shuddered. She had discovered that Sidney was a stickler for detail and that he stood for no foolishness. She was convinced that the only thing that had spared her his wrath last week when she'd sent in her order late was that Sidney's work load was heavy while he was trying to open his chain of Chinese take-out fast-food places.

"You're a long way from Sidney here in Ketchikan," Nick said soothingly. "He'll never be the wiser if you sell a few cookies. What will you do with the profits?"

"Oh, I'm not going to keep them. I consider all this cookie-baking part of 'product development' for Sidney Pollov Enterprises. Bagel Barn sells bagels for a meal, and we sell tea or soda pop for drinks, so why not sell cookies for dessert? That way people can get a whole meal at a Bagel Barn, and any part of it would serve as a snack. I don't see how I can lose money. After I test-market cookies here, maybe other Bagel Barns will want to try selling them.''

She thought Sidney would appreciate her initiative. It pleased her to take steps to make Bagel Barns even better than they already were. She couldn't wait to prove to Sidney that she was worthy of the trust he'd placed in her.

''If you were my employee,'' Nick said, leaning toward her and crooking his arm nonchalantly around the back of the bench where they sat, ''I'd give you a bonus for inventing these chocolate-chip cookies. But since you're not, how about dinner tonight?''

''That's bonus enough for me,'' she said, allowing herself to snuggle into his arm for a moment before they both headed their separate ways.

On Thursday, Nick and Davey left for Juneau and Davey's appointment with Dr. Whitmer. This time Nick, rather touchingly in Martha's view, made his itinerary clear before he left. He told her the name and telephone number of his hotel and the name of the psychiatrist. He told her where he and Davey would be likely to eat dinner. He left no loose ends, no room for suspicion, and he made a date for her to come to Williwaw Lodge again to spend the day with him and Davey on the Sunday after his return.

Almost as much as his elaborate explanations about his whereabouts, the invitation to the lodge pleased her. She had begun to feel comfortable and at home there. And she loved the wild beauty of the scenery.

Martha missed Nick while he was in Juneau with Davey, but this time he was only gone for two days. On Sunday morning she flew with Nick and Davey to the lodge, where they had a picnic that was cut short by a sudden rainstorm.

''I take it that the visit to Dr. Whitmer was a success,'' Martha said as she and Nick set up the chessboard on the table in front of the blazing fire he'd built in the fireplace. Davey sat playing with his Tonka trucks and cars on an oval braided rug on the other side of the room. From time to time Davey would stop and pop another of Martha's chocolate-chip cookies into his mouth from the bowl beside him.

''Our visit was very encouraging,'' Nick said. ''We mapped

out a plan for separate counseling sessions for Davey and me and one for Davey and me together every two weeks. Because we live so far away, Dr. Whitmer will spend a little more time working with Davey in each session than he normally would with his local clients, but he thinks that we can eventually get to the bottom of Davey's problem. Davey likes the doctor a lot, which helps.''

"What does he think Davey's problem is?"

Nick hesitated. After Martha had told him how a particular trauma had affected one of her mother's kindergarten students, he had known what to tell the doctor about Davey's case. He had vowed never to speak of what had happened to Davey, but he'd known he had to tell the psychiatrist in order to help the boy. That was different from discussing Davey's trauma with Martha, however. He couldn't tell her. To tell her would be to betray an old friend.

He swallowed, and if Martha detected any mental turmoil on his part, she didn't let on. "I'm not quite sure," he said, rationalizing that this was not quite a fib. It was mostly true, after all.

"Davey's always looked so sad," whispered Martha as she watched Davey wheel his cars and trucks around the edge of the rug. "Since he's been seeing Dr. Whitmer, I think he looks less tense."

"Yes," Nick said, glad that she was focusing on Davey and not on what they had been talking about.

As they watched, Davey reached into the bowl where Martha's cookies had been and scrabbled around for another. But there were no more. He had eaten the last one.

He pulled himself up on his knees and peered into the bowl. When he saw that all the cookies were gone, he looked dismayed.

"Don't say anything," Nick whispered. "Don't speak."

And so Martha sat motionless, watching the thought processes flit across Davey's face. Left to herself, she would have said to Davey, "I'll get you more cookies," without his having to ask her. Like everyone else, Martha had fallen into the habit of doing things for Davey because she knew he would not ask.

Nick held his breath. He didn't know why he had chosen this moment to withhold something that Davey wanted; he had never tried it before. Davey stood up, picked up the bowl and marched over to where Nick and Martha sat.

He raised his eyes, thrust out the bowl, blinked at Martha and said, "More."

Chapter Ten

It didn't surprise Nick that Davey loved Martha's chocolate-chi
cookies. Davey had always loved chocolate in any form. Wha
did surprise him was that Davey liked them so much that h
was moved to ask for more.

But Nick didn't question Davey. He and Martha put a fev
more cookies in Davey's bowl and waited breathlessly to see
he'd again ask for more cookies when the bowl was empty. H
did.

In his rejoicing over Davey's addition of a new word to hi
vocabulary, Nick almost didn't allow himself to hope that th
was only the beginning, that Davey would eventually talk lik
other children. And yet he kept watching for signs. He was cau
tiously hopeful that Davey's speaking a new word was the be
ginning of a new stage in development for Davey.

Dr. Whitmer had suggested that Davey needed more stimu
lation from other children than his isolation at Williwaw Lodg
provided. Nick accordingly sent Davey with Hallie to spend
day in town now and then with Wanda, where Wanda's tw
youngest grandchildren might provide the stimulus that Dave
needed. Three weeks passed, and they all waited for Davey t
speak more words. Nothing happened. Except for his visits wit
other children, his pattern remained the same. Davey still spok
only four words.

Most of the talk that went on was between Nick and Marth
in their reestablishment of communication after his secret trip t
take care of Elsa Long. By this time, the talk between Nick an
Martha was good. Very good. They were picking up the line

of communication again. And yet Nick knew that Martha didn't quite trust him. Despite her sharing of his happiness that Davey now knew another word, despite the returning ease of their relationship, trust was slow to rebuild.

Nick admitted to himself that he really couldn't blame Martha for her wary attitude. He had the uncomfortable feeling that she was watching and waiting for him to make another misstep. This annoyed him and made him self-conscious when he was around her, but he understood it.

He had tried to see his leaving town from her point of view, and he knew that if he had been in Martha's place he would have felt the same way. What if she had disappeared suddenly without a word, had skipped out on a commitment to eat lunch with him and then returned several days later only to inform him that she couldn't tell him where she'd gone or what she'd been doing? He'd have suspected the worst, wouldn't he?

What the two of them needed was extended time together, time away from Davey and the Bagel Barn and other extraneous influences. They needed time alone in which to recapture the trust, pleasure and companionship of those first happy weeks when they had fallen in love.

Nick racked his brain to come up with a way to isolate the two of them. He discarded the idea of a long hike in the wilderness because he didn't think Martha was ready for it. He considered proposing a camping and kayaking trip together on the Salmon River and discarded it for the same reason.

And then he thought of the perfect outing. The *Tabor*, his father's old fishing troller. The *Tabor* was where Nick went when he wanted to be alone. On the *Tabor* he could feel far away from problems and their evasive solutions. On the *Tabor* he could begin to feel whole again and communicate within himself. Or with another.

Nick could send Hallie and Davey to stay with Wanda for a few days; that would not only provide the stimulation Davey needed, it would be a nice vacation for Hallie, too. Martha could get Randy to take over at the Bagel Barn. She'd been talking about how she hadn't had much time off since she'd arrived in Ketchikan and about how capable an employee Randy was.

He and Martha would go away on the *Tabor* for a few days, and then everything would be all right between them. Martha

would again be convinced that he truly loved her, and awa
from Faye's or Hallie's prying eyes they would be able to ex
press their love in the way that it should be expressed. Physi
cally.

The physical expression of their love was what he wanted
and what she wanted, too, in her heart of hearts. Nick understoo
why Martha hung back. He knew that their lovemaking woul
be important to her, and that she worried about walking awa
from it at the end of the summer. But he also understood tha
he loved her, and loving her, he desired her. He would romanc
her; he would win her. They'd worry about the end of the sum
mer later.

THE COFFEEPOT WAS PERKING on the small diesel-fueled stov
in the tiny galley, and the boat's engine vibrated the smooth fi
planking of the *Tabor*'s deck. Nick had already pumped th
bilge and was presently hauling anchor. He turned off the winch
and the anchor, thickly coated with mud, clunked heavily agains
the bow.

He joined Martha in the wheelhouse and accepted a mug o
coffee from her hands. It was dark, foggy and damp on th
Tongass Narrows in this hour before dawn, but he and Marth
were preparing to leave like any other fishermen anchored i
the Ketchikan harbor.

"Are you cold?" he asked.

Martha, bundled up in a bright yellow windbreaker, with he
curls peeking out from under its hood, shook her head an
clasped both hands around her steaming coffee mug. She smile
at him. "No. I feel wonderful." The cold, bracing air made he
feel healthy and robust.

Nick smiled back at her, not minding the chill himself an
marveling at how she could brighten even the darkest of morn
ings.

They were going to be real fishermen on this trip, althoug
that wasn't the way Nick had originally planned it. He had en
visioned a pleasure trip, drifting with the tides, reveling in eac
other's company. He was surprised to find out that wasn't wha
Martha wanted at all.

"I can't imagine being out there on the wide ocean with nothing to do," she told him when he first brought up the idea.

"Wouldn't you enjoy a vacation from work? A few days away from the Bagel Barn?"

"Of course, especially with you. But I'm used to filling every minute. I'd go stir-crazy on a boat, Nick." He was surprised that she didn't mind being away from work or leaving the Bagel Barn in Randy's hands. What she minded was the inactivity. Well, he could handle that.

"Then I'll show you how I used to make my living. We'll do some trolling for salmon while we're out there. That should keep us both busy."

She became so enthusiastic over salmon trolling that he was surprised. She wanted to know what it was like to fish for this staple of the Alaskan economy, she said. She wanted to experience living as a fisherman for a few days. It would be a new experience for her, one that none of her friends had had.

Martha was always surprising him, making events out of happenings that should have been ordinary, being interested in things in which no other woman he knew had ever evinced an interest. Most wives and girlfriends of the fishermen he knew hated, or at best only tolerated, the sea and what it represented, because it took their men away from them for months or weeks at a time; they never tried to discover its allure for those who fished it. But Martha was different, and he was glad.

Now their rapidly churning wake separated them from the receding shore of Ketchikan. Wispy white swatches of fog clung to the mountainsides, and faint streamers of gray light lay across the tops of the spruce trees. Nick grasped the wheel in one big hand and cradled his coffee mug with the other.

Martha rested her head against his shoulder as they cruised past other fishing boats with lighted galleys. A flock of petrels swept across the crests of the waves ahead. Nick couldn't remember ever having known such peace and contentment in all of his life.

As they watched, the eastern sky became a ferment of changing color. Gradually the dawn layered itself up from the horizon like successive, ever larger layers of pastel-colored tissue paper, at last tearing away to reveal the bright orange sun.

Martha was overwhelmed by the wild majesty of the scene

surrounding her. The far-flung mountain peaks were gilded by
the first light of morning, and the lights of Ketchikan winked in
the glossy black waters of the Narrows.

"Beautiful," Martha said, her shining eyes taking it all in.

"Yes," Nick said, gazing at her rapt face, but he wasn't re
ferring to the scenery.

Nick took it easy handling the *Tabor* out of the Narrows,
aiming for one of his favorite fishing grounds off the coast of
nearby Prince of Wales Island. The *Tabor* rocked steadily on
ever-increasing swells, and Nick watched Martha carefully for
the first signs of seasickness.

He soon realized that he didn't have to worry about Martha's
finding her sea legs. She kept her balance with admirable ease,
gliding without a misstep to the stove in the galley aft of the
wheelhouse to check the coffeepot, then returning to insert her
self again into the circle of his arm as he tended the wheel. She
grinned up at him, and little diamonds of mist winked from her
fog-damp hair. He was glad that she was enjoying this.

Once, off the starboard bow, a geyser of steam erupted and a
black-and-white killer whale rolled cumbersomely out of the wa
ter and back again. Martha laughed, treating him to the golden
rippling sounds of mirth that he loved so much. He wished he'd
had his camera in hand at that moment, not to catch the surfacing
of the whale on film but to capture Martha in her laughter.

When the *Tabor*'s fathometer showed a water depth of forty
fathoms, Nick throttled the engine so that its noise sank from
roar to a rhythmic *pocketa-pocketa*. "Time to set out the lines,"
he told her.

The troller *Tabor* was equipped with two long poles that
swung the fishing lines into the ocean away from the boat. When
cruising, the poles were fixed in an upright position, but for
trolling they were lowered and steel fishing line was paid out
and weighted with a fifty-pound lead weight called a cannonball.
From the fishing line dangled as many as eighteen "spreads,"
each with bait and hooks.

Nick put on his oilskins, went outside into the chilly half-light
and methodically began to lower the poles and attach and bait
the spread lines. It was quiet, and there wasn't another boat in
sight. A stiff breeze blew from the west, scuffing the surface of
the sea into peaks of foam.

"I know I'm only a green hand, but what can I do to help?" said Martha as she appeared suddenly at his elbow.

He hadn't expected her to come out of the wheelhouse into the cold and the damp, and he eyed her speculatively. "Think you could check the hooks for me? Make sure the eyes are strong and that they're sharp?" He had to shout so that his words wouldn't be flung away by the wind.

"Sure," she shouted back, ready to prove herself a fast learner.

He gestured with his head. "Go put on those spare oilskins in the wheelhouse. Then come back."

Martha donned the foul-weather gear quickly and hurried outside again. Nick patiently showed her how to check the hooks and how to bait a line, and even though her fingers were stiff with the cold, Martha managed to get an approving "Good work!" from Nick when all the lines were out.

When they finished their work on deck, it was a mere seventhirty in the morning. They retreated across the rolling deck to the galley and held their red hands over the warm stove to thaw. Martha's teeth chattered.

"You sound frozen," Nick said.

"I am cold," Martha admitted.

"Maybe this is too much for you. Are you sure you don't want to only chug around out here for a couple of days watching the other boats troll?"

"I want to know what your life was like when you were a fisherman," Martha said firmly. "I want to know how other people in Alaska live."

"You're finding out right now," Nick said with a chuckle before carefully pouring them each another mug of coffee.

Nick turned the radio to the marine weather forecast. He listened soberly as a voice delivered a notice to mariners. When Martha, heedless of the radio's importance, started to speak, Nick held up a hand to silence her.

"Sorry," he said afterward. "I had to hear that."

"Was it important?"

Nick's eyes were hard, his expression grim. "Weather is *always* important here. For pilots and for fishermen." His attitude as he turned the radio's volume knob did not invite further questions or comment.

Suddenly one of the trolling lines began to shake. Nick set his coffee mug down with a clatter and ran outside. As the line was reeled up out of the water, the leaders attached to it appeared, and he slid them out of the way.

"It's a salmon!" he hollered, knowing from the jump of the line, but when the hook appeared above the surface of the water, the bait was gone and the hook was empty.

Martha had run out behind him. The wind whipped her hair in her eyes, and she brushed it away.

"What happened?" she asked at the sight of the empty line.

"Somehow he got away," Nick said.

Despite the disappointment, they kept their spirits up. Nick rebaited the hook and dropped the line into the water again. They went inside, and Martha volunteered to cook breakfast.

She fried potatoes and heated up some moose liver that Hallie had cooked last night. She wasn't accustomed to cooking in a frying pan that rocked back and forth, and she wasn't quite used to Nick's hearty notion of breakfast yet. Right now she longed for a bagel, preferably one sopping with lots of butter and honey. Or even a chocolate-chip cookie. But Nick gulped his breakfast down rapidly. So did she. Something about the sea air whetted her already hearty appetite.

After breakfast they relaxed and listened to other people talking on the shortwave radio. Today the catch wasn't good. No one was catching anything much on this fishing ground, and Martha sensed the painful uncertainty in the fishermen's voices.

"I can't imagine what it would be like to earn a living in so haphazard a fashion—waiting for fish to bite, never knowing what kind of fish are out there, dependent on the radio for company and weather information," she said.

"Sometimes it's really a good life, especially when we're hauling fish in one after the other. No one knows what makes the fish bite one day and not bite the next. If we don't get fish one day, we simply go back and try again the next day. It's not as lonely as it seems. There are all those long winter months when fishermen have to stay in port. A lot of socializing gets done then."

"What a business," Martha said, calculating in her head like the good businesswoman she was. "You must never know if the number of fish you catch is going to pay for your fuel or your time.''

Nick shrugged. ''There are a lot of intangible things to make up for that. A fisherman is entirely his own person. He doesn't depend on a boss or the whims of a big company. He's independent. That's why fishermen do it, in spite of the cold and the storms and the dangers.''

They continued to troll without much luck. Later Nick hauled in some of the lines because he suspected some activity, but they had caught only three cod—unwelcome, since they were trolling for salmon. Nick iced the fish down in the hold anyway; Hallie could put them to good use.

When Nick put the *Tabor* on automatic pilot, there were lots of quiet moments in the galley, waiting. They sat at the tiny table that served for dining, facing each other, occasionally glancing out the window to watch seabirds searching the waves for their supper. Sitting across from Nick, his attention focused on her, Martha felt like the center of his universe. Out here there was no Davey, no Faye, no rumors and no unexplained photos in the family album. Here it was only the two of them on the *Tabor*, suspended between the endless sea and sky.

Had she been a fool ever to have doubted that Nick loved her? Was she a fool for loving him when she knew she'd eventually leave him? Or maybe she was only a fool for telling him that she loved him. Without that particular knowledge, Nick Novak wouldn't know where he stood with her. He'd work harder to please her. He wouldn't disappear from her life for days at a time if he wasn't sure that he'd won her heart.

Now, with Nick sitting across from her and studying her, she didn't doubt that he loved her. The picture of Davey's mother in his photo album didn't matter. Or was she lying to herself, telling herself what she wanted to hear?

She shifted uncomfortably in her seat, and Nick misread her restlessness.

''Bored?'' he asked.

Martha forced a smile. She wanted to talk about what was bothering her, about the gossip and rumors and innuendos and about her own suspicions about Davey's origins. But she was afraid of what she might learn. She didn't want to ruin these few days alone with him. She reminded herself to continue to heed Faye's counsel. Only if she knew him better would Nick open up to her; only then would she learn what she wanted to know.

So she hid her feelings and answered his question. "I could never be bored on the ocean. It changes all the time. There's always something to watch."

Nick seemed not to notice the tension in her voice. She had apparently smoothed things over well, because Nick only grinned approvingly, and Martha resolved to let things go at that.

It wasn't hard to do with the ship's radio chattering, muted by the engine noise. The radio ran continuously, a fisherman's link to the rest of the world. In this case, it was also a valuable ally. They didn't have to talk so much if the radio did most of the talking.

Martha found the overheard topics of conversation on the radio fascinating. Art's wife reminded him via radio to take his pills. Everett's friend Bud communicated in code, telling Everett how many fish he'd caught and where. A message was relayed to Karl Vandergrift that he was the father of a baby girl. The *Vanguard II* reported a man overboard, almost setting in motion a complicated search-and-rescue operation, but only a few minutes later the relieved captain reported the man rescued.

The danger of a man overboard alarmed Martha, but Nick reassured her. "He wasn't in the water long enough to be in danger. What's bad is when a man's overboard in cold water without a survival suit. He can't survive long then. I've fallen into the water on days like this many times. Sometimes I was baiting the lines and the boat rocked so much that I fell. Other times I was just careless."

"Careless!"

Nick shrugged. "It happens. You get to thinking you're invincible, and no man is invincible where the sea is concerned. The worst tragedies arise from situations that could have been prevented."

He stood up abruptly, his eyebrows knit together and his expression dark. She couldn't see his face as he ripped a paper towel from the roll hanging over the sink and began to wipe the cups he had washed earlier. This was one of those times when Nick retreated into himself and became prickly and aloof.

This time Nick didn't stay that way for long, but then he never did. In a moment he seemed to gain control of his emotions, turning to her and saying, "Come on, let's check the lines. Maybe we've caught something."

There was nothing to do but to follow him outside and watch as he hauled in the lines. The port side yielded several cod and a halibut.

"That's our dinner," declared Nick, tossing the halibut to one side.

When Nick pulled up the starboard lines, there were two big king salmon, one a twenty-five pounder, the other weighing at least thirty. Nick let out a cry of triumph.

"At least these two salmon are a positive sign. There are salmon down there, all right. All we have to do now is get them to bite."

Cleaning the fish was messy work, but Martha didn't mind. Nick cleaned them in a trough with his trusty old knife as a bevy of gulls gathered for the free meal. Martha tossed the unusable parts of the fish overboard and watched as the gulls dived headlong into the water after them.

"I've never known a woman who could stand to watch me clean fish," commented Nick as he sluiced down the trough afterward with seawater.

"It's part of fishing," said Martha. "I have many happy memories of going fishing with my father when I was a kid. I guess it's because I'd always try things that my sisters wouldn't, and my father was desperate for a fishing companion. Anyway, I learned to clean fish then. I could still do it if I had to."

"Is there anything you can't do?" Nick teased, his arm around her shoulders.

I can't get you to tell me your secrets, she thought, but she didn't say it. She only pulled him close and felt for a moment the steady thrum of his heartbeat beneath his oilskins, and then she pulled away.

Nick cut the halibut into cubes, and Martha fried them in batter. They ate dinner at dusk while the *Tabor* proceeded under automatic pilot to a sheltered cove near a small, rocky island. Martha cleaned up the small galley while Nick lowered the anchor and made things fast on deck. Then Nick went below to ice down the fish they'd caught.

Here in the cove, where they were protected by arms of land, a sense of calm settled over the *Tabor*. The dying wind rippled the incoming tide into little wavelets. They slapped against the hull, rolling the boat gently up and down.

Martha was waiting for Nick on the foredeck when he emerged from the hold. She wore her yellow windbreaker, and her hair curled gently around her face. Her eyes were a sea gray now, glimmering in the moonlight. Nick went to her and slid his arm around her narrow waist.

"Look," she whispered, pointing toward the shore.

A moose picked its way across the sandy, rock-strewn beach. It lifted its head and appeared to sniff the air. Perhaps it had caught their scent. The big antlers seemed tipped with silver in the faint moonlight filtering through the clouds. They watched for a few minutes more until the moose disappeared into the forest.

Nick's hand tightened around her waist. "Are you ready to go inside now?" he asked gently. It had begun to mist lightly, softening the outlines of the island.

Martha lifted her eyes to his. She had known all along that this moment was coming, and she'd prepared for it. When Nick had asked her to go for a trip of several days' duration on the *Tabor*, she had known that he expected them to sleep together. She had already decided that it was okay, that she was ready. She hadn't known that, faced with the fact of it, she would suddenly feel so shy with him.

He took her by the hand and led her across the deck into the wheelhouse and aft to the galley, where he pulled down a bed that fit neatly over the dinette. She stood aside, wondering what was expected of her. Somewhere outside she heard the muted clang of a warning buoy, but it seemed far away and of another world. Nick turned to look at her, and the love and expectation shining from his eyes was unmistakable.

"If you'd like, I can sleep on one of the bunks below," he offered when he saw her reticent expression.

"I wouldn't like that at all," she replied. Slowly, her eyes never leaving his, she began to unsnap her windbreaker, but then he took over and did it for her. Her knees went slack, but not from the rolling of the boat. She sensed her heart thumping wildly underneath the pullover jersey she wore; surely he heard it, too? From the look of him, though, he was listening to his own heart and what it told him.

She waited while he removed his damp oilskins; he threw their outerwear in a corner and touched her cheek. A wisp of her hair fell forward against his fingers. He bent forward and kissed it.

As his parted lips moved away from her hair, she stared at them, willing them to meet hers. Was it possible to tell from the set of a man's lips whether he was a good lover? She thought it was. The curve of Nick's lips as he brought his mouth to hers was sensual, even erotic.

Her mouth opened beneath the pressure of his lips as his hands dug through her hair. She clung to him, tasting salt, hard put to keep her balance now. A low moan escaped him, and she wondered distractedly how they had managed to avoid love-making for so long. How *she* had managed to avoid this when it was what she had wanted ever since she'd first seen Nick Novak.

He shrugged out of his shirt, which fell to the floor, and began to unbutton his jeans. Though they were still kissing, Martha brushed his hand away. His jeans were the kind with a button fly—a nuisance.

"Now I know why they invented zippers," he whispered as he let her fingers do the work, and her mouth curved upward in a smile.

She eased him out of his jeans, delighting in the warm length of his unclothed body pressing against hers. She touched him and said, "Now I know why they invented these," and he laughed before stifling her with a kiss.

He tugged her jersey out of her corduroys and, releasing her lips, shimmied it over her head. His big hands momentarily cupped her rounded breasts before he found the front clasp of her bra and released it. The wisp of nylon fell away; her breath seemed to catch in the back of her throat as his fingers slowly explored her nipples.

Without his help, since he was busy elsewhere, Martha unzipped her corduroys and slithered out of them. By this time he was nibbling at her shoulder.

"Wait," she said, the word bordering on a gasp.

"I've waited too long already," he told her, continuing to do what he was doing with consummate skill.

She slipped out of her underpants.

"I guess it *was* worth waiting for," he said, his eyes gleaming as he looked at her, all of her. And then he swept her into his arms, held her close for a single perfect moment when their heartbeats rose and merged, and gently lowered her backward onto the bed.

She wrapped her arms tightly around him and gloried in the sensation of her face against the taut muscles of his chest. The weight of his body pressed upon her. They lay like that for a long time, drinking in the exquisite sensation of being held in each other's arms. The stubble of his beard bit into her cheek, and his arms beneath her were strong and warm. His hair was sweet with the scent of the sea.

Gradually their burgeoning awareness grew into an insatiable physical hunger. She arched upward so that he could slide his arms out from under her; he propped himself on his elbows so that his hands could cup her face while his eyes searched hers for one memorable moment.

"Martha, my dear Cheechako, I love you so much," he said, his voice firm and strong. His eyes were bright with sincerity, and she didn't think he was holding anything back. Everything that he was to her seemed revealed in the gold-flecked depths of those eyes—friend, confidant, admirer and now her lover. *Her lover.* And she did love him so much.

"I love you too," she said, her voice a mere whisper.

His fingers enclosed her breast, and he bent his head to savor the nipple. Her legs slid instinctively around his as he murmured love words against her lips; she was staggered by her body's powerful response to him. She was talking, answering his whispers with little cries of her own, incoherent cries of joy. Her excitement incited his, and with the suddenness of a storm at sea they were caught up in the swift fulfillment of their passion. At its peak he cried out, and she cried tears of joy, and he held her close and kissed them away.

Afterward, after they had lain quietly together, their legs intertwined, their cheeks touching, their breaths mingling, Nick said, "That was a little too fast for my taste. But I wanted you so much that—"

Martha silenced him with a kiss. "We both wanted each other so much," she amended, her voice breaking with emotion.

He smiled and curved his body over hers, marveling at her velvety warmth, at her fragrant, soft skin, at her silvery eyes telling him so much more than words. Her hands delicately caressed the contour of his back, soothing him in her own rhythm, a rhythm that rose and fell with the stirring of the sea. The creaking boat rocked gently beneath them, secure in its mooring; Martha rocked gently beneath Nick, equally secure.

For the moment they could both forget that this wasn't forever, that it was only for now. For the moment, it was enough.

Chapter Eleven

Nick stirred drowsily and batted at the weight on his chest. Davey...Davey must have climbed in his bed during the night and was lying across him. He struggled up out of the fuzzy depths of sleep and mumbled something about going away. He woke up completely when a surprised female voice said, "That's the most unflattering wake-up call I've ever heard!" The weight shifted and arranged itself on his shoulder; its hair tickled his ear.

He opened his eyes to see Martha smiling up at him.

"Martha," he murmured, remembering now. They were on the *Tabor*, anchored off some secluded island. Last night they had made love. Over and over, it seemed to him. Or had that been a dream?

"Four times?" he inquired hesitantly.

"Five," she said, nestling into him and making it perfectly clear that she had no intention of moving.

"Five times," he agreed. They had been awake half the night. No, not awake all that time; they had alternately fallen asleep and fallen upon each other for hours. He had been insatiable. *She* had been insatiable. Like all her enthusiasms, this one had been strong. Lucky for him, he thought.

He finally noticed the sunbeams because they sparkled so prettily on Martha's dark hair. He half sat, removing his fingers from where they stroked Martha's rose-tipped breast to shove aside the flimsy drapery at the window over the bed. The world seemed bathed in sunlight, a rare commodity in these parts. The sun seemed like an omen of a bright future.

He returned his hand to Martha's breast. She snuggled closer in encouragement and he drifted his hand lower. He could feel the outline of each of Martha's ribs, which was surprising because Martha ate so many chocolate-chip cookies. Not to mention all the bagels she consumed at the Bagel Barn. Thinking of food, his stomach commented on its empty state. Martha giggled against his neck.

"Time for breakfast," he announced unnecessarily, swinging his feet over the edge of the narrow bed. Martha reached for him, unwilling for him to leave. She looked rumpled and contented, replete with love.

Martha wore no makeup at all, and her hair curled endearingly in ringlets all over her head, like Shirley Temple's in all those old movies. Nick knew she probably considered herself an Ingrid Bergman type, and he thought she'd do something to change her hair if he told her what it looked like, so he didn't mention it. He merely kissed the tip of her breast, tweaked her big toe and got up.

She lifted herself on one elbow, holding the sheet up in misplaced modesty as she watched him. "How can we eat breakfast? What used to be the table is now the bed."

"I'll take care of it," he promised, tugging on his jeans. He left the top button unbuttoned.

"Sexy," murmured Martha, touching the button.

"Comfortable," he said, although if Martha thought leaving the top button of his jeans unbuttoned was sexy, he'd gladly leave it unbuttoned all the time.

He heated oil in a pan and fried cold sliced oatmeal. Martha wrinkled her nose at the sight of it, but she roused herself enough to peel a couple of oranges as she sat in bed. He brought plates of the oatmeal and little sausages, and they wrapped themselves up in the bedclothes and balanced their plates on their knees.

Their activity the night before had left them hungry enough to down enough fried oatmeal for four people. Considering his bias against anything sweet for a morning meal, Martha was pleased that Nick allowed her to put maple syrup on hers.

"Fried oatmeal," she said over and over, not believing that anyone would actually eat fried oatmeal for any reason.

"So what's your idea of a good breakfast?" he asked.

"Bagels. Bagels with cream cheese, bagels with salmon, bagels with peanut butter, bagels with honey—"

"Never mind, I get the idea," he said, finishing the last of the oatmeal and unceremoniously dumping their dishes in the sink. He wrapped his arms around Martha and set about kissing the remains of the maple syrup off her lips. It was a tougher job than he anticipated, and it ended up having complications that took over an hour to complete. By that time it was noon, and Nick decided it was too late to do any trolling.

"So what will we do all day?" Martha asked, as innocently as could anyone who had found a man who seemed capable of making love for hours and hours at a time.

Nick only laughed.

The water in the cove where they had anchored last night was lightly crinkled now, shining in the sun like yards and yards of billowing blue cellophane. A flock of squalling gulls pursued little fish near the shoreline, plummeting into the water and flying up again; the air vibrated with the sound of their wings. Otherwise, everything was quiet, pristine; the island seemed like an untouched corner of the universe. There was no sign of the moose they had spotted onshore the night before.

The sunlight was so balmy that Nick said, "Let's go for a walk on the island."

Martha agreed, and they dressed and packed a light lunch in a waterproof satchel that Nick slung around his waist. They were anchored a hundred feet offshore, so Nick lowered the *Tabor*'s small dinghy into the water. Martha climbed in and luxuriated in the bow while Nick rowed, and in a few minutes they were walking on the beach.

A faint brine-scented breeze moved off the water, ruffling the needles of the tall Sitka spruce trees. Many boulders, their sides furred with moss, littered the beach. Rocks crunched beneath

Nick's and Martha's feet as they walked, swinging their hands between them.

Martha bent over, looking for the footprints of the moose. She didn't see any.

"They've been washed away by the tide," Nick said. He tugged at her hand and they headed inland on a path the moose might have taken.

"What if we run into a bear?" Martha asked with some apprehension.

"We'll stand still and talk softly. That's what you're supposed to do when you meet one," Nick told her.

Martha shuddered. "You can stand still and talk softly if you want to," she said. "I'm going to run screaming for the dinghy."

"Do that and you'll end up being some bear's dinner."

"You know what, Nick? I can't imagine what I, Martha Rose from Indiana, am doing on some remote island in Alaska discussing what to do if I meet a bear. A *real* bear. The only bear I've ever seen was in a zoo. Just think, I thought San Francisco was strange, but there all I had to worry about was the man who called himself a Video Jukebox and people who believe that crystals have magical powers. That all seems tame compared to Alaskan bears."

Nick turned her to him and kissed her lingeringly on the lips. "I'll tell you what you're doing here, Martha Rose. You're making love to me."

"No, I'm not," she protested, pushing him away with a quick glance into the surrounding underbrush to see if a bear was watching.

"Oh, yes, you are," he said, chuckling softly as he brushed aside her cotton cardigan sweater and began to unbutton her blouse.

"No, I'm—" She was silenced by his lips.

He pulled her down to a fragrant bed of leaves, and bright purple fireweed danced above their heads as they lay together beneath the gracefully swaying spruce trees. It was, fortunately, a warm day, and as they shed their clothes they also shed their inhibitions. Kissing Martha, Nick thought as he kissed her over and over, was one of life's most delightful pleasures. And beyond her lips there were other things, too. Her breasts, so round and full. Her thighs, so white and firm. Her feet, high-arched and beautifully wrought. Her hands, which she never had been able to keep still and which certainly did not remain still around him. They explored him bit by bit and with growing confidence.

It was a long time before Martha said, "Nick?"

"Mmm?"

"What about bears?"

"What about them?"

"I don't like lying here at the side of the trail like meat in a trap. I think we should go."

He traced her eyebrow, raised in worry, with a gentle fingertip. "I don't, but if you're that uncomfortable with it—"

"I am, Nick. I'd rather be on the boat."

"I thought it would be nice to get off the boat for a while," he said.

"It is, and it's beautiful here. But I really am scared of bears, Nick!"

She finally convinced him, and they slowly dressed after a fashion. There were certain items of clothing that Martha didn't bother to put back on, and Nick carried his shoes in his hand. They made their way back to the beach, unable to control their laughter.

"If my friends at the boutique could only see me now!" giggled Martha. Her shirt was buttoned all wrong, her corduroy were littered with fragments of dead leaves and her hair was a corona of curls standing up all over her head. She hadn't brought any makeup along on the *Tabor* except lipstick, and she hadn't bothered with that today.

"You might start a new fashion trend," Nick said, soberly but with an amused glint in his eye.

"I've certainly seen worse," Martha replied, giggling. "Remember when everyone was wearing torn-up sweatshirt cropped short and hanging off one shoulder?"

"No," Nick said with a certain wryness in his tone. "That must be a fashion that didn't penetrate all the way up to Ketchikan."

"How about men's boxer shorts worn over a pair of leggings? Did you ever see that in Ketchikan?"

"No man I have ever known ever wore his underwear over a pair of leggings," Nick swore.

This inspired a fresh gale of giggles. "No, silly. Girls wore men's boxer shorts over tight leggings. We sold boxes and boxes of boxer shorts in the boutique."

"Men's boxer shorts?" Nick looked frankly horrified.

"Yes, white ones, and don't look so aghast. It was a big item at that time. The girls used to tie-dye them."

"Good grief, and people think Alaska is uncivilized. We only have bears here, not girls who wear— Martha, are you sure you're not putting me on?"

She walked on tiptoe so she could reach his nose to kiss it. "No, I'm not putting you on. What are we going to do when we get back to the boat?"

"Guess."

Martha laughed and skipped ahead of him. "Oh, Nick. We can't do *that* all day."

"We can't?" he said in mock distress. "Why not? We've been doing it almost nonstop ever since last night."

"Yes, and I've decided that you're an absolute sex fiend."

"Me? Oho, that's a good one. Who was the one who practically— Hey, look at that eagle over there! I wish I'd brought my camera!"

Martha, who had been walking backward, turned to look. A large eagle was swooping toward the sand in an attitude of attack. The sight of the eagle's sharp extended talons frightened Martha, and she let out a loud involuntary "Oh!"

The eagle, startled, swerved off course and spiraled high into the air.

"What's he attacking, can you tell?" Martha asked, grabbing Nick's arm.

"I don't know. Maybe there's a fish washed up on the beach."

"Let's look," Martha said, keeping a watchful eye on the eagle. It still circled overhead, assessing them.

They rounded a large boulder and came upon a cowering

small animal huddled amid the seaweed in a niche on the other side.

Nick stopped in surprise. "Why—it looks like a sea otter pup!" he exclaimed.

Martha knelt in the sand. The animal was about as long as her forearm, and it was plainly frightened.

"What's it doing here?"

Nick's eyes scoured the beach. "I don't know. I don't see any sign of its mother, do you?"

Martha shook her head. "If we leave it here, Nick, that eagle will surely get it."

Nick bent down to inspect the pup. It didn't have a scratch on it, but it was clearly immature and too young to be on its own.

"Something must have happened to the mother," he reasoned. He looked around to make absolutely sure that she wasn't waiting nearby, but even a walk in both directions on the beach produced no sign of her. The eagle hovered threateningly, waiting for them to leave its prey alone. Nick cast a small stone at the eagle and it flapped away to perch on the skeleton of a dead tree nearby. Martha knew that as soon as they left the eagle would be back to reclaim its meal.

"Oh, Nick, let's take this little fellow back to the boat," she cried. It was a pathetic little creature and so scared.

"There are all-too-few sea otters left since the fur trade nearly wiped them out," Nick said. "We shouldn't take the chance that the eagle might get this one." Quickly he removed his shirt. "Let's see if he's afraid to be picked up," he said.

The animal quivered in fear as Nick scooped it from its niche in the rock. He wrapped it quickly in his shirt and held it in his arms. Its rapid heartbeat thudded against his arm. Although it was still frightened, the animal made no move to bite or scratch.

"Come on," Nick said. "We'll rescue it. I can call the Fish and Wildlife Service office and find out what to do with it. Maybe there's a colony of them nearby where this little fellow should be released."

On the way back to the *Tabor*, Martha had to hold the sea otter while Nick rowed the dinghy. She was quickly captivated by the creature's furry little face. It lay quietly in her arms, staring up at her like a baby. It resembled the pictures she'd seen of sea otters lying on their backs in the water and smashing shellfish on their stomachs with a rock. She found herself clucking to it and talking to it, much to Nick's amusement.

"Must be your mothering instinct," he commented when they were back aboard the *Tabor*.

"I didn't know I had any," Martha said.

"Of course you do," Nick said, suddenly serious. "I could tell that on the day you dug earthworms with Davey."

"I never had any urge to mother an earthworm, Nick."

"But you certainly acted as if you knew how to mother a little boy," he shot back.

Martha turned the sea otter to Nick, self-conscious now that she knew that Nick had discovered something about her that she hadn't even known herself.

"This animal needs a name," Nick said after installing the sea otter in a galvanized tub with a few inches of seawater in it.

"A name," Martha repeated thoughtfully.

"How about Bear?" suggested Nick. "Since you were so scared of seeing one."

"All right," she agreed. "Bear is a terrific name for an otter." They both laughed, and Nick went to the refrigerator in the galley to get some milk. He was reasonably sure that Bear wasn't old enough to have been weaned from his mother.

They soaked a rag in milk. Bear wouldn't take it at first, so they added a bit of sugar to the warm milk. Before long, Bear was sucking on the rag as though he was ravenous.

"What do you think happened to Bear's mother?" Martha asked.

"Maybe a predator got her. But baby sea otters stay so close to their mothers that I don't know how Bear could have escaped."

"Do you think there's a chance she'll turn up?"

Nick looked doubtful. "Sea otters are remarkably capable mothers. They carry their babies on their backs as they swim, or they hug them to their breasts, and if they get separated the mother comes at the baby's slightest little whistle or bark. If she were in this vicinity, she would have been with him.''

"Will he survive?"

"It looks like he's going to eat. If he can survive on cow's milk, and if we have enough milk, he may just make it."

They remained anchored in the cove that night. Bear's feedings necessitated getting up several times that night. Whenever the sea otter got hungry, he uttered a series of short, sharp yelps.

"No wonder sea otters don't like to get separated from their pups," grumbled Nick as he wearily stumbled out of bed and went to the refrigerator for more milk. "The way Bear barks is pure punishment."

Martha, warm in a nest of sheets and blankets, murmured something unintelligible. She tried to sleep through this feeding, since it would be her turn to get up next time.

She didn't really mind taking care of Bear, she thought dreamily as she snuggled him in her arms later. The little sea otter fell asleep, and in the dim light of the lamp over the stove, Martha cradled Bear and watched Nick. Nick slept with his mouth open, which, surprisingly enough, seemed to be an endearing trait. *It's amazing the kind of things you can forgive when you're in love,* she thought. And then she thought wryly, *Even unexplained business trips.*

When Bear awoke, sucked at the milk-soaked rag again and then clambered to get out of Martha's arms, she put him in the galvanized tub in the middle of the galley floor and crept into bed beside Nick. As soon as it was quiet, Bear began to shriek indignantly.

"My turn?" Nick asked sleepily.

"No, it's still mine," Martha said, tumbling out of bed again. She wrapped Bear in a dry towel. He gurgled contentedly, and she tried to walk him around the galley, but the galley was so small that she could only walk two steps in either direction, stepping over Bear's tub each time. Bear chose that moment to nod off, but when she tried to put him down he objected again.

The warmth of her body seemed to be what Bear needed. Finally Martha decided there was nothing to do but take him into the bed with her and Nick.

As soon as he was curved in the protection of her body, the baby sea otter let out a contented sigh and fell sound asleep.

Nick awoke early the next morning, and, forgetting about Bear for the moment, he stretched luxuriously and slid his hand up Martha's back. Except that it wasn't Martha's back, unless Martha's back had grown sleek and hairy during the night. Nick opened his eyes not to the welcome sight of Martha's smiling face but straight into the snout of a curious baby sea otter.

The otter regarded him calmly and twitched his whiskers. Martha lay on the other side of Bear, breathing in the deep, measured cadence of someone who wasn't planning to wake up for a while.

So Nick lay back on the pillow and Bear crawled up onto his chest.

"I think I liked yesterday morning better," Nick said, closing his eyes against Bear's unwavering stare.

Martha found them like that when she woke up later. She shook Nick awake and scratched Bear on the stomach. It should have been the other way around, thought Nick as he awakened.

"What's for breakfast?" Martha said brightly.

"How about roast filet of otter?" suggested Nick, pushing Bear over to her side of the bed.

"I know your penchant for hearty breakfasts, Nick, but that's going too far," she said. "Isn't it, fella? Isn't it?"

Disgruntled, Nick slid across her and padded to the refrigerator. He peered inside. There was halibut left over from last night.

"We'll have halibut," he decided. "There's not much milk left though. Bear drank most of it."

Martha dressed herself and then warmed the milk. Bear frolicked in the galvanized tub. Despite the presence of the tub, Martha and Nick managed to work efficiently around it. They engineered an embrace while the halibut was frying and a kiss while the rag was soaking in milk.

It wasn't what Nick had had in mind, although he told Martha, "I guess if we wanted leisure, we should have gone for a cruise on the *Trondheim*." He bent and scratched the sea otter on the top of the head. It was a cute little thing, he admitted to himself as he found his resentment toward Bear fading away.

Nick became concerned that cow's milk might not be the correct diet for a baby sea otter, so they left Bear on the *Tabor* and took the dinghy over to the island to dig clams for Bear to eat. They didn't know if he'd eat them or not, but they had fun digging them. They also looked for signs of Bear's mother, but none were to be found.

"I think he's an orphan," Nick said later after Bear had surprised them by eating the clams.

"Well, he's eating. That proves he can get along without his mother."

"Maybe. But I'd worry about letting him go off on his own. He's not big enough to take care of himself."

"We're almost out of milk. I don't see any little corner stores around here where we can buy any, either." They stood at the deck railing, and Martha cast a glance at the island, which was a perfect example of what people meant when they described a place as rugged.

"I have canned milk in the cupboard. It'll last us until we find a store."

Martha turned to Nick and rested her hands on his shoulders. Her hands linked behind his neck, and he kissed the tip of her nose. "When are we going to look for one?" she asked.

"We'd better head back to Ketchikan, Martha, if we want Bear to survive. I need to find out exactly what diet he should have. Once the canned milk is gone, we're out of milk. I hate to cut our time together short, but—"

"I know," she said, resting her cheek against his.

"There'll be other times. In fact, we'll do this again whenever you can get away from the Bagel Barn. Okay?"

She smiled up at him. How like him to take the plight of a lost sea otter pup to heart. He had selflessly taken turns feeding Bear. He had decided they should see if Bear could eat clams. He had taken the orphaned animal's situation on as his responsibility, and she was glad he was the kind of man who would do that.

"Maybe I'll be able to get away again in a week or so. How about you?"

"I'll make time," he promised.

And so for Bear's sake they cut their getaway short, heading back to Ketchikan and Mooseleg Bay and Davey and the Bagel Barn.

"SO HE'S KIND TO ANIMALS, is he?" Polly said, sounding as though she was calling from right next door when in fact she was still in San Francisco.

"Yes, it's one of his redeeming qualities," Martha said with irony.

"I can't believe you really went away with him on his boat."

"I *had* to, Polly."

"It sounds like one of your impulses," Polly said.

"No, I thought it over carefully. I wanted to give him a chance. I love him, and he loves me."

"Oh, Martha."

"Well, I'm not the type to fall in love often, you know. Five, six, seven times in a lifetime—that's enough for me." Polly, she knew, had been in love many more times than that.

"Is that a joke?"

"Sort of. You know that I've only had a couple of boyfriends I really cared about. But Nick is special. He's different from any of those. I've grown to love him very much, and—"

"Martha, if you say you love him, I believe you. All I can say is that with his mysterious background, you must love him tremendously if you can get serious about him."

"I do love him."

"You've told me you love him three times in this conversation. That's enough. Time to change the subject—how is the chocolate-chip cookie recipe coming along?"

"Oh, fine. I haven't made any more changes. Randy started to sell my cookies at the Bagel Barn and they're selling, well, like hotcakes."

"Sigmund and I went to one of Sidney's new Chinese take-out places the other night."

"How was it?"

"Too slow for a fast-food place. In a place like that, you should be able to wok in, pick up the food and wok right out again. It took them fifteen minutes to find the fried rice."

"I'm glad you can joke about it. Let's hope the service improves, for the sake of my future position with Sidney Pollov Enterprises."

"By the way, Sidney called here the other day and wondered where he could find you. He said he'd been ringing your apartment in Ketchikan and you didn't answer. He even tried to find Randy, but there weren't any Randy Gallahorns in the phone book. He asked me if I knew Randy's husband's last name. I thought Randy was a guy."

"Randy's husband?" Then Martha realized what must have happened. She laughed. "It's all right, Polly. Sidney must think Randy is a girl. And Randy lives with his mother, who has remarried and has a different last name."

"Why on earth does Sidney think Randy is a girl?"

"Oh, it's a silly rule he has about hiring only women to work in Bagel Barns. I never got around to informing him that Randy is a teenage boy. Hey, Polly, I'll call you next week. I hear Nick coming up the steps."

"Right. Good luck, Martha."

"With what?"

"Everything, but especially Nick. And if you ever want to talk about anything, I'm here."

"Thanks, Polly. Talk to you soon." She hung up just as Nick came in the door.

He kissed her, then pulled away. She knew at once that he had something on his mind.

"I'd like to take you out to dinner tonight," he told her with a worried frown. "But I don't know if I can."

"Is something wrong?"

"I have to go over to Wanda's. One of Wanda's grandchildren called my office at the cannery and left a crazy mixed-up message with my secretary about Wanda's falling downstairs and having to go to the doctor. Hallie and Davey were visiting Wanda today, and neither of them was there when I called back.

I couldn't make heads or tails out of the message, so I want to see what's going on.''

"I'll go with you," Martha said.

"No need for that. I'll drive over to Wanda's house and call you if I can't get back in time to take you to dinner, if that's all right with you.''

"Sure," Martha said. "I wanted to change clothes anyway. I spilled hot chocolate down the front of these jeans this afternoon.''

"If you'd been wearing your apron like Sidney said—"

"Never mind that. I think wearing jeans in a place called a Bagel Barn makes sense, and Sidney's checkered apron looks plain silly over jeans." She grinned up at him.

He kissed her goodbye. "I'll call you soon," he said before ducking out the door.

But it wasn't soon, and when he did call he sounded exasperated.

"Wanda fell down the steps to the basement, just a short fall, but she put out her hands to break her fall and broke a wrist. Hallie drove her to the doctor, and he was out. Wanda sat around in pain until he showed up. She's just had the cast put on her wrist, and Hallie is trying to cook supper for all these grandchildren of Wanda's. I've decided that the best thing to do is to leave Hallie here and take Davey home.''

"I'm so sorry," Martha said. She had met Wanda once and liked her.

"Not only that, but Hallie doesn't think Wanda can manage here by herself, and she wants to stay for at least a week. I don't feel that I can leave Davey, though, not with all these other kids around. He's smaller than most of them, and they can get pretty rowdy, especially if Wanda isn't right there to correct them.''

"What are you going to do?"

"I don't know. We left Bear at Williwaw Lodge this morning with a large supply of clams and oysters, but he's due to run out of food, so I have to go home and feed him. I want to take Davey with me, but Bear and Davey together are a lot to handle alone, and—'' Nick was interrupted by a crash and a loud wail.

"You see what I mean about how the kids get out of hand," he said.

"Why don't I come to Williwaw Lodge with you? I can at least look after Bear while you take care of Davey. I could even spend the night if you'd like."

"What about work tomorrow?"

"You have to come into town to go to the cannery, right? I'll come in with you on the *Tabor*."

"Davey could go over to Wanda's tomorrow, I suppose," Nick said. "When the bigger kids are out playing or fishing or whatever, he'll play with the younger ones as usual." A hurried consultation with Hallie ensued.

"Hallie says it's a good idea for you to go to Williwaw Lodge. She says that the sheets for the guest room are in the bottom drawer of the dresser."

"So I have Hallie's approval, do I?"

"I'm sure. In more ways than one. She's always said I needed a woman around the place. Hush, Hallie, you're embarrassing me," he said in an aside to his housekeeper.

"What did she say?"

"Never mind. I'll pick you up in a few minutes."

Martha hung up the phone in a bemused frame of mind. She could have sworn that Hallie had said something involving "married" and "a wife."

Chapter Twelve

Nick and Martha arrived at Williwaw Lodge to discover that Bear was crying and out of food. Davey leaned over the pen Nick had contrived for Bear in a corner of the kitchen, petting Bear while Bear barked and whistled and Nick unloaded more clams and oysters from the *Tabor*.

"Being in the seafood business certainly has its advantages," he said as they watched Bear floating in his collapsible bathtub and eating clams. Bear was almost completely weaned now and existed mostly on solid food.

Martha was inspecting the jar of earthworms she and Davey had dug up some weeks ago when Davey suddenly said, "More oysters, Nick! Bear needs more!"

She almost dropped the jar in surprise.

Nick regained his composure first. "Yes, Davey, Bear certainly does need more oysters. Here, I'll give him some." He tossed a few more oysters in the tub. Davey clapped his hands in glee as Bear gobbled them down.

"I didn't know Davey had been talking like that!" Martha remarked in an undertone after drawing Nick aside.

"No more than the usual four words. That was the most he's ever said. It's the closest Davey has ever come to normal speech!" Nick beamed excitedly.

"What should we do?"

"Just respond normally. Act as though he's always talked. We'll reward Davey by giving him more leads, more questions he might want to answer. Like this—'' More loudly this time, Nick said, ''Would you like to put the oysters in the tub next time, Davey?''

But Davey only nodded his head up and down. His eyes lit up with delight, though, as the oysters fell from his hands into the water and Bear splashed after them.

''Davey, time for your bath,'' Nick said after a while.

''Bear,'' Davey said. It was clear that he wanted Bear to take a bath with him.

''No, Bear has his tub and you have yours,'' responded Nick.

''Bear!''

''No, Davey.'' Nick took Davey firmly by the hand and led him away to the bathroom. Davey followed with only one backward glance at his pet. After his bath, Davey again ran back into the kitchen to see how Bear was faring. Bear regarded Davey with soulful eyes, twitching his whiskers and looking altogether lovable.

''Davey has certainly taken to Bear,'' Nick said. ''He spends lots of time just watching him. Hallie says that he's responded to Bear better than anything else she's ever tried, even other kids.''

''Davey may feel intimidated by other children,'' Martha said, thinking of the hubbub at Wanda's house. ''An animal is probably much less threatening. It doesn't talk, so it's like him. Bear is good for Davey.''

Davey went to bed shortly, and Nick piled logs in the fireplace and lit a big fire. He and Martha sat in front of it, holding hands and sharing thoughts.

''This is what my mother and father used to do when my brothers and I were kids. I used to get out of bed at night and find them in front of the fire, talking and holding hands. I thought it was silly and sappy then.'' He smiled.

''And now?''

''Now I think it's sweet and sentimental,'' he admitted. ''I've never done it with anyone else.''

This admission surprised her. ''Surely you've brought other women here,'' she said.

''No,'' he said. ''After my brothers married, it was just my dad and me and Hallie at Williwaw Lodge. And after my father died, it was just Hallie and me. I never knew a woman I'd feel comfortable bringing here.''

"Why, Nick,'' Martha said, touched at his admission.

"You know what Hallie said tonight when you and I were talking on the phone,'' he said in a low voice.

"What?''

"She said she'd always hoped I'd get married and bring a wife to Williwaw Lodge. She said if she were going to choose the woman, it would be you.''

Martha hardly knew what to say. She and Nick had never even talked about marriage, and he seemed to be signaling her in an oblique way that he was ready to talk about it.

He took her in his arms, and she surrendered to his kisses. The fire crackled and blazed, and the room was bathed in golden light.

Marry Nick? she thought, but then the idea dissolved and swirled away, eclipsed by the joy of being with him. When it occurred to her again much later, she was sure that he couldn't have meant it.

HALLIE INSISTED that she couldn't leave Wanda, so Martha was still living at Williwaw Lodge two weeks later. She slept alone in the guest room; Nick worried about the effect it would have on Davey if he woke up to find Martha in Nick's bed. Martha agreed with Nick. She didn't want Davey's burgeoning development to be blocked by anything she and Nick might do.

And Davey was becoming more outgoing day by day.

He began to talk haltingly in sentences by the end of the second week Martha was there. They were short sentences, and sometimes he didn't speak for hours. His infrequent smiles were brief, but at least he was smiling. But the most promising sign was that Davey was beginning to communicate with words, and his eyes were beginning to lose that unexplained hidden pain in their depths.

Hallie, with whom Davey stayed at Wanda's during the daytime when Nick and Martha were at work, was ecstatic at this turnaround in Davey's behavior.

"It's because of you, Martha," she said. "You're so warm and friendly—so *good* with him—that he couldn't help responding."

"No," Martha demurred. "Davey's not talking because of anything I did. If Davey has improved, it's because of his visits to Dr. Whitmer. And maybe because of Bear."

Davey continued to open up to the little sea otter in a way that neither Nick nor Martha would have believed possible. The first thing Davey did when he arrived home at the lodge every evening was to dash into the kitchen to see how Bear was doing. He clapped his hands to applaud Bear's antics; he dug clams on the beach for Bear's dinner. He would sit holding Bear as long as Bear would be still, stroking Bear's silky gray-brown fur.

When Nick took Davey to Juneau to see Dr. Whitmer for their next appointment, Nick came back with glowing reports.

"Dr. Whitmer told me about something called pet therapy," he told Martha. "Psychologists have found that lots of people respond to pets when they don't respond to anything else. Elderly people who are lonely or unhappy often become more optimistic after they get a dog or a cat. Kids with behavior problems or trauma in their backgrounds begin to feel more comfortable about themselves when they have a pet. Dr. Whitmer thinks that Bear is playing an important role in Davey's development."

"I thought you weren't going to keep Bear," Martha said.

"I've agreed to let the fish-and-wildlife people release Bear in a colony of sea otters when he's old enough," Nick said. "I don't know how to break the news to Davey that Bear will leave us eventually."

Martha, who had spent time getting to know both Davey and Bear, said, "Let me talk to him about it."

"All right," Nick agreed.

Martha found a book about sea otters in the children's section of the Ketchikan library, and she brought it back to Williwaw Lodge one night. Davey listened with wide eyes as she read it to him.

The book told about the life cycle of sea otters, and it showed wonderful color pictures of a newborn sea otter and one that had just been weaned. The one that had been weaned looked just like Bear, and Martha pointed out that soon this bigger otter would go away and start a family of its own.

"Bear will go away someday, too," she told Davey. "He will grow up and want to be with other sea otters."

"Not today," Davey said with a worried look.

"No, not today. After a lot of tomorrows, though. Bear will want to go play with his friends in the ocean, like you go to play with your friends at Wanda's," Martha said.

"Oh," Davey said. He patted the picture on the page of the book. "This looks like Bear."

"Maybe Nick would take pictures of you and Bear together so that you'll always have a picture of him. We could hang the picture in your room."

Davey grinned at that.

"Why don't you go ask Nick to take a picture of Bear while he eats tonight? And of Bear's sitting in your lap while you rub his stomach?"

"Okay," Davey said, and he ran away to find Nick.

Martha closed the book, hoping she'd said all the right things. It was so hard to know with Davey. Communication was so new to him and he was so much in the habit of concealing his feelings that she wasn't always sure if she was getting her point across. Tonight had gone well, she thought, but only time would tell.

Nick took several pictures of Bear alone and of Bear and Davey together. Martha bought frames for the pictures, and they hung the best ones on the wall of Davey's room. One night while Bear was napping, Davey, under Martha's direction, sat at the kitchen table and pasted the other pictures of Bear in a big scrapbook.

"How do you know how to do all the things you do with Davey?" Nick asked.

Martha shrugged. "Having a mother who taught kindergarten probably helped. Mother was always thinking up ways to teach her students. I helped her sometimes with the preparations, like mixing buckets of tempera paints and binding construction paper into scrapbooks for the kids."

"You're a natural-born mother," he said, thinking that when he'd first observed her on the dock in Ketchikan looking so glossy and sophisticated and assembling bagels so efficiently he never would have guessed it.

"My only connection with children so far is that I'm an honorary aunt to my former roommate's daughter," insisted Martha, but nevertheless, Nick's admiration for her ability to handle Davey couldn't help but grow.

As for Martha, Davey was rapidly becoming one of her enthusiasms. She could hardly wait to see him running down the steps at Wanda's house when she and Nick picked him up every evening.

"He adores you," Hallie insisted when she accompanied Davey out to the car one time.

"Oh, I like him a lot, too," Martha said, understating the facts. To tell the truth, she had fallen in love with Davey's pudgy little cheeks, his almond-shaped eyes, which were so often brightened by a smile these days, and with the attention she got from him.

She who had never particularly desired children, who had never wondered what it would be like for milk to issue from her breasts, now delighted in the curve of Davey's backbone nestled in the crook of her arm. Martha knew now why people wanted kids. The unquestioning adoration in their eyes when they gazed up at you, the funny little things they said and did, and what she had begun to think of as their *cuddability* when they snuggled against you to be read to at bedtime—all these things brought a new maturity and understanding to Martha that she had never experienced before.

She explained to Nick that she had coined the word *cuddable* to be applied to Davey, but Nick only laughed and said that if anyone was cuddable it was Martha. She was glad he felt that way, but a child was infinitely more cuddable than she was, she was sure.

All the while she was forging this incredible new bond with Davey, Martha continued to run the Bagel Barn. The running of the business continued to be a challenge, and she enjoyed dealing with her customers. She had become friends with Randy, who never ceased to amaze her with his versatility and originality.

For example, one morning Martha walked up the dock after arriving on the *Tabor* with Nick and Davey to find a new sign posted on the side of the Bagel Barn. The sign said Free Cookies Tomorrow.

She confronted a grinning Randy with an incredulous look on her face.

"What in the world are you doing, Randy, promising free cookies tomorrow?"

"Oh, it's just a way to get customers to stop. They're going to be curious, right? And the sign says Free Cookies Tomorrow, right?"

"Well, yes, but—"

"So if the sign always says Free Cookies Tomorrow we don't give away free cookies today. Tomorrow is always tomorrow. The sign always *says* it'll be tomorrow. And they'll have to buy the cookies today to find out if they want to come back for free cookies tomorrow. Most of our passengers come off cruise ships, anyway. They won't be back the next day."

Martha stifled a laugh. This was one case in which she couldn't allow Randy's spirit of enterprise to prevail.

"Take the sign down, Randy," she directed. "I'm much more interested in the cookies we'll sell today rather than the free ones we're giving away tomorrow, even if tomorrow never comes."

Chagrined, Randy took down the sign and replaced it with one that said Chocolate-Chip Cookie Special. That day they sold more cookies than on any other day.

"I'll have to double the recipe again tonight," Martha said. "It seems as if I just can't bake them fast enough."

"Your cookies outsold the bagels today," observed Randy as he thumbed through a stack of five-dollar bills.

"They've caught on with the townspeople, too," Martha said. "I used to think that the locals bought them just to get a look at the woman Nick Novak is seeing, but they keep coming back for more, so I guess that's not it."

"They love the cookies," Randy said with a shrug. "You should be proud of yourself for developing the recipe."

"I don't know," Martha answered. "I'm getting tired of baking cookies. It used to be more fun when I lived alone in my apartment. Baking the cookies was something to fill the lonely hours. But now that I'm at Williwaw Lodge with Nick and Davey, it's all I can do to bake enough."

Martha enlisted Nick and Davey in her cookie-baking efforts. Davey, who still loved chocolate better than anything except perhaps Bear, was a help in fetching spoons and utensils. Nick could mix the recipe and do almost everything that Martha could do, although it took him longer. Together they spent every night in Hallie's little kitchen baking batch after batch of chocolate-chip cookies. The aroma of cookies filled the air at Williwaw Lodge. Nick loved it.

"This old lodge finally smells like I've always thought a home ought to smell," he told Martha.

"I guess it's better than the smell of fish," she said with a little laugh, because that was how the cannery smelled. Nick could only agree.

All in all, Martha's presence had made a big difference at Williwaw Lodge. Whereas before Nick had had to force himself to visit with Hallie after Davey had gone to bed, he now looked forward to that quiet period as a time when he could be alone with Martha. The atmosphere at the lodge since Martha had arrived was cheerful. It was never tense. If a problem arose—for instance, when Davey once refused to take his bath and lapsed into a temper tantrum—Martha handled it with characteristic understanding and efficiency.

"He's only communicating," Martha said afterward. "It's not as though Davey has tantrums frequently. He's learning how to let his feelings out. He's using a tantrum to tell us what he thinks of something. If we keep encouraging him to communicate verbally, he won't have temper tantrums anymore."

Martha's instincts were astonishing. Upon reflection, Nick agreed that she was probably right. Even a temper tantrum was more reassuring than Davey's former stony silence, which had worried Nick so much.

Hallie showed no signs of returning to Williwaw Lodge. Wanda's cast wouldn't come off for weeks, and without the use of one hand Wanda couldn't very well keep up with the care of her five grandchildren. Hallie told Nick that if he was smart he'd keep Martha at the lodge forever.

Nick had begun to think the same thing himself. He just didn't know how he was going to bring it about, that was all.

WEATHERWISE, the last Monday in July was one of the worst days since Martha had arrived in Ketchikan. A smoky fog settled over the town, and air traffic was restricted. The wind whistled through cracks in the Bagel Barn and tore around the buildings of the town, driving sodden refuse ahead of it. To top it all off, Martha felt the beginnings of a sore throat.

"We might as well go home," Randy said in discouragement as he stared unhappily at the boats heaving against the dock. "We won't get too many customers anyway."

"A couple of cruise ships are going to arrive today, not to mention the ferry," Martha replied stubbornly. "There's no point in missing out on any customers." She hated to give up before the day even started.

"All I can say is that I hope our customers like soggy bagels," Randy said.

The tenders from the big ships arrived one by one, disgorging only a nominal number of passengers. They straggled up the ramp looking like wet rats, but nevertheless eager to see the sights for which Ketchikan was famous—its Totem Heritage Center and its fish hatchery. Martha and Randy sold many bagels, but as usual they sold even more cookies.

Martha was dispiritedly counting out change to a customer when she saw a familiar dapper figure walking rapidly up the ramp from a ferry that had just docked. The man was particularly noticeable because he seemed to be in a hurry, while the other passengers meandered listlessly through the rain, huddling under dripping umbrellas as they unfolded their new street maps.

"That's Sidney!" exclaimed Martha as a feeling of dread clamped down on her. She'd had no idea that the busy Sidney ever indulged in surprise visits.

Sidney approached the Bagel Barn like a man with a mission. "Martha! How're things? Not so busy today, right? I thought I'd drop by, see how things are going! I was looking over the town of Sitka for a new Bagel Barn, I couldn't catch my flight out of there because of the weather, and I had to take the ferry instead. The ferry stops here, so I thought to myself, 'Sidney, you'd better say hello to Martha.' Say, is there anywhere nearby where we can talk business?" He noticed Randy inside the Bagel Barn for the first time. "Hey, who are you?"

"I'm Randy," Randy said, sticking his hand out the front of the Bagel Barn. Sidney's eyebrows flew up, and for one awful moment Martha was afraid that Sidney wasn't going to shake Randy's hand. He did, though, just in time.

"I suppose I have some explaining to do," Martha said. She was prepared to back Randy up one hundred percent. After all, Randy was the perfect employee for the Bagel Barn; if it weren't for Randy, sales wouldn't be as good as they were.

"Well, let's find a place out of the rain," Sidney said with the first hint of grumpiness she'd ever detected in him.

Martha took Sidney to the café where she and Nick so often went for chili. She realized as soon as they sat down that it had been a mistake. Sidney couldn't find anything on the menu he wanted to order, and he proclaimed that chili interfered with his digestion. He looked exhausted, and for the first time Martha noticed that skin drooped from his jowls. Finally they both ordered a cup of coffee, and Sidney said abruptly, "All right. What's with Randy?"

"He helped me put up the Bagel Barn when I first got here, and I hired him because I needed someone. I had a hunch he'd be a terrific worker. And he is. Why, he's—"

"Never mind, never mind. You know I want pretty girls working in my Bagel Barns. Fire him."

Martha blanched. Surely he didn't mean it.

"I can't do that," she said. "I could never find another employee as helpful, as enterprising or as loyal as Randy."

"Randy. Do you know that I thought he was a female? I thought it was spelled R-A-N-D-I or something cute like that."

"Sidney, I *need* Randy."

"Never mind that. Get rid of him and find a girl. A pretty girl like you. Which brings up another thing. Why aren't you wearing a dress and the checkered apron like you're supposed to?"

"Everybody wears jeans in Ketchikan. It's a casual place. Anyway, jeans are fine to wear in what is supposed to be a representation of a barn. And the apron looks silly with jeans, believe me. In this weather I needed my windbreaker, so that's what I'm wearing."

"Martha, Martha. Girls—women, I mean—who work in my Bagel Barns wear dresses and aprons, and that's that."

"It seems to me you should be more flexible and let the conditions at each Bagel Barn dictate the correct way of dressing." Martha regarded Sidney coolly; he might be her boss, but he had promised her a certain autonomy in running this Bagel Barn, and she was using good judgment in making her decisions.

"You let me decide what my employees wear. Stick to business, Martha."

"I *am* sticking to business."

"Your sales figures look good, Martha. I'll say that for you." Sidney whipped a sheet of paper out of his briefcase and began to read off a series of figures. "You should be proud of how well you've done these first few weeks," he continued. He consulted another sheet and scowled. "I notice your order for lox is way down. Any explanation for that?"

"I'm selling Alaskan salmon on the bagels; it's smoked with alder wood by a local firm, and the customers love it." She sat back, ready to accept the praise she was sure would come her way.

"Alaskan salmon, huh? What's wrong with plain old lox?" He narrowed his eyes and waited.

Martha quickly explained how tourists loved Alaskan salmon and how lox wasn't really salmon but trout. All the selling points that had worked on her didn't make any difference to Sidney.

"I don't know about this, Martha. It sounds like a good way to ruin a perfectly good bagel." He took a sip of coffee and grimaced. "Tastes like turpentine. I should've ordered something else."

"Sidney, I'm proud of my business decisions. For instance, the chocolate-chip cookies. I was going to wait to tell you about this, but since you're here I'll tell you now. I've developed this wonderful chocolate-chip cookie recipe, and I've been selling the cookies at the Bagel Barn. I package two giant cookies in cellophane, sell the package for two dollars, and so far the packages of cookies are outselling the bagels almost two to one. I'm going to keep on selling them, too." Again she waited for his praise. After all, everyone else had praised her cookies. Why shouldn't he?

Sidney sputtered and appeared, for once, to be speechless. His expression settled into one of violated outrage. "*Cookies?* You're selling these cookies you make in *my* Bagel Barn?"

"Yes, and they're good, too. You'll have to try them."

"But you say they're outselling bagels!" He appeared incredulous.

"Sidney, they're making money! It's an original recipe! And I developed them on my own time! Why, I think it would be a good idea if we hired a bakery to bake the cookies from this recipe in quantity and shipped them fresh to every Bagel Barn in the country!"

"That, Martha, is the most ridiculous thing I ever heard! Cookies at a Bagel Barn? You must be crazy!"

"Sidney, didn't you hear me? They're making money! They're delicious!" Martha couldn't believe that Sidney didn't like her idea.

"I'm outraged that you would begin to sell these cookies of yours in one of my Bagel Barns without my consent. That's insubordination as far as I'm concerned. Add that to the fact that your weekly orders have come in late a couple of times and you can see that I have good reason to be annoyed with you." Sidney, his manner totally changed from what Martha remembered, glared at her over his coffee, which was now cold.

She was even more stunned when Sidney stood up from the table in the booth and tossed a few bills down on the scarred Formica. "I'm going back to San Francisco. You get rid of that Randy and stop selling the cookies. I don't want to get the locals mad at us, so you can keep on selling the Alaskan salmon if you insist. I'll expect your orders on time in the future.''

With one final glance of total fury, Sidney stomped out the door.

Chapter Thirteen

Feeling sick to her stomach, Martha leaned her head on her hand and wished that Sidney had never come to Ketchikan. Sidney's visit had been a total disaster. If only she'd had some inkling that he was coming! Where was the authority he'd promised her? She had no authority at all if she couldn't make decisions concerning the Bagel Barn she managed.

What was she going to do? She couldn't fire Randy. Aside from the fact that he was doing a wonderful job, she felt a certain loyalty to him, just as she was sure Randy felt toward her. And her cookies—her delicious cookies! Why wouldn't Sidney even try one?

She roused herself out of her misery, pulled on her damp windbreaker and went running through the rain back to the Bagel Barn. If it wasn't too late, she'd insist that Sidney taste one of her cookies, just one. Better yet, she'd give him some to take on the ferry with him. Surely she could convince him that they ought to sell cookies in Bagel Barns.

But when she arrived breathlessly at the Bagel Barn she saw the ferry steaming out of the harbor, its wake widening as it left the dock behind.

"Did Sidney stop by here on his way back to the ferry?" she asked Randy.

Randy looked perplexed. "All he did was stick his head in the door and shout, 'You're fired!' What did I do wrong, Martha?"

Martha sank against the counter. "Nothing. Except perhaps be born a boy."

"*What?*"

Martha sighed. "Randy, Sidney has this prejudice against hiring men to work in the Bagel Barns. He wants pretty *girls* who wear dresses and aprons." She gestured down at her windbreaker and blue jeans. "You can imagine," she said ruefully, "what he thought of this outfit."

Randy's eyes bulged. "Gee, Martha, did he fire you, too?"

She shook her head. "No. But he said I can't sell cookies anymore."

"Not sell cookies? That's unbelievable!"

"Well, that's what he said. I'm supposed to fire you, stop selling cookies and wear a dress and the red checkered apron."

"I guess I don't have a job then," said Randy, his perplexity turning to sadness. "That's too bad, 'cause I've always liked working here."

"Wait a minute," Martha said. She didn't like this. She didn't like anything about it. She didn't believe in sex discrimination of any kind. And she wasn't going to fire Randy.

"But you said—"

"Never mind what anyone said. You still have a job here, Randy. And I'm not about to stop selling cookies. Let's close up now. You'll report to work tomorrow as usual." Briskly she shoved the cream cheese and jelly into the refrigerator; she gathered up all their unsold cookies and stored them in plastic containers.

"Are you sure, Martha?" Randy said as she locked up. He looked so forlorn as he stood beside her in the softly falling rain that it only strengthened her resolve.

"I'm sure," she said, before hurrying off to the cannery to meet Nick.

"WHAT ARE YOU going to do?" Nick asked, staring at the plastic containers of cookies that Martha had piled on his desk. In the background clattered the noise of the cannery, but in Nick's office, with the door closed, it was quiet enough that Martha could hear the ticking of the clock on the wall.

"I'm going to pay Randy out of my own pocket," she said. "Is that wise?"

"My expenses are minimal. Sidney provides the apartment and the car; I was saving most of my money so that I could rent or buy one of those old Victorian houses I liked so much in San Francisco. I can afford to pay Randy."

Nick leaned back in his chair. It creaked. He tried to think. He didn't know if Martha was making the right decision.

Finally he cleared his throat and spoke. "That's very kind of you, Martha. What if Sidney finds out? He made it clear that he wants only pretty women working in his Bagel Barns."

"Pretty *girls*—that's what he said," Martha replied bitterly. "He always calls women *girls*."

"Nevertheless," Nick said patiently, "he won't like it if he finds out that you've kept Randy. It could cost you your job."

Martha's eyes sparked with defiance. "I don't care. It isn't right."

"He's still the boss. Bagel Barns are his business. You work for him."

Martha shook her head. "Maybe I don't really want to work for him anymore," she said. "Maybe I wouldn't be happy working for him."

"I'm not sure you can decide that on the basis of Sidney's surprise visit today."

Martha shook her head impatiently. "Nick, when I go back to San Francisco I'll have a lot more contact with Sidney. He's not the way I thought he was when I met him. Now he's being totally unreasonable. Today I saw a tyrant, not a levelheaded, reasonable businessman. I didn't like the Sidney I saw today, Nick. I didn't like him at all."

The clock ticked on, and Nick sighed. "It's your decision, Martha." His voice softened. She looked so disillusioned, sitting across from him in her wet jeans and with damp curls fringing her forehead. "You know, my dear Cheechako, I don't want you to leave at the end of the summer. If you're not working for Sidney, you won't have to leave." The words hung in midair. He waited to see what her reaction would be.

Martha leaned back in her chair and rubbed her eyes. "Nick

I can't talk about that now. I can't take any more heavy discussions today.''

"Whatever you say," he said lightly. He stood up and came to stand beside her chair. His hand reached out and massaged her shoulder for a moment. It slid up to her neck, where it cupped her nape, and then he bent and kissed her lingeringly on the lips.

"You shouldn't kiss me, Nick. I'm getting a sore throat."

"I'll take my chances," he said. His eyes linked with hers. In them she saw interest, concern and a love that he never tried to hide. She was suddenly grateful to him for all the happiness he'd brought into her life. She had felt incomplete before she'd known him, and she hadn't even known how incomplete she'd been.

"Oh, Nick," she said, reaching out to wrap her arms around his waist. He knelt in front of her and held her close for several moments. She rested her head on his broad shoulder.

"You've had a hard day," he said tenderly. "Let's go somewhere and have a quiet meal, just the two of us."

"Not Davey?" They usually picked Davey up at Wanda's if they were going to eat in town, and Davey went with them. This had ensured a steady diet of McDonald's hamburgers, because Davey was getting to like them almost as much as he liked chocolate.

"Not Davey. Just you and me in a nice, quiet, candlelit restaurant. We'll talk this over at length. Would that help?"

"Yeah," Martha said, disengaging herself from his embrace. "I'll go to the ladies' room and try to get myself looking half-decent first, and maybe I'll calm down a bit. I'm so keyed up that I can hardly think straight."

"A glass or two of a good wine might help that," he said with a smile.

She looked at him, and it seemed to her that she'd never get enough of looking. He was a tall, rugged, handsome man, and he was in love with her. She knew the way his ears stood out from his head, the cowlick on his crown, the whiteness of his teeth in the dark. When she was with him, it was all she could do not to be touching him every minute, because touching him was such a tantalizing pleasure. She had known it would be from the first moment she'd seen him, and she remembered how she'd longed for his touch at first. Now she could touch him anytime he was near. It was a luxury she would never be able to take for granted, and just to prove that she wouldn't she reached out and laid her finger against his arm.

He looked at her questioningly.

"I just wanted to touch you," she explained, and by the answering look in his eyes she knew he understood. He understood everything, always.

Thank goodness Nick understood, Martha thought a few minutes later as she stood before the mirror in the cannery ladies' room and tried to run a comb through her tangled curls. Without him she'd feel so alone here in Ketchikan.

It was strange about Sidney. He didn't seem like the same person she'd known back in San Francisco.

She gazed into the mirror with dawning awareness. The person who stared back at her wore her hair in haphazard ringlets that were drying stiffly all over her head. She wore no eye makeup at all, and her lipstick seemed to have disappeared. Her skin was no longer milk white; instead it was turning a pale amber color, though how she could have become suntanned in this place where it rained most of the time, she couldn't imagine. Instead of one of her former color-coordinated outfits, she wore a windbreaker and a pair of jeans so faded that once she would have thrown them out. Who was this Martha Rose?

Sidney had changed. There was no doubt about that. But the most peculiar thing was that Martha had changed too. She wasn't the same person who had arrived in Ketchikan. She was someone entirely different.

And her own metamorphosis was even harder to understand than Sidney's.

MARTHA DIDN'T FIRE RANDY. And she didn't stop selling chocolate-chip cookies. She stopped selling them at the Bagel Barn, though.

This was Nick's idea.

"You know," he said one Sunday afternoon when they had

taken Davey to see the totem poles at Totem Bight Park, "you may have to be like Raven in Tlingit mythology." All the way to the park Nick had regaled them with Native myths, much to Davey's delight and Martha's mystification. "Never mind," Nick had said. "The totems will help you understand."

But Martha didn't even pretend to comprehend the stories the Native totems told; their carved images weren't always readily identifiable as the beavers or fish or whales or ravens that Nick told her they were. Now he was telling her she should be like Raven. How?

"I'm not even sure what question to ask you after a statement like that." She smiled up at him and slid her arm through his. A totem loomed over them, casting a shadow in their path.

"In the Tlingit legends, Raven outwitted Eagle. That's because Raven knew how to change his form, you see." Nick's teasing smile invited more questions, but she sensed that he was half-serious.

"I don't know what in the world this has to do with anything, Nick," Martha said as she kept an eye on Davey, who was trying to shinny up one of the totems by planting one sneakered foot firmly in the mouth of what Martha thought must be Wolf. Or was it Raven, changed into Wolf? While Martha was mulling this over, Nick retrieved Davey. Then, with Davey skipping along the path in front of them, Nick explained what he meant.

"You could outwit Sidney by selling your cookies at my salmon store. That way you still get to sell your cookies, only in a different way. You may have to change their form, like Raven did his. Instead of packaging two large cookies for an immediate snack, offer smaller cookies in a bag or box so that the tourists can easily carry them back to the ship the same way they carry the salmon they buy from me."

"That way I won't be selling them at the Bagel Barn, so it won't make Sidney angry," Martha said.

"Right. And it would be wrong to deprive people of those cookies now that you've perfected the recipe. Why, Hallie tells me that Wanda's grandchildren are spoiled for any other kind of cookies. They only want to eat yours."

Martha had been offering a steady supply of cookies to

Wanda's grandchildren since Hallie had been living at Wanda's house. The children managed to tuck away several dozen cookies a day.

"What about the profits? I've been turning them over to the Bagel Barn, you know."

"Start your own business, Martha. You keep the profits."

"My own business? You understand how I feel about that after what happened to my father's business," Martha said. "It scares me. I don't want to take the chance."

"I thought you told me you were a creature of impulse."

Martha gazed at the white-capped mountains in the distance. The sun, bright enough to cast a shadow only minutes ago, was shrouded in clouds. She thought carefully before she spoke.

"I've never been a creature of impulse where business is concerned," she said. "Not when it involves my own money. I don't have much money to invest in supplies now that I'm paying Randy his salary out of my own pocket. I'd need packaging for the cookies, which might be an expensive outlay. I'd need to buy flour and chocolate chips and all the other ingredients, which I was paying for with Bagel Barn money while I sold them at the Bagel Barn."

"Hey," Nick said gently. His eyes bespoke confidence in her, which she found reassuring. "I'd like to be your business partner."

"My business partner?" Surprised at this kind of encouragement, she stared at him, trying to figure out if he really meant it. It appeared that he did. He put his arm around her and kissed her on the cheek.

"Sure," he said easily. "It's a small investment of capital, and I know it'll pay off. You can buy me out later when you're making money."

"I hardly know what to say," she said in confusion. This was totally unexpected, and yet she was encouraged by Nick's faith in her. If he didn't think her cookie business would succeed, he wouldn't offer to bankroll it, would he?

"Think of it this way," urged Nick. "With our cookie business, you won't be subject to the whims of a boss. Remember what I told you about why fishermen like leading their kind of life? It's the same reason I enjoyed fishing for a living. It's a way of being self-sufficient and independent. This cookie business could make you independent, too."

Her recent experiences with Sidney's unreasonableness had certainly soured Martha on working for someone else. And she trusted Nick's business acumen. She hesitated, though, caught up in doubts.

"Martha?"

"I don't know, Nick. I just don't know what to say about it."

"Say you'll do it," he urged. "Be a creature of impulse."

Martha thought for a moment. She loved knowing that people enjoyed eating her cookies. *She* enjoyed eating her cookies. She had come a long way in the development of the perfect chocolate-chip cookie, and it would be foolish to stop now just because of Sidney.

She flung a smile up at Nick. His personal involvement, his faith in her, made all the difference. And he was right—the money she'd have to invest wouldn't be so much if it was a joint venture. The business wouldn't require much inventory; supplies could be bought as she went along. Also, right now she had her job with Sidney Pollov Enterprises to pay the bills in case this new venture failed.

"Okay," she said recklessly. "We're partners."

"Partners," Nick agreed. They shook hands. "Oh, heck," Nick said. "That's much too formal." And he pulled her into his arms and kissed her in front of a group of tourists.

"Are they on their honeymoon?" piped a little girl's high-pitched voice before someone shushed her.

Nick and Martha pulled apart self-consciously and let the group pass them on the path.

"Back to our discussion," Nick said when the group had rounded a bend in the path ahead. "Let me take care of the packaging. I deal with a packager who ships me boxes for packing my salmon, and I'm pretty sure he can come up with some kind of simple cookie box on short notice. You won't need sales help, because my salespeople in the store will sell your cookies right alongside my salmon."

"Salmon and cookies, isn't that a strange combination?"

"Maybe, but it doesn't matter. We also sell newspapers and saltwater taffy made by a friend of Hallie's. We cater to tourists, and I'll sell whatever is popular with them. I don't have hidebound rules like Sidney does. And your cookies will encourage the local people to come into my store, which is something I'd like to see. I have a feeling that unless I have something to sell besides salmon it's going to be a long, cold winter at the store."

What if I'm not here to bake my cookies in the winter? The thought struck Martha with the force of a southeasterly gale. She was supposed to leave soon after Labor Day, and she couldn't bear the thought of being separated from Nick.

Despite her feeling of adventure at the prospect of beginning a new business with Nick, the thought ruined the rest of the outing for her. She was quiet and withdrawn, and she was grateful that Davey talked a lot on the way back to Williwaw Lodge. The sun stayed behind the clouds, almost as though it was wary of coming out.

Martha had a lot of serious thinking to do, and she needed to start now.

OVER THE NEXT FEW DAYS, Martha did think about her future plans. But she found it easy to be distracted when she was increasingly caught up in sharing Nick's life in the present.

She had not known that it was possible to lead such a life. Certainly nothing had ever prepared her to wake up to such big-scale bold beauty right outside her window every morning. Nor had she known what it would be like to live so far removed from other people.

Here on Mooseleg Bay, nothing other than the occasional chatter of a boat's engine from far across the water disturbed the silence. Oh, occasionally there were the throaty cries of arctic loons or the slap of their wings on the waves as they frolicked in the whitecaps. Or maybe the peace would be disturbed momentarily by the crashing of a porcupine through the surrounding thickets. But there were few man-made sounds.

Martha gloried in the wealth of wild fruits they picked on Nick's land. Sweet pickings were bountiful. There were bright blueberries, crunchy cranberries, salmonberries, raspberries and more. Berrying was always fun, because Davey had such a good time trying to pick more berries than either Martha or Nick. Here nature gave freely of her bounty, and all one had to do was take it.

Martha learned to pick cow parsnip for salads and to cook wild rhubarb. Hallie, who still lived with Wanda, directed her in this and the results were encouraging. Martha learned to eat dandelion greens that Nick cooked, and she learned that the leaves of nettles were edible. She helped Nick take care of Hallie's garden, and she discovered that she enjoyed grubbing in the dirt while Davey swung from an old mooring buoy hung by a rope from a nearby spruce.

Nick showed her and Davey how to pan for gold in the stream. He brought little rocker boxes out of the shed, boxes that his father had made for him and his brothers, and he demonstrated how to shovel sand and gravel into them so that the boxes would separate tiny flakes of gold from the gravel. They found only a bit of gold, not enough to amount to much, but Davey carried it around in an old pill bottle, whipping it out at odd moments to admire the shining flecks within.

Nick showed Martha some gold nuggets he had found when he was a boy. The largest one was about half the size of her thumbnail.

"Are they worth much?" she asked.

Nick shrugged. "Only a fraction of the gold mined in the world is placer nuggets like these, so these nuggets would cost more than gold at the open-market price. I've hung on to these because of their sentimental value. That I found any at all was a fluke. If this stream were known for its gold, my father wouldn't have remained a fisherman all his life. There's gold in Alaska, but not here at Williwaw Lodge. Too bad, but that's the way it is." He wrapped the nuggets up in a handkerchief and put them in back in a drawer.

Martha was pleased to discover that flowers bloomed at the lodge all summer long. The soil was acidic, and it supported daffodils, rhododendrons and azaleas as well as delphiniums and dahlias. The flowers brightened the place on gray days. One thing for sure—with all the rain, the flowers never lacked water.

"I could stay here forever," Martha sighed one morning as she stood with Nick on the rhododendron-bordered front porch of his cabin, watching the sun tinge the clouds pink beyond the mountain peaks in the distance. She had just awakened and hadn't been able to resist coming outside to feast her eyes on the blazing display of colors as dawn flickered up from the tops of the mountains.

Nick kissed her neck. "Do you mean that? Really?" he asked. He wrapped his arms around her to keep her warm. He'd always assumed that Martha would eventually tire of Ketchikan or Alaska or the isolation of Williwaw Lodge.

"Yes, I mean it. I don't mind the rain, and I don't mind the clouds, and I don't mind the chill. I love everything about this place," she said fervently. "I love not straightening my hair, and I love not fussing with my clothes. I love not feeling as though I have to put on a style show for people who couldn't care less."

"I almost think you mean it," he said, looking down at her in surprise.

She regarded him with a long, level look. "I wouldn't say it if I didn't mean it, Nick. It's a comfortable way to live, and this has to be one of the most beautiful spots on earth."

"I've always thought so," he admitted, but Martha's declaration set him wondering. Did she like Williwaw Lodge well enough to stay forever? To quit her job with Sidney and live with him and Davey? To marry him?

He had never thought he'd find a woman who would appreciate Williwaw Lodge the way he did. Women found life in Alaska difficult, he knew. In Alaska you could be attacked by wild animals, frozen in icy waters, drenched by perpetual rain. You had to battle ice and snow and hordes of mosquitoes, and if that wasn't enough to test your endurance, there was the williwaw wind sweeping down off the mountainsides.

And then there were the little towns, some of them no more than clumps of small buildings with rusting snowmobile parts strewn outside. As for running a household, it was difficult even in one of the more civilized places like Ketchikan. Everything cost so much because everything had to be shipped in from

Outside. No, this wasn't the kind of place where most women felt comfortable. This he knew from past experience.

His best friend Hank's wife hadn't stayed on in Alaska after Hank died. She'd taken her three kids and headed back to the Lower Forty-eight, where she lived now. But then, he wasn't sure that Nancy had ever wanted to live here.

The only reason she'd come to Alaska in the first place was that she'd fallen in love with Hank while he was in the service, and once married there had been no alternative except for her to follow him back here. Hank and Nick had always known they'd be partners on a fishing boat someday, and that was the only way Hank knew to make a living once his enlistment in the navy was over.

So Nick had watched his best friend's wife sour on Alaska, and in only a few months, too. She'd poured her heart out to him many times in her loneliness. But Nancy was Nancy. Nick knew Martha well enough to realize that she was a different kind of woman.

For the first time in his life, Nick Novak had met a woman who wasn't pretending to be something she wasn't. He was sure that he had fallen in love with the real person inside Martha Rose, not someone who was trying to live up to his expectations. He had expectations, of course. But Martha, the real Martha whom he had come to know, met his expectations by being herself.

With every day that passed, Martha seemed to find something new and different to love about her surroundings. If it wasn't a hike up Deer Mountain, it was trolling on the *Tabor*. If it wasn't chocolate-chip cookies, it was Davey. Nick had grown accustomed to Martha's bright-eyed eagerness to know and to do and to see. He was used to the merriment that always seemed to simmer just below the surface of her. He couldn't imagine how he would ever manage to get along without Martha Rose in his life.

Would she marry him? He didn't know. But, cautiously, Nick began to hope.

Chapter Fourteen

Martha began selling her cookies in Nick's Front Street store, and she didn't notice any drop-off in sales. If anything, she sold more. Baking the cookies became such a burden that she began to inquire about people who could be trusted to bake them exactly to her recipe.

"That's easy," Randy said when she asked him. "My sister could do it. She's home all day with a tiny baby, and she'd like having the extra income." And so Randy's sister Edith became Martha's adjunct baker, working out of the kitchen in the little cinder-block house she shared with her husband and her baby.

Nick, through his supplier, found boxes printed with a flower design, and these proved to be the perfect container for Martha's cookies. She baked smaller cookies and packed a dozen nestled in a tissue-lined box. A dozen cookies seemed to be the perfect number for tourists from the cruise ships, whether they were buying them for a picnic in one of Ketchikan's recreation areas or taking them back to the ship.

When a cook from one of the smaller cruise ships asked if Martha could supply the ship with twenty dozen cookies each time it docked in Ketchikan, Martha knew she was on to a good thing. She sent free boxes of her cookies to other, smaller cruise ships, too, and she received two additional orders. At that point she hired Randy's other sister to bake cookies in her home.

"It's a good thing I have this cookie sideline," she told Nick one night at the lodge when they sat going over the accounts for their business. "If I didn't, I wouldn't be able to pay Randy this week."

"Why not?" Nick asked, his pencil poised over a column of figures.

"My paycheck didn't come in the mail today the way it usually does. I'm supposed to be paid once a week. This is the second time it's been late."

"Have you tried to find out what's holding up your checks?"

A frown creased Martha's forehead. "I called Sidney's office in San Francisco both times, several times in one day, and his secretary always says that Sidney is out of the office. Of course, he can't call me here at the lodge, but still..."

"You think he's giving you the runaround?"

"Maybe. But my check finally arrived four days late last time. Let's see what happens this time."

"If it doesn't get here, what are you going to do?"

Martha smiled. "I guess I'll just bake more cookies," she said.

During this time, Davey continued to progress. He had days when he talked more than other days, and some days he proved to be a real chatterbox. He still played with Bear, and the little sea otter remained a treasured member of the household.

"What will we do when it's time to send Bear away?" worried Nick. "I'm planning to release him at the end of August."

"Davey needs another pet, Nick."

"How about a puppy?"

"We could use the puppy to wean Davey away from Bear," Martha said, and accordingly she and Nick began to speak of the time when Bear would go, soon after Davey got his new puppy.

"A puppy? I'm going to have a puppy?"

"The best puppy I can find," Nick told him as Davey clambered into his lap.

"After Bear goes," Martha added for good measure.

All Davey could talk about after that was what it would be like when he got his new puppy. He told everyone—the other kids at Wanda's, and Hallie, and even Nick's secretary at the cannery—that he was going to get a new puppy.

"This puppy is the second-best thing that ever happened to Davey, and we haven't even got him yet," Nick said one day when he and Martha thought they had heard enough about the new puppy to last them a lifetime.

"What's the *first*-best thing that ever happened to Davey?" Martha asked.

"You," Nick said unhesitatingly as he pulled her to him and kissed her. "He didn't begin to talk until after he knew you."

"You're forgetting Dr. Whitmer's influence. And Bear's," murmured Martha against Nick's chest.

"No, I'm not," insisted Nick. "They don't have the particular gift you have of giving of yourself." Martha, whose lips were seeking his by this time, didn't reply. It was Nick to whom she wanted to give of herself at that point, and in the way that they knew best.

Sometimes, when Davey begged to stay with Hallie at Wanda's all night, Nick agreed. On those nights, he and Martha occupied the double bed in Nick's bedroom. If she lived here permanently, Martha knew, this would be her room as well as Nick's. And then she brought herself up short, realizing that she was thinking of marriage, and she'd never thought of marrying anyone before.

One night, after Nick had fallen asleep, she couldn't stop herself from thinking how wonderful it would be to be married to Nick. It would be fun to wake up to his smile, to open her arms to Davey when he and the puppy—the new puppy that Davey didn't have yet—romped into the bedroom in the morning. It would be lovely to lie beside Nick all night, watching him sleep openmouthed beside her as he did now and loving the way he looked.

She slid close to him, deliberately snaking her smooth leg up his to wake him.

"Mar—" he said, fuzzily and incompletely, and she maneuvered herself so that her legs wound around his. He rolled over on top of her and she snuggled her face into the curve under his chin. She found a fold of skin to nibble. By this time Nick was alerted to the fact that Martha wasn't sleepy, and he sank his face in her hair and whispered, "I've always considered myself fortunate that you're a creature of impulse," before moving his lips in a circuitous route that led him to her moist mouth and other exciting places.

Martha let her fingers drift over the rugged jawline, rough now with unshaved stubble, past his temple into his bronze-brown hair. Her hands cupped the shape of his head, floated downward to his sinewy shoulders, grazed the taut muscles of his back. She trembled beneath him, and he felt her tremble, and it was as though the earth moved.

Which could be what was happening, considering Alaska's inclination toward earthquakes.

"I think I felt an earthquake," he said, only partly joking, but Martha shifted beneath him and whispered, "No earthquake. No world. You make it all go away," and then he laughed deep down in his throat and said, "We've done away with the world. Let's get rid of the universe, too," and she said, "The whole galaxy," and then she tensed beneath him so that he knew he had better get serious about it.

Afterward, when they lay spent, when she could speak, she said, "I feel as though I've been sucked into a black hole," and he felt her smile against his chest.

"Ah, Martha, I suppose that two people in love always think they're the only ones who ever felt so magnificent together. But the two of us are more than magnificent. When we make love, there are no words to describe how I feel." He traced her collarbone with a forefinger, marveling at the silkiness of her skin.

"I know," she said.

"I feel as though I'm opening up to you in all sorts of ways. I lose my boundaries. I don't know where you begin and I end."

"Does that frighten you?" Martha wasn't sure why she asked that question. Maybe it was something in his tone of voice.

"A little. I've never wanted to be so honest with anyone before. I've never felt as though I wanted to unreel my whole life and say, 'Look, this is Nick Novak—what he was like, what he is now, what he is going to be,' but I feel that way with you."

She reached up to caress his cheek. "Dear Nick. Thank you for feeling that way about me. It makes me happy to know."

They fell asleep then, still wrapped in each other's arms. In the morning they made love again, slowly and yet passionately. And when he left her on the dock at the Bagel Barn, he kissed her tenderly right in front of Randy.

"We'll go away this weekend, okay? I'm sure I can talk Hallie into spending the weekend at the lodge. We'll go out on the *Tabor*, and this time I don't want to do any trolling. I don't want to do anything but drift and dream with you."

Today was Thursday. That meant they'd leave Saturday morning. They'd have both Saturday and Sunday to spend together.

"I'll line Randy up to take care of things at the Bagel Barn," Martha promised, and she spent all day daydreaming about how wonderful it would be to be on the *Tabor* again, just the two of them together.

But they didn't go. Nick stopped by the Bagel Barn late that afternoon. Martha knew as soon as she saw his tense expression that something was wrong, terribly wrong.

"Is it possible for you to spend the weekend in town at your apartment?" he asked tersely.

Martha took in his distraction, his rumpled hair and the crease between Nick's worried brown eyes.

"Why, yes, I suppose so," she said. "What's happened? Is something wrong?"

It was as though a knife fell between them, cutting their line of communication.

"Something's wrong, yes, but it doesn't concern you." He hesitated.

"Davey? Is Davey all right?"

"Davey is fine. Martha, don't ask me any more. I can't talk about it, do you understand?" His eyes raked her face, begging for understanding, but Martha couldn't give it. She didn't understand. And she knew that something momentous was about to occur and that she wouldn't like it at all.

"I have to go out of town," Nick said, biting off the words sharply. "I don't know when I'll be back."

"But what about going away on the *Tabor*?" she cried involuntarily. She couldn't help it; her disappointment was so keen.

"It'll have to wait," Nick said.

"Nick—"

"I'll talk to you when I get back," he said. For one long moment his expression seemed to beg her forgiveness, but then he turned on his heel and headed toward the cannery.

Randy saw the tears in Martha's eyes.

"Martha, if I can help in any way..." he began.

Martha shook her head vigorously. The tears threatened to spill over. "No, I'll be okay," she said.

"If you want me to close up the Bagel Barn for you while you leave, I'll be glad to," he offered.

"No," Martha said, and methodically and automatically she went about her usual tasks. She wouldn't cry yet. She'd wait until she got back to her lonely little apartment.

But when she finally reached her apartment, she didn't cry. She was too angry for that. All his talk about wanting to be open with her, about wanting to unreel his life so that she'd know everything about him, meant nothing if he didn't follow through by confiding in her now. He'd said that he felt like being completely open with her. If that was true, then why wasn't he?

Nick had convinced her that he loved her. She believed him, despite this new incident. Now more than ever she wanted to know his secrets. She had to know, if she was going to make the decisions she knew she must face.

How could she marry Nick Novak when she had so many unresolved questions about his mysterious past?

"How's Davey?" Billy Long asked as he and Nick hurried through the creaky swinging doors at the hospital in Petersburg.

"He's talking now, Billy. He's making great progress."

"Is this because of his visits with the psychiatrist in Juneau?"

"That's part of it. But there are other things, too," he said, not knowing how to tell this man who was Davey's uncle about Martha and her effect on Davey. He decided not to mention Martha, at least for now.

Elsa Long lay in her hospital bed, each breath a painful rasp.

She was covered by a white thermal-knit blanket, and her hands, worn and corded with blue veins, were folded across her chest.

"How bad is it?" Nick asked in an undertone as he stood gazing down at her small, leathery face.

"Granny is very old," whispered Billy. "I never know if she'll make it. Last time we expected her to die, and you know what happened. She made it through all right."

Elsa opened her eyes. "If you're going to say something about me, don't whisper. Say it so I can hear it," she snapped. Her voice was weak, but there was no doubt that she understood what was happening.

"Nick's here, Granny," Billy said.

"Nick," Elsa said. "Is Davey all right?"

Nick sat down by her bed. "Davey is fine. He's talking now, Elsa. Not a lot, but enough."

Elsa closed her eyes. Nick wasn't sure whether she had fallen asleep or was merely gathering her strength for more words.

"Something important," she said, her tone so low that he had to bend close to hear her.

"Yes, Elsa?"

"I want you to adopt Davey." The old woman paused and licked her dry lips. Her eyes pleaded with Nick. "Will you?"

Nick already thought of Davey as his. He supposed he had thought of the boy as his very own since he'd first held him in his arms a few months after the accident. He didn't have to think it over.

"Of course I will adopt him," he said slowly. "Of course."

"You are a good man, Nick Novak," whispered Elsa.

Nick thought she had fallen asleep, but she opened her eyes again. "Take care of the arrangements now, Nick," she begged. "I can die happy if I know my grandson is legally yours."

"If there's time—" Nick began.

"There's time. A lawyer. Billy will find you one. I'll sign anything I have to if it means Davey will be your son."

Nick rose to his feet. He patted Elsa Long's hand awkwardly.

"Davey is already mine," he told her. "He's been mine for a long time now."

A hint of a smile passed over Elsa's lips. "I know," she said.

Afterward, when Nick and Billy were talking over a cup of coffee in the hospital cafeteria, Billy said, "You mean it, Nick? You'll adopt Davey?"

"I love that kid like my own," Nick said. "He's lived with me for more than three years. It's crossed my mind many times that I'd like to make it legal. I didn't ever bring it up because I thought it might be hard on Elsa. Yes, I'm going to adopt Davey."

Billy's relief was obvious. "I'm glad, Nick. Me and Gloria, we don't have much money. We can't take on raising another kid on top of raising our own two teenagers. For you to bring up my sister's baby when he's no kin to you—well, I'll always be grateful for your generosity, Nick."

"Don't thank me," he said, embarrassed by Billy's gratitude. Nick shoved his coffee cup away and stood up. "Let's go find a lawyer who can tell me what I need to do," he said, clapping Billy on the shoulder.

Nick called Martha that night. He had known she would sound cold, but he hadn't been prepared for her words to chill him like a dunk in the winter ocean.

"I don't understand anything," Martha said unhappily. "All I know is that this is the second time this has happened, Nick."

"I know," he said miserably.

"First you tell me that I'm the only woman you ever wanted to be honest and open with, and then you run off on some unexplained errand that takes several days. When will you be back?"

"I'm not sure," he said.

"Why aren't you?" She deliberately put the screws to him, knowing that he was squirming on the other end of the phone line.

"I can't go into it. Trust me, Martha, that's all I ask."

Martha let out a sigh of complete exasperation.

"Nick, I hate it when you won't communicate with me. We were doing so well together. Remember the utter frustration you felt when you would talk with Davey but he wouldn't talk with you?"

"Yes, of course," Nick said.

"Well, I feel the same way now. The worst thing is that *you* could talk to me if you wanted to, but you won't." She was breathing rapidly now, caught up in the fervor of her own words. She so desperately wanted him to confide in her, but she felt as though she was failing in her attempt to convey her need to him.

Nick knew she was right. When she described her feelings, he understood all too well what she was going through. Yet he was helpless to respond the way she wanted.

"Martha, I love you and I miss you," he said, knowing that she expected more than love and longing. She expected honest communication, and that was much harder for him to give right now.

There seemed to be no point in continuing to force a conversation that could hardly be termed a conversation.

"Love isn't enough," Martha said with firm finality. "Goodbye, Nick."

She hung up the phone. Sadness, mingled with bitter disappointment, trickled through her. Faye had been right. Polly had been right. Everybody had been right except Martha, whose misplaced trust in Nick had only made her miserable again.

A knock sounded on the door. When Martha opened it, Faye scooted in. From the puffy look of her short hairstyle, she had obviously just come from the hairdresser, and she was smiling happily.

"I haven't seen your light on in such a long time, I thought I'd drop in and say hello. Dr. Andy and I came back from the boondocks yesterday where we saved a guy's life. He'd crashed his plane on Tilkotsu Glacier, and—but Martha, what's the matter?" Her smile faded when she noticed Martha's agonized expression.

Martha sank down on the couch. "Sit and talk with me, Faye, or I'll go bananas." Her futile conversation with Nick still echoed in her ears.

Undone by Martha's lusterless eyes, Faye sat down and regarded her friend with an expression of concern. "It's Nick, isn't it?" she asked.

"Yes, it's Nick. He's gone away again, Faye, with no explanation and no questions allowed."

"It sounds to me like having a romance with Nick Novak is

only slightly less painful than having a root canal," observed Faye with a wry shake of her head.

"You and Polly both tried to warn me, but I wouldn't listen. I was in love with him, head over heels, not knowing that Nick was the heel!"

"I thought everything was going so well."

"So did I. Apparently it wasn't." She paused, blinking her eyes rapidly to hold back the tears as she remembered yesterday morning, when they had been alone at Williwaw Lodge and he had made love to her so sweetly and tenderly. How could she have been wrong about him?

"Martha, it sounds like he only wanted a playmate while you wanted a soul mate, and never the twain shall mate. What are you going to do?"

"Go back to San Francisco the way I originally intended to do."

"You mean you had changed your mind? You really thought you might stay here?"

"I haven't been happy working for Sidney, and I'd thought that with my new chocolate-chip cookie business, maybe I'd stay on in Ketchikan."

"And now you won't. Oh, dear." Faye heaved a big sigh. Then she brightened. "Martha, what you need is a distraction. And do I ever have one for you. You know those nine other men in Alaska who are supposed to be yours? Well, one of them is looking for a date tonight, and there's no reason why it can't be you. He's not an Alaskan but what does it matter? Why don't you get dressed up, and we'll go out on the town."

"Faye, no. I don't feel like it."

Faye grabbed Martha's hand and pulled her to her feet. "Of course you feel like it. These two fellows are brothers of the pilot whose life Dr. Andy and I saved this week. They're here in Ketchikan waiting to catch a flight out of town tomorrow. One is almost my age, and one is considerably younger. I *was* going to take the younger one," she said with a twinkle, "but you can have him."

"Nick might call," Martha said, although she doubted it. She wasn't at all sure she wanted to talk with him, anyway, in light

of what she was beginning to regard as her firm decision to
return to San Francisco.

"It would do Nick good to wonder where you are. Go put on
one of those pretty dresses you never wear anymore." She gave
Martha a shove toward the bedroom.

"I'll be back to get you later," Faye called as she left. "And
I'll have Lloyd and Greg with me, so be ready."

Martha tried her best to force her hair to lie in its former
smooth, uncurly state. She daubed her eyelids with eye shadow
in a shade called antique rose; she slathered her eyelashes with
two coats of mascara. She put on a blue silk dress with wide
lapels and, eschewing the carved ivory bracelet Nick had given
her, slipped all her gold bangles on her wrist. When she looked
in the mirror on the back of her bedroom door, she recognized
herself as the person she'd once been. Unfortunately she now
radiated a chic that seemed inappropriate for her. She felt as if
she was dressed up in somebody else's costume. She was half-
frightened by this ghost of her former self. Quickly she opened
the door, concealing the mirror so she wouldn't have to look.

The man Faye had provided was almost as tall as Nick, and
he had blue eyes that lit up when she walked into the room. His
name was Greg, he was an attorney in Los Angeles, and he
frequently traveled to San Francisco on business. Besides, his
ex-wife lived there with his little girl. Maybe he'd come to see
her sometime when he was in town—after she went back to live
there, that is. Martha forced a smile and wondered why she had
let Faye bring her along.

Faye was obviously smitten with Lloyd, who was also tall
and also had blue eyes and who was clearly impressed with
Faye's vibrant personality. While they were hitting it off so well,
there wasn't anything for Martha to do but to talk with Greg,
and although he was nice, their personalities didn't produce any
sparks.

Martha's mind wasn't even engaged. She kept thinking about
Davey and about what he and Hallie must be doing now. When
it was seven o'clock, she knew that it was time for Davey's
bath. When it was seven-thirty, she knew Davey would be telling Bear good-night. When it was eight, she knew that Hallie

would be tucking Davey into his bed. And when it was nine, she knew that if she and Nick had been together at the lodge they would have been sitting in front of a brightly burning fire, telling each other about their day.

Her loneliness for Nick grew until it was a large ache clenched around her heart. It didn't matter that they were in one of the nicest cocktail lounges in town or that they later moved on to eat prime rib at her favorite Ketchikan restaurant. It didn't matter that she was surrounded by people and noise and was the recipient of eager, seductive glances from Greg. She wanted Nick, and no one else would do.

Afterward the four of them went dancing, and Martha, unfamiliar with her high heels, stumbled over Greg's feet as she tried her best to follow his lead.

"I guess we just don't dance the same way," she apologized after she had practically skewered Greg's instep with one of her spike heels, but he only laughed graciously and slid his arms around her again.

"If I were going to be here a few more nights, we could practice our dancing," Greg murmured in her ear.

She didn't respond because she didn't want him to get the idea that she ever wanted to see him again.

When the men took them back to their duplex, it was plain that Faye intended to ask Lloyd to come in for a nightcap. Greg apparently expected Martha to invite him in, too. She couldn't. She wouldn't.

"What should I do?" she whispered frantically to Faye as she mounted the steps together.

"Tell him...tell him you have to bake cookies," Faye whispered, so that's what Martha did.

"I thought maybe I'd get a taste of these famous cookies of yours," Greg said forlornly as his brother disappeared into Faye's apartment.

"Wait here," Martha said, and she returned with a bagful of the latest batch. "Here," she said, all but shoving them out the door.

"I'll call you next time I come to San Francisco," Greg called as she closed the door, but she didn't bother to answer. San

Francisco seemed very far away at this point. She couldn't even remember what the place was like.

The phone rang, and her heart leaped. She stood beside it, her heart pounding the breath out of her as she debated whether or not to answer it. When she did give in and picked up the receiver, it was a wrong number.

She sank down on her bed and buried her face in her hands. She loved Nick Novak. What was she going to do?

Chapter Fifteen

Elsa Long died three days after Nick arrived in Petersburg.

No matter how much they had all expected it, her family wasn't ready to accept the fact that she was gone. Billy Long broke into tears, his wife Gloria sobbed, and their two children cried, too. Nick had his hands full comforting them.

Nick had consoled them once before, after the accident when Dolores and Hank had been killed, so he felt as though he was an old hand at this. He was the one who made the funeral and burial arrangements for Elsa. He was the one who paid for everything. He didn't mind, because he was jubilant over Davey.

Davey was going to be his. All the necessary forms for the adoption had been completed and would soon be filed by the attorney he and Billy had found. It wouldn't be long before Davey was really and legally Nick's son.

Of course, Nick had felt from the first as though Davey belonged to him. He wondered, though, how he would handle announcing that Davey was now his. Or should he keep the vow of secrecy he had made to himself after the accident? Should anyone have to know Davey's change in status?

He was well aware that plenty of gossip circulated around Ketchikan about the boy's origins. He even knew that many people considered him the boy's natural father. Maybe, for the sake of his own reputation, he should have set everything straight in the beginning when Davey had come to live at Williwaw Lodge.

But he hadn't, and for good reason, too. He'd had to protect Hank and his family. Nick thought a lot of Hank's wife Nancy; she was a fine and lovely person. He wouldn't have hurt her for the world, especially when she was still grieving inconsolably over Hank's death.

Nick hadn't regretted what he'd done, at least not until recently. One thing was for sure, keeping Hank's secret had certainly landed him in hot water with Martha. She'd been furious when he'd called her.

How could he explain everything now? And to whom would he explain it all? Who could still be hurt by his revelations? Nancy, who now lived far away? The children of her marriage with Hank?

Nick tossed and turned all night, trying to divine the answers to these questions. When morning finally came, he still didn't know what he was going to do.

One thing was paramount in his mind by the time he stepped off the plane in Ketchikan. He had to reconcile with Martha before he did anything else.

He'd square things with Martha and let the chips fall where they may. But first he'd better catch some sleep. He was hollow-eyed and exhausted after everything that had happened in Petersburg.

"HANG IN THERE," Polly said over the telephone.

"That's not what you said last time," Martha said.

"Yes, well, that was before I knew you were absolutely crazy about the guy. It was before you went and stayed with him at his lodge—what's the name of the place?"

"Williwaw Lodge," replied Martha faintly.

"Martha, you know this doesn't sound like you. Living in a place called Williwaw Lodge where the only live things you see besides Nick and Davey are porcupines and moose and where you can't even wear a decent dress."

"I've changed."

"I'll say. Anyway, if you've changed so much for this guy, and if you love him as much as you say you do, and if you're convinced he loves you—"

"I was," Martha said. Now she didn't know what to think.

"Then you ought to stick around and find out what's going on. You might not like it, but it should be an interesting story, maybe more interesting than those stories we read in *Cosmo*."

"I've already reserved a seat on a flight back to San Francisco next week. I decided yesterday that since I hadn't heard from Nick for a couple of days I might as well cut my losses and get out of here."

"I thought he was your business partner!"

"He is, but I could handle all our business by mail. I've got these people baking cookies for me in their houses, and I can communicate with them by phone. I could ship them the supplies like Sidney does me, and——"

"Oh, gosh, Martha, I almost forgot what I called to tell you. I read in the paper that Sidney has filed for bankruptcy!"

"Bankruptcy!"

"Yup. Here it is, it's in the business section of the *Chronicle* today. 'Sidney Pollov Enterprises has filed under Chapter eleven.' That's what it says. It says that Sidney was overextended trying to start this Chinese take-out food business, and the whole shebang is going under. Which means you don't have a job."

Martha felt weak. No wonder she hadn't received a paycheck for the past two weeks. No wonder Sidney hadn't answered her phone calls. Now all she had left was the cookie business.

"Martha? Are you all right?" Polly demanded.

"Just shocked, that's all. And yet not surprised. I had an idea things weren't going well for Sidney. He seemed awfully tense when he came here to visit."

"Maybe you'd better hang on to that reservation on the flight out of there next week. You might need it."

"I'll have to talk with Nick," she said heavily. "I'll have to decide whether to keep on with the cookie business or find another job—or both."

"I'm so sorry about your job, Martha."

"Maybe it's for the best," she said unhappily.

"Hey, when you come back to San Francisco, you're welcome to move in with me. Sigmund is still here, but he doesn't sleep in the guest room. We'll love having you here.''

''Thanks, Polly,'' Martha said, but the thought of living in a household that included Sigmund and his crystals didn't appeal to her in the least. In fact, San Francisco and its trendiness no longer held any attraction for her, she realized with a sinking heart. Even its fogs seemed feeble in comparison to the magnificent mists that rolled into Ketchikan off the Tongass Narrows.

Come to think of it, going back to her former way of life in the Lower Forty-eight was totally unappealing. Martha could no longer imagine painting her eyelids in shades such as navel orange and jaded green; she didn't ever want to wear expensive but shoddily made clothes of rayon just because they were dictated by the whims of some fashion editor. She had grown to appreciate the simple things in life, such as flannel shirts, hikes on the mountain, kisses in the rain and the laughter of a child.

Now that she didn't have a job with Sidney Pollov, she'd have to get on with her life somehow. But how?

She'd better talk with Nick before she made any firm decisions. She could keep it businesslike if necessary, and after this last disappearing act of his, it looked as if she'd have to. She didn't see how she could resume a personal relationship with him, never knowing if he was planning to run out on her.

She'd talk with Nick. But first she'd have to find him.

HIS SECRETARY at the cannery told her that Nick was back from his trip, but he wasn't there when she stopped by to see him.

She went to Wanda's house, and Hallie told her that Nick was back at Williwaw Lodge, that Davey was still with her, and that if Martha wanted to talk to Nick she was perfectly welcome to use the shortwave radio in Wanda's kitchen.

''No thanks,'' Martha said, shuddering inwardly at the thought of Wanda's large household hearing the things she had to say to Nick.

She went to help Randy, who was dismantling the Bagel Barn on the dock. ''I wish I could get out to the lodge,'' she fretted to Randy, who as usual knew exactly what was going on between her and Nick.

"No problem," he told her as he slid bolts into a plastic bag. "My cousin can take you in his boat."

Randy apparently had a relative for every purpose, thought Martha as she huddled in the bow of his cousin's runabout, braving flecks of spray that the wind blew off the water. And it was a good thing, or she'd never be able to surprise Nick like this.

"Thanks," Martha said when the boat had dropped her at the dock at the lodge. She tried to press some money into Randy's cousin's hand, but he only waved it away and headed back out into the bay. Martha stood on the dock, gazing at the log cabin and recalling all it had meant to her. Then she squared her shoulders and marched up the slope to the door.

She knocked, and the door swung open. Nick blinked under her hard, penetrating stare.

"Martha! I heard the boat, but I thought it was a sports fisherman anchoring in the shallows. What are you doing here?"

"I came to talk to you," she said, watching him. "May I come in?" He still had exactly the same effect on her; her mouth went dry and the hair on her arms stood on end. If only they could get this over with!

Nick scratched his head. He wore an old sweatshirt and a pair of jeans. His feet were bare. He looked tired. There were purple half circles beneath his eyes, and his hair was tousled. He looked as though he'd just awakened from a nap.

Once inside, she slipped out of her windbreaker and hung it on a peg beside the door as she had so many other times. She swung around to face Nick.

"I've lost my job, Nick. I won't be working at the Bagel Barn anymore."

"What happened?" His heart went out to her; she looked overwrought.

"Sidney Pollov Enterprises has gone bankrupt. Polly called and read me the news out of the San Francisco *Chronicle* a couple of days ago. Since then Randy and I have been dismantling the Bagel Barn. I haven't received any instructions from Sidney, but that seemed like the best thing to do.''

"We still have our cookie business, Martha. You can expand it, start selling cookies in other resort towns in Alaska, not just in Ketchikan. And the cruise-ship business—don't forget that. You've barely scratched the surface. Cruise ships will make three hundred stops in the Ketchikan harbor next year, and some of them will be your best customers.''

"I'm going back to San Francisco next week, Nick. I'm here to see if you think we can work this cookie business out together long-distance.''

He stared at her, completely taken aback. He felt as though the air had been struck from his lungs. "Martha...'' he said. He realized that they were still standing in front of the door.

"There's no point in arguing with me,'' she said, surprised at the way her voice gave no hint of the strain and anguish she had suffered in order to come to her decision.

"Martha, let's sit down,'' he said, indicating the couch. Martha sat. He pulled up a wooden footstool, handcrafted by his father, so that he sat directly in front of her. He reached out and took her hands in his. She pulled them away.

He dragged a hand through his hair. It made it even more tousled. Martha aimed her eyes at the fireplace, the pictures on the wall, anything so she wouldn't have to look at him. She found herself thinking about the way he slept with his mouth open. It seemed a stupid thought to be having when she was trying to disengage herself gracefully from their relationship.

"I have a reservation on a plane for San Francisco. I'm leaving next week,'' she said. She no longer wanted to go there, but she had no choice now. Besides, she'd already bought her ticket.

"We can't possibly run this cookie business long-distance,'' Nick said. He paused, searching for the right words. He cleared his throat. "What I really mean is that I don't want to,'' he said finally.

"Then consider the business dissolved.'' She knew what she would do. She would go back to Kokomo and start a cookie business there. She had lots of friends in Kokomo who would welcome her with open arms and open mouths, the better to feed them cookies. The nice thing about being in the cookie business was that you could sell cookies anyplace. Everyone loved cookies, especially her cookies. She loved cookies. In fact, she wished she were eating one right now instead of sitting here with Nick and—

"Martha," he said, and it sounded as though he were a long way away instead of sitting in front of her looking distraught. "Martha, you're crying."

The tears rained down on her hands, falling as gently as the Ketchikan rain. The difference was that they were warm. The rain—the real rain—was always cold.

He gathered her into his arms, staggered at the thought that he had hurt her so much. And she was ready to leave. She had bought an airplane ticket. She wanted to dissolve their business.

His brain whirled in painful circles. He squeezed his eyes tightly shut and tried to think. He was terrified at the idea of living his life without her. His days would be unbearable if they were unpunctuated by her loving looks and her vivacious laughter. Life would be meaningless for him without Martha.

Now was the time to reassess the meaning of his promise to Hank. As he thought about it, he realized that he had to break that promise now. It was time to violate what he had always considered a sacred confidence.

He kissed her cheek. Her tears were salty on his tongue.

"Dear Cheechako," he said, knowing at last that he was doing the right thing. "I should have told you everything long ago. I was being loyal to the wrong person, someone who has been dead for years." He stopped and moistened his lips. His eyes searched her face. He saw love, and he saw pain. He couldn't let her go on hurting.

"Listen," he said gently. "Listen to the story I have to tell you."

And then he began to tell it for the very first time.

NICK'S CHILDHOOD FRIEND, Hank Patton, returned from his stint in the navy ten years ago with one goal in mind: to be a partner with Nick in a fishing venture. It was what the two of them had planned to do ever since they were boys growing up together in the wilderness on Mooseleg Bay.

Nick was already working with his brothers and his father on their Novak and Sons fishing fleet, but it was easy enough for him to be in business with Hank at the same time. The two of them bought a small troller at a bargain price, and Nick divided his time between the trollers of Novak and Sons and the boat he co-owned with Hank. It was a good system; that way, Nick got along with his father and brothers all the better. They had no quarrel with Nick's going into business with Hank. Dan and Fred had long known that that was what Nick wanted to do.

Nick was still unmarried, but Hank brought his wife Nancy, a pretty nineteen-year-old brunette he'd met in Corpus Christi, Texas, back to Ketchikan. Nancy had a hard time adjusting to Alaska, a place she'd never seen before her marriage except in pictures. It was an environment that the shy, gently reared Nancy could scarcely have imagined.

Nancy Patton found Alaskan men too rough and Alaskan women hard to get to know. She missed her family. She hated the rain; she longed for sun. It was no secret around Ketchikan that Hank and Nancy's marriage was in trouble almost from the time Nancy first set foot in Alaska.

But Nancy was pregnant when she arrived, and looking forward to motherhood. Hank became busy with the boat, which he and Nick had named the *Puffin* after the black-and-white birds that inhabit the rocky cliffs of Alaska's coastal waters. The baby was born, a girl, which disappointed Hal. He'd always longed for a son.

Hank's disappointment in their firstborn only made things harder for Nancy, who spent a great deal of time alone with their baby in their little house in Ketchikan while Hank and Nick were out highlining. Nancy decided that the best thing to do was to give Hank the son he said he wanted, but when their second child was born only a year after the first, it was another girl.

Nick grew to like Nancy, and when Hank didn't pay much attention to his growing daughters, Nick, with his love of children, found himself naturally gravitating toward them. He rode Kitty on his shoulders and he pushed Dina in her stroller while

Hank watched television or read the newspaper. Nick was aware of Nancy's extreme misery.

"If only I could go back to Corpus Christi for a while," she said to Nick one day when he'd stopped by to talk with Hank and found Nancy with her eyelids swollen from crying and the kids screaming and looking neglected. "It's been raining every day for a week; I can't take the kids to the park. This place is driving me crazy, Nick. If only I could go visit my parents and sit in the sunshine."

"Why don't you go this summer?"

"I mentioned it to Hal, and he said we can't afford it." She twisted her wedding band nervously. Nick had never seen Nancy so unhappy.

"I'll talk to Hank about it," Nick promised. Then he went to Hank and told him that instead of splitting the profits they made on the *Puffin* half-and-half he'd be willing to take less. Nick, after all, didn't have a family to support, and he was assured of his income from Novak and Sons. Hank argued, but when Nick made it plain that Hank's larger share of the profits would make it possible for Nancy and his daughters to fly to Corpus Christi for a long visit with her family, Hank reluctantly agreed.

Nancy came home from Corpus Christi with a renewed determination to make her marriage work. She became pregnant again shortly after her return, but to her disappointment and Hank's, their third child was another girl. They named her Joanne. And Hank and Nancy began to have bitter fights over almost everything.

Nick never knew exactly how Hank met Dolores Long. He began to suspect that Hank had a woman hidden away somewhere when Hank began to insist that he'd rather take the *Puffin* out alone, freeing Nick to spend more time with his father and brothers. Hank and the *Puffin* began to be gone trolling for longer and longer periods of time. Sometimes when Hank should have been available Nick couldn't reach him on the radio.

Hank became distant, remote. Sometimes he forgot things that Nick told him. He was easily distracted. At first, Nick attributed this change to Hank's troubles with Nancy. It didn't take long for Nick to realize that there was more to it than that.

Hank did a foolish thing, and afterward Nick thought that Hank must have wanted to get caught so he could confide in someone. It was clear that his deception was exacting a painful penalty of guilt.

Hank and Nick, out on the *Puffin* trolling for salmon, dropped anchor one night in a remote area off Kuiu Island. It wasn't where they normally anchored when they fished these particular grounds, and Nick had been uneasy about maneuvering the *Puffin* in so close to land.

"It's all right, I've been here before," insisted Hank, and so they anchored not far from shore. They ate dinner in the tiny galley as usual and listened to the radio, but it seemed to Nick that Hank seemed more alert, jumpier than he'd ever been before. They turned in early, and Nick awakened once in the night to hear the familiar sounds of the dinghy being lowered into the water. Groggy with sleep, he paid no attention.

But later he heard more sounds, and this time he was fully awake. A glance at the other bunk told him that Hank wasn't there. Nick stumbled onto the foggy deck to find Hank rowing toward the *Puffin* in the dinghy. He had clearly gone ashore earlier. It was just before dawn.

Nick silently helped Hank load the dinghy aboard the *Puffin*.

"Mind telling me where you've been going out here in the middle of nowhere?" he asked mildly.

"Nick, I can't," Hank said, looking guilty.

There was a long silence. During that silence, Nick added two and two and got the answer. He turned away in disgust, unable to speak to his friend.

"Nick, don't tell anyone. Don't tell Nancy," Hank begged, running after him, the sound of his boots a hollow echo on the deck.

Nick could scarcely contain his contempt. "I can't believe you'd do this to her," he gritted through clenched teeth.

Hank looked miserable. "If you knew the anguish I've been through over this," he pleaded, "you wouldn't judge me. Nancy and I haven't been getting along for a long time, but I won't leave her. She'd have a hard time taking care of herself and the three kids."

"You're all heart, aren't you, Hank?"

"I love Dolores. And she loves me. Maybe I can set things right eventually, but for now this is the way it has to be."

Nick refused to discuss it any further at that point, but later Hank told him the whole story.

Hank had started seeing Dolores frequently in Petersburg, and the beautiful young Tlingit woman with long flowing hair and skin the color of antique ivory had quickly become an obsession. Hank worried that someone from Petersburg would tell Nancy about Dolores, so Dolores moved into an isolated cabin on Kuiu Island, where she lived with her grandmother, Elsa. Dolores was a talented craftsman who carved walrus ivory for the tourist trade, and living in the wilderness was quiet and conducive to her work. It was an arrangement that everyone found satisfactory, at least for the time being.

Then Dolores told Hank that she was going to bear his child.

"I want to marry Dolores," Hank confided unhappily to Nick, but Nick refused to listen to such talk. He was concerned about Nancy's state of mind. He suspected that she had turned to drink for comfort. By that time, Hank was deeply in love with Dolores, who gave birth to his long-awaited son. If Hank had any affection left for Nancy, Nick didn't see it, even though Nancy, unaware of Hank's relationship with Dolores, claimed that she still loved him. Nick couldn't imagine how Hank was going to get himself out of the mess he had made of his life.

Hank never had to face that question. One night, when he was out on the *Puffin*, Hank noticed that the red light on the mast was out. He climbed the twenty-foot mast to insert a new bulb. All of a sudden the wind picked up and the boat began to roll violently. The aluminum mast snapped, and Hank was thrown into the cold sea.

Dolores, her son in her arms, rushed out on deck to see Hank struggling to stay afloat in the water. She screamed and ran to the stern, watching Hank trying to swim to it. In the icy water without a life jacket, Hank's strength faded fast. The boat was still pitching and rolling, and great spurts of spray drenched Dolores and her infant son. She tried to throw Hank a line, but she lost her footing on the wet deck and she and the baby were flung headlong into the roiling sea.

Dolores and the child were tossed onto some nearby rocks, where she huddled, barely alive, trying to keep her screaming baby warm. She was unconscious by the time another vessel fishing nearby spotted the *Puffin* as it broke up on the rocks and, looking for survivors, found the mother and child.

"Dolores regained consciousness long enough to tell them what happened," Nick said. "She died of exposure the next day. But the baby lived. Davey was their child, Martha, Hank and Dolores's child."

"Then the picture in your photo album—that was Dolores, wasn't it?" Martha asked in a tentative voice.

"Yes. It was a picture Hank had taken of her. I found the undeveloped roll of film at the cabin where Dolores and Davey lived. I saved the picture of Dolores for Davey so he'll know what his mother looked like. The nude study on the wall over there is of Dolores, too. I discovered it with some of Hank's things at the cabin where he visited her, and I didn't have the heart to throw it away. It's one of Hank's best photographs. She was very beautiful, wasn't she?"

Martha swallowed the lump in her throat. "Yes," she said softly, remembering what she had thought. She was glad to know that Dolores had been nothing to Nick. Just knowing that cleared up a lot of problems.

"What happened to Hank?" Martha asked.

"They never found Hank's body," Nick said with a haunted look in his eyes.

"Oh, Nick," Martha said. "How terrible."

"The worst part is that I had noticed a problem with the red light on the mast a couple days before, but I forgot about it. If I'd replaced the light myself, Hank wouldn't have been climbing that mast when the storm hit."

"You can't go on blaming yourself," Martha said gently.

"Oh, I don't know," Nick said, glancing down at the floor and shaking his head. "I'm pretty good at it."

"Is that why you've been so devoted to Davey?"

He raised his eyes to hers. "After the accident, when the first shock had passed, I realized that I had to take care of Davey for Hank's sake. So a couple of months later I went to the cabin where Dolores had lived with her grandmother, Elsa Long. There I found a toothless old woman who was overcome with grief and who could barely care for herself, much less her one-year-old grandson.''

"And that's when you took Davey?"

Nick nodded. "I'd first met the Longs after the Coast Guard notified me about the *Puffin*'s accident. I was the owner of record, along with Hank, and so I was the person they called first. I met Billy Long, Dolores's brother, at her funeral. After I discovered the conditions under which Davey and Elsa were living after Dolores's death, I persuaded Billy to come and take Elsa home with him.

"I knew he was financially strapped, so I sent him the money for his grandmother's support. I've visited Elsa frequently in the past few years because she's been in and out of the hospital many times. That's where I was those two times when I told you it was none of your business. This last time, I went to bury Elsa. She's gone, Martha. There won't be any more sudden departures.''

"Do you know what I thought? Can you imagine the ideas that ran through my head? I heard rumors, Nick, all sorts of rumors. Half the town of Ketchikan thinks that Davey is your illegitimate son.''

Nick's lips hardened in a grim line. "I'm sorry, Martha," he said. "I really am sorry. But my vow of secrecy came first, even before protecting my own reputation.''

"I was so upset both times when you went away," Martha murmured.

Nick caressed her face with his hand. His eyes, varnished with gold in the fading afternoon light, were earnest. "That was the worst thing," he said. "Not being able to tell you where I was going or what I was doing. I was mostly concerned with keeping the secret so no one would know. I should have trusted you.''

"Now I know what might have affected Davey," Martha said. "He must have been traumatized, even as a baby, by what happened to him when the *Puffin* was wrecked.''

"That's what I think, too. And Dr. Whitmer shares my opinion. I never could tell you before what I thought was wrong with Davey, but when you told me about the kindergarten child your mother taught, that's when things began to slip into place. That's when I began to see how I could help Davey."

Martha's head reeled with the details of Nick's revelations. There was still something he hadn't explained. "What happened to Nancy?" Martha asked.

"As far as I know, Nancy never found out about Dolores or Davey. I managed to hush up the fact that Hank had been with Dolores on the *Puffin.* I was afraid of what it would do to Nancy to find out that Hank had another family."

"Perhaps Nancy would have wanted Hank's son," Martha said.

"No. She was a young widow who was struggling to manage three small children. She was barely coping with them. How could I lay another burden on her? That's why I kept Davey, and that's why I never told anyone whose child he was or where he came from."

"And what happened to Nancy?"

"Her parents flew here from Corpus Christi and took her back home shortly after the accident. She traveled back to Ketchikan a few times to settle Hank's estate, though. Every time she came back, she seemed to be getting along better and better. Last year she married and moved to Alabama. I hope she's happy."

"If Nancy can no longer be hurt by it, then perhaps it's time to tell people what really happened," Martha suggested.

Nick shook his head. "I don't want to tarnish Hank's memory, Martha. A lot of people in Ketchikan remember him fondly. No, I don't want anyone to know. You're the only person I've ever told. You're the only person I ever will tell."

A lot of things made sense now. Nick's constant worry about weather conditions when they were on the *Tabor* was the result of his firsthand knowledge about the tragedy that could strike as the result of an unexpected storm at sea. His sudden silences and aloofness had only been his way of turning off further questions about a topic that he didn't feel free to pursue. His loyalty to his friend Hank must have been very hard on him all these years in terms of his relationship with his family, his friends and the few women he'd dated.

There was something noble in such loyalty, Martha thought. And something caring and compassionate, too. She admired Nick for providing for a destitute old woman who was no relation to him, and for taking on the care of a child who was no child of his.

"I'll never speak to anyone of this, Nick," she said slowly. Her silence was what Nick wanted, and it was probably best for all concerned. After all, she understood Nick so much better now that she knew the circumstances that had been the driving force behind many of his actions during the last few years.

"There's one more thing. I've set the wheels in motion to adopt Davey. Then he will legally be my son."

Martha smiled. "Oh, Nick. That's wonderful. Truly, truly wonderful."

Nick clasped her hands in his. "And there's something else," he said softly.

"What else could there be?"

"I know it's a lot to ask," he began.

"Go on."

"And that Alaska is a nice place to visit, but not many people would want to live here," he continued.

"Not everyone," she agreed.

"And that Williwaw Lodge is very isolated."

"Which has its advantages," she murmured.

"Also, I've never done this before, and I don't know if I'm going to be any good at it."

"You're good at most things, Nick Novak, including kissing. Please kiss me now," she said, and he thought that the combination of laughing bright eyes and upcurved lips must be the most beautiful sight in the world.

He kissed her, and afterward she sighed and nestled her head on his chest.

"Now go on with what you were saying," she urged.

"What I was saying in my roundabout way was, will you marry me, Martha Rose?" He waited.

"Since you like chocolate-chip cookies and you *are* still my business partner..." she began.

"Yes?"

"And since you're tall enough so that if I ever want to wear spike heels again I could, though I doubt that I will want to..." she went on, laughter bubbling up from her throat.

"Mmm-hmm?" He nuzzled her ear for good measure.

"And since I think I could probably get used to eating moose liver for breakfast..."

"No waffles, though. I could stand eating a bagel in the morning, but I hate waffles."

"And because you're kind, compassionate and awfully good with kids and also because you'll make a good father to the many children I intend to have..." she said, dragging it out.

"Mmm," he agreed. Her luminous gray eyes were shining with love.

"And because you are such a good kisser, among other things..."

"Other things," he said, thinking about the other things.

"And since I've developed a taste for kisses in the rain and because I'm madly in love with you and want to live here with you forever and ever, till the glaciers melt and Southeast Alaska dries up into a desert..."

"Yes?"

"Yes, yes, yes, I will marry you, Nick Novak!" she said. Then she murmured, "I thought you'd never ask."

And he replied in relief, "Dear Cheechako, I thought you'd never answer." And he kissed her once again.

Epilogue

Williwaw Lodge
Labor Day Weekend

Polly stepped back to take in the stunning effect of the delicate baby's-breath blossoms she had pinned among Martha's curls.

"You need one more sprig on the left side," she decided, working the spray of tiny flowers into the curls above Martha's ear. "There. How's that?"

Martha looked at herself critically in the mirror over the dresser in the guest room. "Could you move it up a little bit?"

Polly poked gingerly at the flowers. "Better?"

"Much better," Martha said, beaming at her reflection.

"I still don't understand why you didn't want to wear a wedding veil."

"Because Nick says he wants to see my face when I walk up to him before the ceremony."

Polly rolled her eyes. "He really *is* in love with you as much as you said he was. I'm so glad, Martha. And so relieved. If you knew the thoughts that were running through my head during the flight from San Francisco—"

"What did you expect?" Martha asked curiously.

"I expected that this whole wedding was another of your impulses. And I fervently hoped that Nick would show up for the ceremony and not be running off to points unknown."

"Polly, that's all over," Martha said patiently.

"When are you going to tell me where he was those times when he left?"

"Never. Here, hook up the back of this collar, will you?"

Polly moved behind her and expertly buttoned the tiny covered buttons on the back of Martha's high-necked wedding dress. The dress was of white crinkled muslin with delicate hand-crocheted lace insets and leg-of-mutton sleeves. It fell to the floor, and it had no train. Polly had designed the dress to Martha's specifications, and a Ketchikan seamstress had whipped it up. Martha was delighted with it. "Everybody's here," Faye said, peering through a crack in the door. She opened the door and stuck her whole head in when she saw Martha. "Oh, Martha," she said softly. "You look beautiful."

Before Martha could reply, a ball of yellow fluff catapulted through the door, followed by Davey calling, "Come back here, you crazy dog! Come back here!"

The golden retriever puppy, which was only eight weeks old, took refuge in the swirls of Martha's long skirt. Davey dived after the puppy, and the two of them tumbled on the floor, squealing and giggling.

Martha bent over and detached the puppy and Davey from each other. She kept a hand on the puppy, which proceeded to lick her fingers while she straightened Davey's new suit and brushed away a layer of dog hair.

"How about putting Otter in his pen for the ceremony," she suggested to Davey.

"Otter wants to come to the wedding," Davey said.

"We agreed that he could come to the reception, remember? I've put a tray of dog biscuits out on the hearth just for him. But he'll have to stay in his pen for the ceremony."

"The cere— What?"

"The ceremony. When Nick and I marry each other."

"Oh."

"Everybody will have to be very quiet while we're speaking our vows," Martha said. "That's why Otter should be in his pen."

"Well, okay," Davey said reluctantly.

"Davey, I'll help you put Otter in his pen if you'll show me where it is," Faye said with a wink at Martha. Obediently Davey picked up the sprawling Otter and followed Faye out of the room.

"The dog's name is Otter?" Polly said with raised eyebrows.

"That's because we had an otter named Bear," Martha said with a laugh.

"Oh. I guess that explains everything," replied Polly wryly. She paused. "You certainly know how to handle Davey."

"I love Davey."

"Who would have thought you could be so maternal?"

"Not me," Martha said. She looked at her watch. "Are they starting to play music yet?"

Polly pulled aside the curtain and peered out at the slope in front of the cabin. The surface of Mooseleg Bay exploded in little stars where the raindrops hit. "No, the band had to take refuge on the porch. It's raining."

"I thought we'd be able to get the ceremony over before the rain started." Martha said, sighing.

"Maybe it'll stop," Polly said.

"I wonder where Nick is."

"I hear him. He's on the front porch with the band and the judge who is going to marry you. They're placing bets as to how long the rain will last."

Martha sat down on the bed. "The rain may last awhile," she said. She knew this from experience.

Polly let the curtain fall across the window. Again she admired her friend's wedding attire. Martha looked so lovely. "Martha, with all this rain I don't see how you managed to get such a good suntan," Polly said.

"That's not a suntan. It's rust," Martha said.

Polly whooped with laughter.

"Is everything okay?" Faye said, sticking her head in the door.

"Everything is perfect except for the rain," Martha said.

"We can always hold the ceremony inside if the rain doesn't stop soon," Faye pointed out.

"Nick and I want to say our vows with the mountains as sentinels, with the otters and eagles as witnesses, with—"

"Not only are you surprisingly maternal, you're also an incurable romantic," groaned Polly.

"They wrote the ceremony themselves," volunteered Faye before glancing over her shoulder. "Oh, there goes Davey running toward his bedroom with a handful of cookies. It'd be just like him to get chocolate all over his nice new suit." She closed the door and took off after the boy.

"I don't think I've ever been to a wedding quite like this before," mused Polly. "Chocolate-chip cookies instead of wedding cake—now there's an original idea."

"Nick and I wanted this ceremony and the reception to be our very own, a sharing of ourselves with our guests." Martha smiled at her friend reassuringly. "I hope you don't find it too hard to be the maid of honor in such an unconventional wedding."

"Hey, I'd fly to the ends of the earth to be *your* maid of honor," Polly said. She stared through the crack in the curtains at the mountain peaks on the other side of the rainswept bay. "In fact, I think I *have* gone to the ends of the earth. Are you going to be happy here, Martha?" She turned and let her eyes search her friend's face.

Martha smiled serenely and patted Polly's hand reassuringly. "Very happy," she replied.

The gold engagement ring on Martha's hand sparkled in the dim light. Nick had had it made to order for her; a local artist had styled a braid of gold around one of the gold nuggets Nick had panned from the stream here when he was a boy. For their wedding rings, the other nuggets had been melted down and fashioned into matching braided gold bands.

Polly impulsively lifted Martha's hand to admire her engagement ring. "I can't believe it," Polly marveled. "You haven't been nibbling on your fingers. You're not even nervous about getting married!"

"I don't have anything to be nervous about," Martha said with great certainty and tranquillity. Her hands rested quietly in her lap.

"It's stopped raining!" someone called. The musicians, who were friends of Randy's and members of a local string quartet, hurriedly took their positions on the grassy slope in front of Williwaw Lodge. Their guests formed a circle around the judge, who was Randy's uncle, and Nick, dressed formally, walked jauntily down the path clasping Davey's hand in his. Davey's fingers were disengaged from Nick's so that he could fidget impatiently beside Faye. At the first strains of the music Martha had chosen for her processional, Polly quickly kissed Martha on the cheek, grabbed her bouquet of Alaskan wildflowers and, with one eye on the hovering rain clouds, proceeded with undue haste down the path.

"Are you sure you don't want anyone to give you away?" Martha's mother had asked anxiously the previous night when she'd arrived from Indiana, but Martha had told her no, she was perfectly capable of getting herself down the short path to the scenic spot where she and Nick had chosen to speak their marriage vows.

Martha stood now watching her assembled guests from just inside the front door of the cabin; there were Wanda and her five grandchildren, Randy and his mother and stepfather, Hallie, Faye, Dr. Andy, Polly's Sigmund, Martha's mother and her sisters Roxie and Carolyn and their assorted husbands and children, Nick's brothers and their families and a few friends of Nick's. Martha and Nick had invited only the people with whom they wanted to share the beauty of their love and their vows; they had agreed that there would be no pointless paying back of social invitations, and no pretense. How could either of them be nervous when the only people present were well-wishing relatives and dear, dear friends?

All Martha felt now was eagerness to become Nick's wife.

When Polly had reached the end of the path, Martha took the first step forward toward her new life. She proceeded down the neatly swept path gracefully and at a more leisurely pace than Polly. She wanted to savor the experience of being Nick's bride.

It's really happening, Martha thought as her eyes met Nick's. *We're getting married.* All the world for her in that moment was concentrated in his eyes, and she floated toward him, feeling as though her feet barely touched the ground. The wet grass on the edges of the path left a damp ring on the hem of her dress.

The sun ventured out from behind the clouds, casting a golden beam of light down on the assembled participants and guests. The water in the bay shone opalescent in the sun, and beyond the bay the white-tipped mountains rose majestically against the sky. The rain-purified air was lightly scented with spruce.

Nick's eyes were bright and spoke of his love for Martha as she placed her hand in his. Nick and Martha had written their marriage ceremony themselves because they knew that no one else had ever expressed the way they felt about each other. Having learned to communicate, they wanted to start their lives together by saying what was in their hearts and on their minds. And so they began.

"Because you bring me your sweetness and your laughter, and because you made me see the person I could be when I was with you," Nick said.

"Because you are the dream I never knew could be real," Martha said.

"Because the rest of my life is the most precious gift I have to give you," Nick said.

"Because I want to live in your house and mother your son," Martha said.

"Because of the whisper I see in your eyes..."

"Because of the beauty that lives in your soul..."

"Because between us are no secrets..."

"Because we have only love..."

"I, Nick, wish you to be my wife."

"And I, Martha, will be your wife."

"Forever."

"Forever."

Nick slipped the braided gold band, warm from his touch, on the third finger of Martha's left hand. She slipped a larger ring on his ring finger. They stood looking down at their entwined hands, so newly gilded. They were both overcome by the enormity of their emotions.

"Kiss the bride!" called Faye, bringing them back to reality. Nick tenderly brought his hand up and brushed it against the baby's breath in Martha's hair, almost as if she was too fragile to touch. Then his arms went around her and crushed her to him, and the flowers in her hair were tickling his cheek, and he felt the dampness on his face and thought it was Martha's tears of happiness.

"It's raining again!" cried Polly.

"Run for it!" said the cello player, who played a fifteen-hundred-dollar instrument and was loath to have it ruined at a wedding where the principals seemed to find rain an enjoyable occurrence.

There was a great commotion as people simultaneously tried to fold up the musicians' chairs and run for the cabin.

"Look at those two," Sigmund said to Martha's mother once they had reached the haven of the porch.

"They don't even have enough sense to come in out of the rain," Faye said reprovingly.

Nick kissed Martha again. "Well, my Cheechako bride, I guess we'd better go in. Sorry the weather didn't cooperate."

Martha only smiled up at him. Then, laughing, she brushed the rain and the joyful tears from her cheeks and ran hand in hand with Nick to the front porch of the cabin where the small group of guests waited.

"Martha, can I get Otter out now?" Davey wanted to know.

Martha glanced up at Nick, who shrugged and smiled.

"Not before I get a kiss from my new son," Martha said, swinging the boy up into her arms despite the mud on the soles of his shoes.

"It's Mother Martha!" announced Polly gleefully.

"And here are some of her mouth-watering cookies," Hallie said, appearing in the doorway to pass around the platter.

"Mother Martha's Mouth-watering Cookies!" exclaimed Nick. "That's it!"

"That's what?" Martha said, setting Davey on the floor so he could go unpen the dog.

"The name we're going to give to your cookies! Mother Martha's Mouth-watering Cookies! We'll have it printed on the boxes and sell them from Sitka to San Diego, wait and see!"

"Can't you stop discussing business on your wedding day?" asked an exasperated Faye.

A renegade wind cracked around the corner of the house, driving them all inside.

"I can't believe you're really going to live way out here in the wilderness," fretted Martha's mother with a distracted look out the window.

"We're going to buy a house in town," Nick said. "Martha will have a big kitchen where she can test new kinds of cookies, and Davey will have friends nearby to play with."

"And I'm finally going to go live with Wanda," Hallie said with obvious satisfaction.

"We'll stay at Williwaw Lodge on weekends," Martha said.

"And vacations," Nick said.

"That sounds pretty good," admitted a much-relieved Mrs. Rose.

"I'll munch to that," Martha said, and she handed around a tray of cookies.

Later, when their guests had all been ferried back to Ketchikan and Martha and Nick were alone on the *Tabor*, which was anchored in a secluded cove, Martha nestled in Nick's arms in the *Tabor*'s narrow bed and said, "Thank you for such a beautiful wedding."

"Thank *you* for such a beautiful wife," he said.

"Do you wish it hadn't rained during the ceremony?" It was still raining, but softly.

"No. Do you?"

"No. Although for a while there I thought we might have to replace the cello player's cello."

Nick laughed. "We got a little wet," he agreed.

"We kissed in the rain," Martha said.

"And will probably kiss in the rain many, many more times," Nick said.

"Nick, do you know I love you more than—"

"Than what?"

"Than even chocolate-chip cookies?"

He studied her, his eyes gleaming. "Now that *is* a lot," he said. "Is it because I taste better?"

Martha laughed and rested her cheek against his. "I'm not sure," she said.

"Well, why don't you test me out?" he murmured, lowering his lips to hers.

They kissed, and then Martha pulled away. "I forgot to ask you what you thought of Sigmund's wedding gift."

He peered at her in the faint light from the kerosene lantern hanging over the bed. "You certainly picked a strange time to ask," he said. He barely recalled Sigmund's gift; it had looked like some kind of exotic rock.

"Well?"

"It's—uh, nice, I guess," Nick said. "What is it?"

"It's a crystal. It's supposed to improve the vibrations of our marriage."

Nick stared for a moment, then threw his head back in laughter.

"Where," Nick asked wickedly, "are we supposed to put it?"

"On a shelf or something, I suppose."

"What would improve the vibrations is if you would put your arms around me, like this and this," Nick said, demonstrating. "And your head like so, and your legs like so," he continued.

"I think I'm beginning to vibrate already," admitted Martha. Smiling, she lifted her lips to his.

And then the only sound was of the gently falling rain.

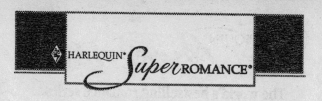

...there's more to the story!

Superromance.

A *big* satisfying read about unforgettable characters. Each month we offer *six* very different stories that range from family drama to adventure and mystery, from highly emotional stories to romantic comedies—and much more! Stories about people you'll believe in and care about. Stories too compelling to put down....

Our authors are among today's *best* romance writers. You'll find familiar names and talented newcomers. Many of them are award winners—and you'll see why!

If you want the biggest and best in romance fiction, you'll get it from Superromance!

Emotional, Exciting, Unexpected...

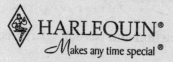

HARLEQUIN®
Makes any time special ®

Visit us at www.eHarlequin.com

HSDIR1

HARLEQUIN *Presents*

**The world's bestselling romance series...
The series that brings you your favorite authors,
month after month:**

Helen Bianchin...Emma Darcy
Lynne Graham...Penny Jordan
Miranda Lee...Sandra Marton
Anne Mather...Carole Mortimer
Susan Napier...Michelle Reid

and many more uniquely talented authors!

Wealthy, powerful, gorgeous men...
Women who have feelings just like your own...
The stories you love, set in exotic, glamorous locations...

HARLEQUIN *Presents*

Seduction and passion guaranteed!

Harlequin® Historical

From rugged lawmen and valiant knights to defiant heiresses and spirited frontierswomen, Harlequin Historicals will capture your imagination with their dramatic scope, passion and adventure.

Harlequin Historicals... they're too good to miss!

HHDIR1

HARLEQUIN®
Makes any time special®

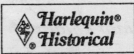
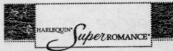

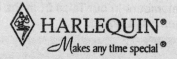

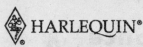